NEIGHBORHOOD WATCH

Also by David Jester

This Is How You Die

The Clinic

Forever After

An Idiot in Love

An Idiot in Marriage

NEIGHBORHOOD WATCH

A THRILLER

DAVID JESTER

Skyhorse Publishing

Skyhorse Publishing books may be purchased in bulk at special discounts for sales promotion, corporate gifts, fund-raising, or educational purposes. Special editions can also be created to specifications. For details, contact the Special Sales Department, Skyhorse Publishing, 307 West 36th Street, 11th Floor, New York, NY 10018 or info@skyhorsepublishing.com.

Visit our website at www.skyhorsepublishing.com.

10 9 8 7 6 5 4 3 2 1

Library of Congress Cataloging-in-Publication Data is available on file.

Cover design by Yiota Giannakopoulou
Cover image credit Pixabay

Print ISBN: 978-1-5107-3123-3
Ebook ISBN: 978-1-5107-3124-0

Printed in the United States of America

Good fences make good neighbors.
—Robert Frost

PROLOGUE

"I've come to kill you."

He laughed, waved his hand dismissively. He had a way of laughing from his nose, a short, sharp exhalation that threatened to expel the mucus from within. It was humorless, sarcastic. It was also smug and irritating—made all the smugger and more irritating by the holier-than-thou smile it preceded.

"Good one. What do you *really* want?" He looked me up and down. Confused. Alarmed. But not entirely sure why. "I'm—I'm kinda busy right now," he stuttered.

"I told you." I repeated slowly, "I am here to kill you."

He rolled his eyes and slammed the door. I heard him mumble to himself on the other side, cycling through a list of expletives before sighing and walking away, the floorboards creaking with every step.

That didn't go as planned.

I knocked again—another sigh, another barrage of expletives. The door swung open and once again I was greeted by the forty-four-year-old Oscar Wilde wannabe, complete with silk nightgown, expensive slippers, and judgmental stare.

He thought of himself as being above everyone else, even though everything he did was for show and everything he said was a lie. He considered himself to be better educated, even though he'd dropped out of school age sixteen to pursue a career in chain-smoking and sexually transmitted diseases. He considered himself more cultured, even though his idea of sophistication was watching *Frasier* and smoking cigars. He was a mid-forties social worker and failed writer who spent his days penning poetry that nobody read, writing a blog that few knew existed, and spouting nonsense to a negligible Facebook following.

He had a job, but he thought it was beneath him. He was a social worker with no social skills, a man who lived to put others down and only went to work every day so he could wallow in their misery, remind them that he was better than them, and subject them to his abhorrent poetry when they were too stoned, drunk, polite, or repressed to stop him.

He was the epitome of a failure, a nobody, but he was too narcissistic to realize it. Friends were few and far between, frustrated with his patronizing tone; girlfriends left when he asked to be treated like a king. His time was spent locked up in a high-rise apartment, drinking cheap bourbon, getting high, and yearning for the day that his slapdash, puerile poetry would be read by millions, and not just a smattering of emo kids online.

"Look, I don't know what you want—"

I grabbed him by the neck and pushed him into his apartment, delighting in the feel of his throat in my hand, the way his eyes filled with horror as his fingertips clawed desperately for release. He was weak, feeble, pathetic, and unable to resist. He toppled over, slipping out of my grasp and hitting the floor hard.

It was barely 8 p.m. and he was already paralytic—stinking of cheap booze and stale weed, just like his cramped, two-bedroom apartment. His eyes were glassy, a stupidly smug and vacant expression still on his face.

"What is this?" he repeated, the smugness slipping away as I retrieved a machete from underneath my jacket.

"I told you," I said, leaning in close. "I'm going to kill you. Now—on your feet."

"Please don't do this." He dragged himself upright, moaning and groaning with each movement. "What is this? Why are you doing this? Please. You know me. I don't deserve this."

"I *do* know you, and you *do* deserve this. That's why I'm here."

He was on his knees now, desperation mixing with the confusion and horror in his eyes. "Please, don't—"

"No more talking!" I thrust the steel blade at him, resting its razor-sharp edge on his forehead, watching a pinprick wound drip down his face like a solitary tear. "On the balcony, now!"

"What do you want?"

I grabbed him by the collar with my free hand, dragged him toward me, and then pressed the blade tight against his throat. "Let's not start that again, eh?"

I shoved him away, he staggered, stumbled, and then righted himself, edging closer to the balcony. The sliding door was already open, the cool air wafting inside. A bong rested on a stool next to the open door, smoke billowing out of the top. There was a bag of weed next to it, a scattering of blue pills around it, and a small baggie filled with white powder. He'd been throwing a party, although he seemed to be the only guest. The apartment stank of solitude. It reeked of a day lost in the abyss of intoxication—smoke, alcohol, stale food, body odor.

In the distance, a bonfire raged, the scent of burning wood polluting the air, filtering into the apartment, and conquering some of those unclean smells.

He turned to look at me—his face a picture of horror, tears in his eyes. "What's this about?" he asked. "I didn't do anything to you. I tried to—"

"—Shut up and keep walking."

"Do you want to make me look like a fool, is that it?"

"Do. As. I. Say."

He swallowed thickly, nodded, and then edged toward the balcony. His gown billowed as he stepped outside, exposing pale, hairy, and surprisingly thin legs. He picked up the bong, turned slowly toward me, and held it out as a peace offering. "Why don't we just sit, chill, and enjoy a smoke?"

I laughed and he joined me, seemingly clinging to the hope that this was still some kind of joke or drug-fueled dream.

For a moment, the horror faded. His tear-filled eyes almost sparkled in the light. His face creased with a hopeful smile.

"Why don't you shut the fuck up and do as I say?" I ventured.

"Please, don't—"

"Turn around."

"Please—"

"Turn. Around."

"I don't want to."

He regarded me for a moment. A cursory glance. Up and down. I could see he was weighing up his options, deciding if he could take me, charge me, knock me down, and escape.

I stepped closer and gestured with the knife to call his bluff. That was enough to convince him. He slowly turned around, his exposed legs trembling, his voice shaking.

"Climb onto the balcony," I told him, the knife still ready to attack.

"Don't make me do this."

"You have two options: You either take one step forward, or you get a machete in the back of your skull. Your choice."

He was whimpering desperately, but he did as I said. He climbed onto the railing, only the lip of the steel structure protecting him from the edge and the drop. He leaned forward to look down and then sharply pulled back.

"Come on now," he said, his voice shaking. "I'll give you anything. Drugs, money. I have a hooker coming later if you're into that sort of thing." He faced me and forced a smile, but it retreated from his face when it wasn't reciprocated. "Just please, stop this."

"Did I tell you to turn around?"

He turned back to the edge and the sheer drop below, his short, sharp exhales leaving a thick, smokelike vapor in the air.

"Please," he muttered again. Shaking his head, fighting a fear that strangled his words. "Please, please, please, I—"

He turned to me again, expecting to see me staring right back, a grin on my face. But I was right behind him, my hands free. "What are you doing?"

"I changed my mind," I said. "I don't want to kill you after all."

"Oh, thank God—"

"It'll be much easier if you kill yourself."

I shoved him and he toppled over the edge. His arms swung madly, his hands grasped desperately, reaching for solid ground, stability. But he was too slow, too weak, too inebriated to make that connection. He disappeared into the darkness. Moments later, I heard the barely audible but unmistakable thud of his body hitting the concrete entrance several stories below.

I waited, listened, expected—hoped. There were no further sounds. No panic, no screams, no shouts or cries.

He died as he had lived—unnoticed by everyone around him.

A few hours after I left the building, the human detritus of his scattered corpse would be discovered by a neighbor returning home from the pub. It would be dismissed as a prank at first, a mangled mannequin left by mischievous kids. Eventually, they would realize they were looking at the remains of their reclusive neighbor. The police would chalk it up to suicide following a drug-fueled depressive binge. Everything that the forty-four-year-old loser had spent his life acquiring, from his ornamental samurai swords to his pages of crappy poetry, would be discarded, pilfered, junked, or forgotten about.

He'd always wanted to make a big impact on the world, and in a way, he'd done just that.

Part 1

1

She stared at her reflection in the window and cursed every inch of it. A clear night, the weatherman had said. Sweltering sunshine all day—a nice, calm, cool breeze throughout the night. It sounded perfect, but he was talking out of his ass.

She'd had her hair done for the occasion. She hadn't devoted this much time and effort to her appearance in years. "You look like a princess, dear," her grandmother had said when she left the house, choosing to walk the short distance to the restaurant.

A princess, she thought to herself, remembering her grandmother's words and the smile she wore when she said them. Fifteen minutes ago, maybe. But fifteen minutes ago, it had been dry. Fifteen minutes ago, the weatherman was probably looking pretty fucking smug. Then the rain started.

She wasn't a princess anymore. She looked like she'd just stepped out of the 1980s and was on her way to a Poison concert.

She growled at the face staring back at her and cursed once more, this time at her luck. Her first blind date ever, her first date in *two years*. The last man she'd been with had tried to change her. He was a geek, an introvert with extroverted tendencies, a man who was one step away from being both an agoraphobic and a psychopath. Their relationship had been short-lived, three weeks of misery, self-loathing, and constantly hoping that she would discover some kind of redeemable feature.

The straw that broke the camel's back came in the form of a double bun and bronze bikini—he had insisted she dress up as Princess Leia, telling her he couldn't get off any other way.

What a charming bastard he was.

That's never happening again, she thought to herself, hoping that her new date would have a fetish for Chewbacca, thus saving both hers and the weatherman's blushes.

She allowed herself a laugh at that. Only then did she see the people on the other side of the glass. Only then did her mind seemingly register that for the last minute or two—when she had been so engrossed in her unintentional perm, laughing, cursing, and doing everything except making faces—a handful of diners had been watching her.

One of those diners seemed more interested than the others, staring intently, hopefully, hesitantly. When he realized she was looking at him and no longer at herself, he turned away.

Abi straightened up, wiped the drizzle off her face, and shook it out of her hair. Then she did her best to smile at him and wave at him. Because although she had no idea what her date looked like, she knew that was him.

That was just how her evening was going. Just how her *life* was going.

Abi kept her head down as she entered the restaurant. She was greeted by a waiter who wore a three-piece suit, with barely a crease out of place. He looked young, fresh. But she knew that by the end of the night that waistcoat would be twisted halfway round his back, that shirt would be soaked with sweat, and he'd be itching to rip everything off and jump into a nice hot bath or a nice cold whiskey.

"Table for one, Madam?"

That was rather presumptuous of him. She thought about asking him whether she looked like a sad, lonely woman who didn't have friends, wasn't married, and enjoyed eating alone on Friday night. But she had just been staring at her reflection and she knew that, minus a few cat hairs, she looked *exactly* like that woman.

"I'm meeting someone," she said. She was proud of that and waited for what she perceived as a smug expression to change. It didn't.

"Are they here now?" He gestured around the restaurant, and she mirrored his actions, though she had no idea why. The man who had been staring at her was now pretending not to look. He was using a napkin to polish a knife, a determined expression on his face as he tried, and failed, to look nonchalant.

"His name is Robert Marlow."

The waiter's eyes scoured a book in front of him, hidden from view by the lip of the wooden desk. "Ah yes, here he is."

The host shifted from one grin to another. Each as disingenuous as the last. "If you'd like to come with me, I'll show you to your table."

He took her straight to the table, where he instructed her to sit, gave her a menu, and then departed. The man who—until a few moments ago—had probably thought she was a well-dressed vagrant smiled and greeted her.

"Nice to meet you. I'm Robert. Although you probably knew that already."

Her cheeks flushed with embarrassment as she tried her best to return his smile.

"Of course. And I'm Abi, although you probably knew that as well."

Abi figured that he also knew she was a little crazy and maybe a little desperate. He'd been staring at her when she had stood outside, no doubt wondering who this crazy woman was, why she was grimacing, and why it looked like she'd been Tasered.

As she sat down and returned his unblinking smile, she knew that she should have stayed home. She had a bad feeling about this one.

If experience had taught her anything, it's that dating just wasn't for her, and blind dating was just asking for trouble.

2

Robert was nice, if a little strange. He worked his way through a repertoire of small talk for the first ten minutes, speaking quickly, barely giving Abi time to answer, and moving to a new conversation as soon as the old one finished. She struggled to keep up. When the waiter came to take their orders, they had been discussing a popular crime drama, but as soon as the waiter headed for the kitchen, Robert jumped into a conversation about literature.

He was trying to impress and desperate to make an impact. He had clearly thought long and hard about how to do that. By the time the main course arrived, he had settled on a single conversation, but it was one that nearly sent Abi to sleep. Apparently, he worked in IT—she still wasn't quite sure what he did and couldn't recall if he'd told her among all the waffling—and had recently moved to the area because of a new job. He said he had spent weeks commuting, before living out of a hotel and then finally deciding to rent a house nearby. It seemed interesting to him, and if those facts hadn't been lost in a mess of awkward conversation, questions, and hesitant silences, she might have found it interesting as well.

Abi thought him to be modestly attractive, and she wasn't deterred by the nervousness. It was something she had sought in previous boyfriends, because she had always associated nervousness with intelligence. Although that probably had a lot to do with her grandmother. "Only smart people get nervous, dear," the old woman often told her. "Smart people worry they're going to sound stupid. Stupid people are too busy trying to sound smart."

She swore like a docker and she could be very crude, but the old woman was incredibly wise and had a way with words.

Abi mentioned her grandmother during dinner, spoke about how the doting guardian had raised her, how she meant everything to her.

"I feel your pain," he told her. "I also lost my parents and was forced to live with a great-aunt. She was crazy but fun. Like Mary Poppins, but with less singing and more diazepam."

"I didn't tell you I lost my parents," Abi had said with feigned suspicion, arching an eyebrow as quizzically as she could and then correcting herself when she realized she probably looked like she'd had a stroke.

That had made him even more uncomfortable. He had shifted self-consciously, averted his eyes, and just when she felt like he was about to apologize for killing off her parents and pigeonholing her childhood in a single careless sentence, she jumped in and saved the day.

"I'm joking. I did lose them," she said. She briefly thought about making a joke about losing them in a supermarket and stopped herself when she realized she couldn't pull it off. She was still smiling at her intended joke when she uttered, "They died in a fire".

His gaze shot to hers, caught her smile, pondered whether it was a joke or not, and then decided it wasn't when she awkwardly turned away.

At that point, he had reached across the table, taking her hand in his.

She had been trying to eat her strawberry cheesecake at the time, so it didn't go as smoothly as he probably hoped, but it was a touching moment, nonetheless. Robert had nice eyes, and she found herself getting lost in them as he gave her a sympathetic stare. It was because of that stare and that moment that she decided not to tell him the truth: she no longer felt anything for her parents.

Maybe she was angry at them, as if it had been their fault for dying. Maybe it was because she had been young and had since had time to heal. Maybe she was just lying to herself and had bottled up the truth. Whatever the reason, the death of her parents felt like little more than a footnote in her childhood.

Abi also considered herself lucky to have been raised by her grandmother, someone she believed to be the strongest and most supportive person in the world.

Her grandmother had convinced her to go on the blind date, actually. She had pushed Abi to respond to Robert's messages on the dating app, one that encouraged users to message, chat, and even meet without profile pictures. It had been the only app she could bring herself to join. She didn't want to let her nosy neighbors know she was on a dating site. She didn't want to announce to everyone that she was single and alone, including her ex-boyfriends, schoolfriends, extended family, and neighbors. She also didn't want to be rejected for being ugly or plain. At least this way she could just pin the blame on her tagline, her geeky profile, or the attempt at humor in her replies.

Abi had been paranoid that Robert would be too weird and that she'd have another messed-up relationship on her hands. She also worried that he would be too perfect, and that she would look like a stuttering, empty-headed troll in comparison. It wasn't like she only focused on the black and white either—she worried about all the gray areas, too.

Her grandmother had been the one to calm her down, to tell her that everything would be okay; the one who insisted that Abi was beautiful and that she deserved the best.

Her grandmother would say anything to cheer her up—to justify her fears, delusions, and concerns. As a teenager, Abi had experienced a crisis after someone called her "average looking." Instead of trying to convince her otherwise, something which would have inevitably failed, her grandmother managed to convince her that average was best. Because, as she put it, "The pretty ones end up pregnant at fifteen, abused at eighteen and dead at twenty-five. The ugly ones end up bullied, ignored, and abused. The world leaves the average ones alone."

Robert had looked just as nervous as Abi felt. He didn't seem capable of maintaining eye contact for longer than a couple seconds. On one occasion, they had stared into each other's eyes in complete silence. He had seemed relaxed at first, but then he flinched, before spending the next few moments looking at everything *but* her while cycling through a slew of small talk.

"I'm so sorry," he had said more than once. "I'm not used to this." She hoped that by "this," he meant the blind date and not human contact, but she suspected otherwise.

Even in the face of all his weirdness—even with the flinching, the stammering, the sweating, and the awkward conversation—Abi felt a mild attraction toward him. She didn't exactly fancy him, and it certainly wasn't lust. If anything, it was pity. But that was more than she had felt for any man in years.

Robert remained on edge throughout the meal. There was something strange about his mannerisms, a conflict—he seemed ill at ease, with the traits of a man who was scared of his own shadow, but at the same time, there were glimpses of confidence, of assuredness. It was almost like he was convincing himself to forget his anxieties and momentarily doing just that, only to remember that it was all an act and then instantly melting into anxiety again.

He seemed drained by the time the check arrived. He offered to pay for it, and after the slightest resistance, Abi agreed. That seemed to lift his spirits, but those spirits were dampened again when he dropped his wallet twice and then laughed awkwardly when the waiter tried to engage him in small talk.

By that time, Abi was ready to call it a night, keen to escape for his sake as well as hers. Mildly attractive or not, she wasn't sure his heart could take it if she hung around any longer.

"Well, it's been good." Robert stood and offered her what seemed to be his first genuine smile of the night, one not born out of fear, nervousness, or humiliation. He was probably relieved it was over. Now he could dry out and calm down. "I'm sorry again for being so awkward. But I promise not to be that awkward next time."

Now it was her turn to flinch, and judging by his reaction, he had seen it. Robert averted his eyes and she felt terrible. He was close enough to go in for the kiss, close enough for her to smell the sweat that had soaked into his formerly white shirt.

He turned back to her, smiled again, and then, just when she was ready to turn tail and run, lest he go in for a kiss, he extended his hand. She shook it, staring into his eyes and trying to resist the urge to wipe her hand on her coat afterward.

"I'd love to see you again," she said.

That had come out of the blue, her mouth rebelling against her brain. It was pity, mercy, and a desperate need not to disappoint, but it was also stupid.

What the hell are you doing?

She felt herself deflate—she had a habit of letting pity get the better of her, even though it had never done her any favors in the past.

She had flashbacks of standing in the corner of her ex's bedroom, doing a striptease dressed as Princess Leia while he pleasured himself and she slowly reevaluated her life.

"That would be great," Robert said. Abi felt a little better when she saw the delight in his eyes. "Do you want me to give you a lift back home?"

"No," she was quick to say.

"Are you sure? I don't mind."

"No," she repeated. "I don't live far. I have booked a taxi." The excuses came thick and fast, canceling out one with the other.

"Well, if you're sure."

Abi smiled politely as he led her out of the restaurant, holding open the door for her. They stood outside, him growing more and more confident, her trying not to stand downwind of him.

"Well, thank you again for a wonderful night," he declared. "I'd love to do this again."

She was already walking away. "Of course. I have your number, so—" she shrugged, trying to maintain her smile "—I'll call you."

—

It was just past 10 p.m. The rain had stopped, the air was cold and wet. Abi loved the dark. She loved the mystery of it, the warmth of it. It was almost romantic. Some of her best memories as a child were of lying in the back of her grandmother's car as she drove through the city at night. There was something so serene and magical about it, helped by the fact that her grandmother hated being distracted when driving, so it was always quiet in the car.

On foot, with the cold air wrapping around her, the lurching, skeletal arms of the overhanging trees looking more ominous than mysterious, and the shadows appearing more threatening than cozy, Abi felt exposed.

She pulled her jacket a little tighter, held her head low, and watched her feet as she walked. She left the glow of the street—where headlights from passing cars placed her in transient spotlights, where heightened voices from drunken revelers hung in the air—and took a shortcut through a park.

She should have felt more ill at ease in the park—branches reaching out to her like the bony, elongated fingers of death, myriad evils preparing to drag her into the shadows—but even in her heightened state, even without the comfort of a car and without the innocence and invulnerability of youth, darkness was still more of a friend than light.

Thoughts of Robert entered her mind, weighing up the pros and cons. The more she thought, the less of a catch he seemed. It wasn't that she was picky, far from it. If anything, she was the opposite, always latching on to the smallest of positives, even if it meant ignoring so many negatives. The problem with Robert was that she didn't know anything about him. He was nervous and average looking, that much she did know, but the rest—his interests, his job, his taste in music—she had no idea.

She was mulling over the date, trying to decipher what he had been telling her about his job, when she heard the footsteps—a succession of heavy thuds. All images of the date dissolved—dissipating into a cold, dark reality—and her mind instantly jumped to the worst-case scenario. Someone was chasing her.

The sound of the footfalls seemed to be getting louder and louder, increasing in volume and speed. The noises syncopated with the sound of her heels clinking against the pavement, but then she stopped. It was almost as if she wanted to hear them better, to convince herself that no one was running after her, that she was hearing things.

She should have known better, because she wasn't hearing things. And now she was directly in their path, a short sprint and a short lunge away.

Abi could almost feel them grasping at her jacket, pulling back on her hair. The image of being pulled into the shadows and assaulted filled her head as the staccato beats of heavy feet continued behind her. Still growing in volume. Louder and louder.

She must have only been standing for a second or two, but it felt like an eternity. It felt like she had waited *too* long. The little girl in her, the one that had enjoyed those long nighttime drives, wanted to dive into the shadows, to curl into a ball and wait for this moment to pass. The woman in her knew that wouldn't work, and it was the woman who acted.

Abi kicked off her heels and ran, her bare feet slapping the cold pavement, her handbag swinging wildly by her side as she sprinted down the dimly lit path. The street, and all of the life and support it contained, was now half a mile ahead of her; the park, vast, empty, and dark, all around her.

The sound of her own labored breathing and her own beating heart blocked out the sound of the chasing footfalls. But she knew they were there, keeping time with her beating heart, keeping her assailant one trip, fall, or stumble away from grabbing her. A stitch burned underneath her ribs—she was fit, she worked out, but she was scared out of her wits and that fear instantly eliminated all those hours of stretching, running, and lifting. The fear sucked the breath out of her lungs; the stitch stabbed at her mercilessly.

She powered through.

The skin on her feet was soft, supple. Every step shook her, every stone went through her. Several times her wayward running took her off the path and into the wet grass and mud that bordered it. She slipped, her stomach sinking as she felt herself stumbling, but she righted herself before she fell.

She felt like she was going to pass out, like she couldn't run anymore, but she didn't want to think about the alternative, so she continued, pushing until she couldn't push anymore, until the anxiety, the fear, and the sudden burst of exercise had caused her lungs to tighten, her throat to burn, and her heart to feel like it was going to burst out of her chest.

Her legs burned as much as her throat and her chest, forcing her to slow down. She grasped for her phone, hoping she would at least be able to punch in the number of the emergency services. That way, if the struggle was long, they might appear just in time to save her life; if it was short, at least they would catch her killer.

But she couldn't find her phone. It wasn't in her pocket where she usually kept it, and she didn't want to stop and search through her handbag. That was the final nail in her coffin. It wasn't going to be her night—it never was.

There was nothing she could do, so she stopped still—better to face her attacker head-on than to let him catch her from behind and take her unawares.

Abi spun around.

3

Abi watched the vapor of her thick, foggy breath as it bellowed out and dissipated like steam from a runaway train. The straps of her handbag pressed into the flesh on her palms as she gripped tight and prepared to swing. It contained all her life, from her makeup to her wallet and to everything else she cared about. It was a mess, but it was heavy enough to do some serious damage.

And right now, it was all she had.

Abi watched as her would-be attacker appeared out of the shadows, stepping into the fog of her heavy breath. He had slowed, knowing the chase was at an end. Abi prepared to scream, to fight to her last breath. Then she saw her attacker's face and quickly began to regret running away.

It was Robert. And he looked even more nervous and sweaty than he had before.

He just stared at her, and she stared right back. He was the last person she had expected to see, and although she knew she should have been relieved, the more she stared and the more awkward it became, the more she wished he had been a violent mugger after all.

"Robert?" she said eventually. "What—" Only then did she see that he was holding her phone in one hand and her shoes in the other.

Her phone wasn't in her handbag after all. She must have left it in the restaurant, and he was returning it, along with the shoes she had left in her wake.

It all clicked into place and she felt embarrassed for running away. She also felt a spark of anger at him for running after her when she was alone in a park at night. What was she supposed to think?

"Oh, thank—thank you." She calmly took her phone and the shoes, holding his stare as she did so. "You're so kind." That's what she said, and judging by the smile on his face, she knew that's what he believed. But that's not what she thought. The words going through her head contained a little more disbelief and a lot more cursing.

But as quickly as those words formed, they began to fade. She reasoned with herself. Partly because she wanted to, partly because at that moment he looked like a small child begging for love. Robert had somewhat beady eyes that always seemed to be downcast, but at that moment, they looked like the eyes of a submissive puppy, and they seemed to be growing wider and wider as she stared into them. He looked a little unsure of himself, no doubt sensing her fear and pondering the ridiculousness of what had just happened.

"I'm sorry about that," he said. "I just—I saw you run, and I just wanted to give you your phone and make sure you were safe."

By chasing me through a park at midnight?

"I understand," she lied.

"I tried shouting to you but—" he shrugged. "You mustn't have heard."

Maybe I was too busy shitting myself and waiting for death.

"And then the shoes . . ." he continued, trailing off, his eyes lowered, avoiding the panic-stricken elephant in the room.

She grimaced as another flare of anger rose in her and then quickly subsided, this time overridden by pity.

"Do you want me to accompany you home?" he asked.

"No, it's—"

"I have the car just at the entrance," he interjected. "I'm actually going this way; we can just walk back and—"

"No. The taxi driver is waiting for me around the corner," Abi said. It was the first thing that came to mind, and she blurted it out. She wanted to avoid getting into a car with him, she wanted to get away from him. And just in case he was planning to rape her, mug her, or kill her, she also wanted to let him know that now probably wasn't a good time.

Robert seemed confused, and she couldn't blame him.

"He said he couldn't meet me outside the restaurant," she added, deciding to run with the lie. "You know what taxi drivers are like."

Robert nodded, an instinctive reaction that accompanied a smile. "So, goodnight then?"

Abi nodded. "Yes. It was great seeing you again." She scrunched up her face. "I mean, because that's the second time I said that, not because we just saw each other again." She smiled. "Even though we did."

He moved in for a kiss, Abi reached out and shook his hand. Squeezing a little more firmly than intended.

It's a good thing he's weird, Abi thought to herself. *Otherwise, I'd feel like an idiot right now.*

Robert turned and left and Abi watched him go. When he had disappeared out of view, into the darkness, she looked down at her feet and then at her phone. She slowly shook her head, not sure whether she should be angry at herself or at Robert.

She dropped her phone into her pocket, slipped on her shoes, and continued on her journey home, walking at a brisk pace in case Robert changed his mind and decided to walk her to her nonexistent taxi.

HER

I could have watched Her all night. There was something about Her—unique, extraordinary, and yet so painfully normal. Her face was plain, uninteresting; yet, when she smiled, her features filled with life, a portrait of thin red lips, soft dimpled cheeks, and bright green eyes. She moved to an anxious, staccato beat, wary of her movements, her pale legs moving with greater haste every time she crossed a halo of streetlight.

It was as if she knew she was being watched; as if she could sense my eyes upon her and knew what I had planned for her.

A rustle in the trees caught Her attention, Her eyes flickering to the source of the sound, Her hand hovering over a small clutch bag, ready to use it as a weapon should she need to. She stuttered, almost skipped, and then continued onward, happy to be clear of the rustling trees, Her subconscious mind warning her of what might lay beneath, even as Her conscious mind registered the sudden gust of wind.

In the unforgiving light of day, she would have been on her phone, lost in whatever distraction she could find, eager to avoid the telling stares of passersby. The device, with its tacky pink case and twee stickers, was her crutch, Her ticket out of the real world and into Her own, the same world she occupied every night when she cuddled up on the sofa with a bottle of wine, a bag of chips, and a cheesy rom-com.

During the day, that phone was the only thing that kept the real world at bay, an escape from something she didn't want to be a part of. In the dead of night, however, it was an unnecessary and potentially dangerous distraction.

She was shy and introverted, scared and vulnerable, but she wasn't stupid. She knew that every small-town horror story began with a young woman walking through the park at night. Quiet parks, though serene, were exposed—a breeding ground for every sadistic, ill-intentioned psychopath. People who preyed upon the lonely, took advantage of the vulnerable, and relied upon distractions and careless disregard for personal safety.

People like me.

During the day, I also faded into the background, out of sight, out of mind, out of suspicion. Social media wasn't my crutch, but it certainly came in handy. You can tell a lot by a person's demeanor, by how tightly they hold their clutch bag as they walk along a deserted park, by how nervously their eyes flicker as they hear a strange sound. Her pale legs suggested that she didn't get out much; her arched back, strong shoulders, and flabby buttocks suggested that while she was fit and strong, she spent a lot of her time sitting and got her exercise in short, intense bursts, probably from home workouts; the state of Her frayed hair and smudged makeup suggested she had been eager at the start of the night but had lost interest a few hours in.

But nothing about the way she looked, from Her intense green eyes to Her thick dark hair and pale legs, could tell me where she worked, what Her name was, who Her friends were, and what Her hobbies were.

Small-town girls have small-town mentalities, hiding their faces, their names, their hobbies, their truth.

Small towns are breeding grounds for depravity—hotspots of degeneracy. In the big cities, this sickness is out in the open and can be found on every corner, from the sex workers forced to sell their bodies by callous, drug-addled pimps, to drug dealers hawking oblivion to the lowest bidders. In small towns, it hides behind closed doors, lurks in the shadows. It's gossip, it's hearsay, it's speculation, but it's hidden.

Social media brings these worlds together. It gives the gossips a platform, a false sense of security—a blinkered, insular, virtual water cooler where they can talk in private while the rest of the world is listening. Thanks to her small-town existence, I knew nothing about her. Because of social media, I had learned everything I could ever need to know.

But this wasn't going to be the night. At least, not for Her.

4

"How was your date last night?"

Abi could have sworn her grandmother was fast asleep. The pensioner had probably been sleeping only seconds before, dreaming about cross-stitching, Robert Redford, and whatever else septuagenarians dreamt about. But as soon as she heard Abi's bedroom door click open and the kettle switch on, she was out of the covers like a sprinter from the blocks, propelled into the kitchen on curiosity alone.

"It was lovely," Abi lied, watching her grandmother shuffle her way into the kitchen and lower herself into a rickety chair. "He was sweet."

"Sweet? This isn't preschool, dear. You're thirty-four. You want handsome, adventurous, dangerous—"

"Like Granddad?" Abi asked, placing a pot of coffee on the table. "*He* wasn't dangerous."

"You clearly never saw him cook, dear." She coughed loudly and cleared her throat. "Your granddad was a fucking liability. Granted, that's not the sort of dangerous you want, but I'll take it over *sweet* any day."

Abi rolled her eyes. Her grandmother was crass at the best of times, but she peaked in the morning, before the caffeine, pain pills, and blood pressure meds worked their magic.

"Ah, come on, he can't have been that bad."

"Did he ever cook for you?"

"No."

"And you're still alive. Those things are not mutually exclusive, dear. Your Granddad could have burned a salad." She took a cautious sip from a cup of scolding black coffee, cleared her throat, and then met Abi with a questioning stare, her gray eyes boring through her.

"Anyway, you're changing the subject," she said. "Tell me more about this fella."

Abi shrugged. "I don't know what to say."

"Was he handsome?"

"He was okay, I suppose, nothing special."

"Was he funny?"

"He had a sense of humor, but he was very nervous. Sweated a lot."

"Sounds like quite a catch."

Abi couldn't help but smile. "He wasn't that bad. Just a little weird, is all."

"Weird can be good."

"Maybe. But . . . I don't know. I got the sense that there was something going on underneath all that sweat and anxiety. Couldn't tell if he was sizing me up, pitying me, looking for an escape, or . . ." Abi finished with a shrug.

"Or thinking about how your skin would look on his lampshade?"

Abi smiled.

"Are you going to see him again?"

Abi shrugged. "Maybe."

"Maybe, dear? First you tell me he's a weird, sweaty idiot; next, you tell me 'maybe'?" She took a noisy slurp of her coffee. "You're a strange one, Abi Ansell. I'm all for getting you laid and clearing those vaginal cobwebs—"

"Jesus Christ, Grandma."

"—but this guy sounds like a serial killer in the making. Get rid before your nipples end up in a jar on his mantelpiece."

"That's unfair," Abi said, trying to hide her amusement. "He wasn't that bad." She looked away from her grandmother as she spoke, unable to make eye-contact as she blatantly lied to her. The truth is, she never wanted to see Robert again. And not just because they had no chemistry and she didn't fancy him—their date had ended in such a humiliating fashion, she'd be happy to discover he'd just slipped off the face of the planet and she never had to think about that moment again.

"What was his name again, dear?"

"Robert, something," Abi said, returning her eyes to her grandmother's accusing stare. "I forget his surname."

His full name was Robert Marlow. Abi knew that, but she didn't want her grandmother to know it. Partly because it suggested she knew a lot about him, mainly because she didn't want her grandmother stalking him. The nosy pensioner had a habit of following Abi's unsuccessful flings on Facebook and Twitter, mocking them every time they posted a shirtless selfie or made a typo.

The Martha Ansell Twitter account had become somewhat notorious in the local area. Nasty Gran—the old-lady equivalent of Angry Grandpa, but with an acerbic sadism that convinced her fans she was at least twenty years younger. She didn't use her real surname or give any hints as to her real location, and her profile picture was a particularly unflattering image of Margaret Thatcher, but it still concerned Abi.

Every day, the account received a deluge of direct messages, and every week Martha became embroiled in a bitter battle of words with a succession of trolls. One of her biggest adversaries, a man who called himself TheMarvelBuddha, regularly sent her tirades of vile insults, to which she replied with her own equally vile and equally obscene insults. Their exchanges had become legendary in the local area and grew more abusive and more personal with every message.

"And how did the date end? Did you kiss him?" asked Martha, Twitter's favorite sadist.

"Not really."

"What do you mean, *not really*?"

"Well, I mean, I think he tried to kiss me, but I didn't want to, on account of the sweat. So . . ." she shrugged, drank a sip of coffee, and then looked at her grandmother over the rim of the cup. "We shook hands and he chased me through the park."

Abi's remark was met with bemused silence, punctuated only by the slurping sounds Martha made when she sipped her coffee. Her grandmother had a way of knowing everything, as if she could see right through her, but this one stumped her, and Abi found herself enjoying the rare look of bemusement on her weathered face.

Before Martha could reply, Abi stood and checked the time on her phone. "I have to get to work. I have a few deadlines to meet. Any plans for today?"

"As it happens, I have a date," Martha said proudly, sitting up straight.

"Really?"

"Don't sound so shocked, dear, there's life in these old bones yet. I can still get down with the young folk. And I mean that in more ways than one," she winked, an exaggerated movement that reminded Abi of a stroke poster she passed on her way to the post office. "Seventy is the new fifty, don't you know." She rose to her feet, still looking smug with herself as her granddaughter looked on, shocked and appalled. "And close your mouth, dear, it's unbecoming."

Abi began her day with a workout. She wasn't one of those people who enjoyed working out and somehow got a kick out of it. If it weren't for her job and the fact she spent all day hunched over a laptop, she wouldn't do it. But it was the only thing keeping her active, fit, in-shape and, possibly, alive.

She stretched, jogged on a treadmill for twenty minutes, did some ab exercises, and then lifted weights—biceps and back today, shoulders and chest tomorrow, legs the day after. After an hour and a half in her home gym, tucked away in a bedroom that would have been a guest room if she had any friends, she ate a protein bar, took a quick shower, and then got to work.

The relaxation she felt after a workout was one of the only things she enjoyed. It also made those first few hours of work more bearable and made her feel less guilty when she tucked into a carb-heavy midafternoon meal.

Her workday always began with a check of her emails. She deleted the ones trying to sell her illegal medications and weight-loss supplements, followed by the emails from Nigerian princes. She unsubscribed to emails from a marketing company for what must have been the fourth day in a row, skimmed over a delivery confirmation from UPS, and eventually whittled the forty-three messages down to nine.

In the past, this is when her work would have begun in earnest, but among the emails from clients—some happy, some demanding—three messages quickened her heartbeat; three messages she could barely bring herself to open.

Work stress wasn't an issue. Demands, deadlines, requests for edits, payment problems; it was all par for the course. But anything involving her personal life—anything to do with relationships and even friendships—put her on edge.

Abi was fourteen when she got her first boyfriend. It was a time of confusion, chaos, uncertainty—she saw him as something different in her monotonous life, someone who could change things for the better, but in the end, he made things worse.

Matthew Graves was eighteen, handsome, ambitious, and charming. He had aspirations of being a rock star and he promised her the world. Abi would be his "star groupie," as he put it, and she would follow him all over the world as he strutted his stuff on the biggest stages.

Matthew performed his first-ever gig in a local club as Abi watched in awe from backstage. He finished the gig on a high, convinced that his band was going to be the next big thing just because a few dozen locals clapped them offstage. He left her the next morning, telling her that he "couldn't be contained" and simply wasn't a "one-woman man," believing that there would be a procession of beautiful women following him around every night.

Matthew was a poorly educated imbecile with delusions of grandeur—a far cry from the rock stars he idolized and the person he dreamed of becoming. Or, as Martha succinctly put it several years later when his dream ended and he wound up stacking shelves at Asda, "Did he forget he was the bassist? No one wants to fuck the bassist."

Abi didn't want to admit she had been naive in falling for a chauvinist pig with the aspirations of Axl Rose and the face of Freddy Krueger; she didn't want people to think he was the reason her life seemed to stagnate.

Abi reluctantly dragged the mouse cursor away from the emails that made her both excited and anxious. She checked her client emails instead and spent the next few minutes confirming some details regarding a job in New York, before sending payment details to a client in Dubai.

"Why so anxious?" she said aloud to herself. "You open a hundred emails a day. You can do this." Abi took a deep breath, hovered over the emails once more, and then quickly ignored them, choosing instead to communicate with a client in Sweden.

The only thing Abi had ever truly enjoyed was writing, so she spent the previous decade writing short stories, poems, and essays—doing everything she could to improve her craft and give herself a way to vent. After years of keeping her work to herself—scribbles on notebooks, documents saved on USB drives—she'd finally gotten a chance to turn her hobby into a career. She got a job writing for a regional newspaper, leaving reviews for restaurants, hotels, and shops. Everything was written under a pen name, and she enjoyed the feeling of being someone other than herself, of being able to say what she wanted without feeling that deep pang of guilt and shame that seemed to follow her around.

One job led to another, and another, and another. Every day, when Abi opened her computer, checked her emails, and began work writing copy for whatever magazine, newspaper, or advertising company was paying her bills that week, she remembered that decision and those years of hard, isolated work. She hated Matthew, she despised his band, and she also hated herself for letting him get to her, but at least she'd gotten a career out of it, at least she was more successful than he was.

Abi finally plucked up the courage to open the email that had been staring her in the face all day. With her heart dancing to the same beat as the previous night, when her sweaty admirer had chased her through the park, she clicked the first email titled, **"TrueConnexions: New Message."**

5

The first email was from Robert. As soon as Abi saw the name, her heart stopped fluttering and immediately dropped to the pit of her stomach. It had been sent the previous night:

Hey Abi. Robert here. I just wanted to say that I had a great time tonight and hope you did too. Maybe we can do it again sometime? xxxx

Onto the next email, her nerves and her expectation returning, her heart rate increasing.

Hey Abi, me again . . .

You've got to be kidding me, she thought to herself.

The message had been sent two hours after the first one and was also several sentences longer. The same man who hadn't asked Abi any questions relating to her hobbies and didn't even know what she did for a living, droned into a monologue declaring how he couldn't sleep because he was thinking about how great she was and how perfect they were for each other.

Abi skimmed through the message and then moved on to the next one. She wasn't anxious anymore; she didn't feel a twinge of anticipation. She was annoyed. Five minutes earlier, she thought she'd been contacted by three new potential suitors, three men who found her succinct and anxiously written profile to be endearing, three men who thought she was interesting and wanted to arrange a date with her.

Instead, she was on the receiving end of a tirade of awkwardness from a perspiring pervert with the social skills of a toddler.

"Let me guess," she said, cursing under her breath as she moved on to the next email. "I wonder who this could be from—" she opened the email "—and there we have it."

Hey Abi, it's Robert again. During my outpouring of adoration last night, I forgot to ask you on a date. I have a busy week, but maybe we could do something on the weekend?
Robert xxxx

Abi quickly closed her emails and turned her attention to her tasks for the day, all while hoping that Robert would treat her silence as a sign that she wasn't interested. The last thing she wanted to do was write an email spelling it out to him. She would rather agree to go on a second date than subject herself to something so awkward.

An hour later, a knock at the door interrupted her rhythm, bringing her to a stop in the middle of a paragraph. Over the years, she had developed an almost automatic process when it came to writing, like a musician who closes their eyes, shuts off their mind, and lets muscle memory take over. It was the only way she could spend all day writing tedious content without throwing the computer out the window or going on a crime spree.

As she crossed the hallway leading to the front door, she walked into a wall of perfume emanating from her grandmother's room. The smell hit her lungs like a wall.

"Jesus Christ, Gran, what are you doing in there?"

"I told you, dear. I have a date. I'm getting ready."

"It stinks!"

"It's *your* perfume, dear. I can't help it if you have terrible taste."

Abi began to respond but quickly decided against it, choosing instead to open the door and let some of the smell out.

A rotund UPS driver stood on the other side, waiting for her with a fake smile.

"Delivery for—" he paused to check his tablet, "Mrs. Abi Ansell?"

"Ms.," Abi said, taking the tablet.

He smiled apologetically as she hurriedly signed the screen.

"Quite a big house you got here. Nice area too," he said, looking around and gesturing to the many houses that lined either side of the cul-de-sac. "Nice neighbors."

Abi shrugged. "It's quiet, that's all that matters."

"You're right about that. *Ms.*" He tapped the brim of his cap, nodded politely, and then left, leaving her with a genuine smile that was much warmer and more handsome than the one he wore when she'd opened the door. Abi found herself watching as he left, allowing her mind to run away from her, but as he made it back to his truck and disappeared inside, she was met with a sight that dragged her right back to reality.

It was Robert. And he was staring straight at her.

6

Abi was motionless as Robert approached. He wore the same awkward smirk from the night before—the same one she had seen through the glare of the streetlight after he had chased her through the park.

He was only a few feet away, but every step brought an avalanche of panicked thoughts.

Has he tracked me down?

How did he get my address?

What does he want from me?

Is he here to kill me?

Those thoughts disappeared almost as quickly as they came, replaced by self-doubt and pity:

Did I inadvertently tell him my address?

Is this my fault—did I lead him on?

Does he think he can move in with me? Is this how dating works now? One date, one handshake, and then, bam, roommates? I mean, it's been a long time—

"Hey Abi! What are you doing here?"

Robert's question dragged her away from her chaotic thoughts. She uttered a few strangled words in reply, almost without realizing it, like her mouth had gone AWOL. He gave her a puzzled look and Abi just doubled down on her smile, hoping that would do the trick and stop him from making a dinner suit out of her skin.

"So . . . do you live here?" Robert asked.

"Here? No, no . . ." She shook her head for effect. "Why—why would you think that?"

He looked down at the large parcel in her hands and then at the door to her house.

She followed his gaze. "Oh, you mean *here*? Yeah, of course." She laughed at the absurdity of her previous statement, stopped when her throat made a strange choking sound, and then tried her best to hide it. Before she could stop herself, she began humming a random tune and then staring down the driveway, as if something had caught her eye.

Robert followed her gaze, looking from the driveway to the box and then back at Abi. He looked like he was on the verge of an embarrassment meltdown, but not if Abi beat him to it.

"So, it looks like we're neighbors now," he said after prolonged pause.

"Neighbors?" Abi said, the awkwardness replaced by shock. She took a step back, cradling the parcel under one arm and reaching for the door with the other. If he moved forward, she was prepared to swing and run.

Robert nodded and pointed to the house next door. "I just moved in this morning."

"This morning?"

"Yes. I had no idea you lived here. Isn't that uncanny?"

"Yes," Abi said slowly. "*Uncanny.*"

"I only signed the agreement last week, but I should have all my stuff in soon, and until then," he shrugged, "I guess I'll have to rough it." He laughed. Abi didn't reciprocate. "I know where to come if I need a cup of sugar though, eh?"

"I don't eat sugar," Abi said, too quickly for her liking. It was true, but as soon as she spoke, she wished she could take it back. A few moments of awkward silence passed and then she tried to do just that. "I mean, I take my coffee with a sweetener instead. And lots of milk. But you don't need to know that. Funnily enough, my grandmother is the complete opposite. Three sugars. Black. Crazy, right?" Abi laughed and made a snorting sound, feeling the need to continue in the hope he didn't notice. "She says she likes a little sweetness to balance life's negativity and a little bitterness to remind her she's not Mother Teresa. And yet, somehow, she made it past seventy without keeling over!"

Robert looked shocked, concerned, and scared all at once. He waited for silence to descend, and when he was confident that she had nothing to say, he asked, "Your grandmother lives with you?"

Abi nodded. "She's old, needs support, you know how it is."

Robert offered a confused smile suggesting that he *didn't* know how it was. "Anyway," he said eventually, the awkwardness getting too much for him as Abi inadvertently found the escape she had desperately hoped for. "I'll leave you to it. But it was nice meeting you. Again, I mean. It was nice *seeing* you again."

Abi mumbled a reply that even she didn't understand and then ducked back inside.

"Oh, and I don't know if you've seen," he called just as she was shutting the door, "but I sent you a few messages. If you have the time, just . . . you know."

"Okay," Abi said abruptly.

She shut the door and heard his muffled salutations on the other side as she watched him through the peephole return to his house.

"Neighbors," Abi said softly. "*Neighbors.*"

She placed the parcel down on the floor just as her grandmother emerged from her bedroom, dressed to the nines, plastered in makeup and smelling like a Turkish brothel.

"Well, dear, it's time. Somewhere out there there's a gorgeous, super-fit copper waiting for me." Martha hiked up her skirt, threw her handbag over her shoulder, and winked. "And I've been a very naughty girl."

Abi shook her head. "You've got to be kidding me."

Abi spent the rest of the morning napping, her mood and her energy taking a nosedive after the promising morning had turned sour. Several hours later, she woke to find her grandmother standing over her as she lay on the couch, one hand on her hip, a grimace on her face.

"What's wrong?"

"Do you want to know what's wrong? I'll tell you what's wrong."

"Okay."

"Men are bastards. That's what's wrong."

Abi rose from the couch and stretched, hiding a smile in the crook of her arm. "Your date went well, then?"

Martha shook her head, indignation still plastered over her face. "He said I was too old. Too old! He also hinted that I was too weird."

"Hinted?"

Martha nodded. "Said I was '*bonkers,*' as '*mad as a box of frogs,*' and I quote, '*too fucking much for me.*'"

"That's more than a hint."

"He also said that I lied on my profile. A liar—me! Can you believe that?"

"And did you?"

"Maybe, but that's beside the point."

"Wait a minute, what profile?"

"The cheek of the man!" Martha continued, ignoring her granddaughter.

"Are you on a dating site?"

Martha continued, "I said to him, 'Well, it takes one to know one; your profile said you were fit and handsome.'"

"You didn't?"

"I did."

Abi groaned inwardly.

"Just wait 'til Twitter hears about this," Martha nodded assertively. If Abi knew her grandmother, and she did, she would spend the rest of the day ranting on social media and then doing everything in her power to make her date wish he'd never met her.

"Maybe you should stay clear of the internet for now," Abi said, keen to avoid the drama. "We may have bigger issues to address."

"Oh?" Martha looked very interested all of a sudden, her anger turning to curiosity. She tapped Abi on the leg, ushering her out of the way before sitting down on the sofa next to her. "What's the problem, dear, clients giving you shit?"

"No, it's Robert."

"The sweaty psycho from last night?"

"The same."

"What does he want? Has he been sending you dodgy messages? Dick pics? I've had a few of them myself, you know. You'd be surprised how eager men are to wave their junk around, and most of them really don't have anything to brag about."

"Nothing like that," Abi said. "I mean, yes, he sent me quite a few messages last night, and they were a little desperate, but nothing obscene."

"Shame. So, what's the issue?"

"He moved in next door. I saw him when I was collecting a parcel and had a . . . let's say, *awkward* conversation with him. Big coincidence, right?"

"*Creepy* coincidence. How long you been talking to him?"

"A few weeks."

"Did he seem . . . overly keen?"

Abi shook her head. "Not really, at least not until last night."

"Then he's probably fine, dear."

Abi always felt better when talking to her grandmother. She didn't always say the right things, or the most sensible things, but there was an air of confidence that always won her over. Abi also knew that whatever happened, her gran would be there to back her up and fight her battles.

"Maybe I should give him a chance," Abi pondered. "I mean, how bad can he be? Assuming he isn't a serial killer."

"He chased you through the park, mail-bombed you, and then moved in next-door, all in the space of a few hours. I'd say that was a pretty big assumption to make, dear."

"You said he was fine!" Abi protested.

"I said *probably*, dear. He could still be a raving lunatic."

Abi sighed. "If it's not the weirdos like Robert, it's the assholes like Matthew Graves. I don't have much luck, do I?"

Martha audibly gagged at the sound of that name, making her intense displeasure known. "I remember that turd," she said, looking off to her right, no doubt daydreaming about disemboweling him. "He was a real piece of work."

"Tell me about it."

"A shit stain on the Y-fronts of humanity," Martha said.

"I suppose . . ."

"A black, rotten smudge that serves only to darken everything that is pure."

"That's surprisingly poetic for—"

"A cunt of the highest proportions."

"And there we are."

"You really shit the bed with that one, dear."

"Yep."

"I don't know what you were thinking," Martha continued. "Too young, too stupid, too horny. That's the problem with teenage girls, no self-respect. They'll fuck anything in tight pants."

"So, what do I do with Robert?" Abi asked, keen to change the subject.

"You should ghost him, dear."

"What?"

"It's when you ignore someone and block them out of your life completely."

"I know what it is, Grandma, but how do *you*?"

Martha looked pretty smug with herself. "I'm still in touch. Just because I'm old doesn't mean—"

"You've been on TikTok again, haven't you?" Abi sighed and shook her head. "Anyway, I can't do that. He lives next door. If I ignore his calls, he'll show up at the door."

"Then bring someone else on the scene," Martha said. "Another man. Make it clear that you're not interested by inviting someone else around and letting him see."

"So, your answer to my problem is to get a boyfriend? The very same thing that I've been trying to do all my adult life and the very same thing that got me into this mess?" Abi laughed, a little more harshly than intended.

"Well!" Martha tried to stand quickly and dramatically but failed on both accounts. "If that's how you treat someone who tries to help," she wobbled and flinched as soon as she was upright, "then fuck you, dear."

"I'm sorry, Gran," Abi said, her frustration disappearing just as quickly as it had appeared.

"I know you are, dear," Martha said with a strained smile, looking unsteady on her feet. "Now, go get my pills, I think I just popped a hernia."

NECKBEARD

I detested everything that he stood for, everything that he was and everything that he would ever be. People can change, people can grow from nothing and become something, but those rules don't apply to everyone, and the exceptions are easy to spot. The man with the neckbeard was one such exception.

He lived alone in a two-bedroom flat; one room reserved for his mattress, plonked on the filthy, worn-thin carpet, and his clothes, hanging from every surface like tattered curtains; the other for his collection of action figures and comic books. The aptly named living room was where he spent most of his time, from watching porn on his dusty 32-inch TV, to eating takeout and frozen meals while slouched on his vomit-colored, food-stained sofa.

The kitchen was filled with all the usual suspects, including an oven and dishwasher, but the dishes piled high in the sink and only the fridge and microwave were in use. A fish tank rested on the kitchen windowsill, but the water was jet black and the sides of the tank were covered in a thick layer of grime—fit for bacteria but not for fish. The bin overflowed with takeout boxes, plastic wrap, and food, each stacked on top of the other like a disgusting game of Jenga, daring anybody to retrieve a piece and avoid the whole shit pyramid from crashing down.

Neckbeard called it "lived in," and a desperate real estate agent might agree, but to everyone else, it was uninhabitable, condemnable. He had spent his youth locked away in his mother's house, tucked away in the basement where he had been free to do what he wanted when he wanted and without consequence. He could have taken a steaming dump on his pillow, pissed on his shag carpet, and ejaculated over his posters of Megan Fox and his mother would have still cleaned it up without complaint.

"Boys will be boys," she might say if she saw the state of his apartment.

And if she wasn't dead.

In his head, he was a stud. A rock star. The man that every woman wanted to be. He was lonely not because he looked like the runt of the Mansion family and stank like he'd been fucking a bag of ferrets, but because women were "too stupid," "too blind," or just didn't know what was best for them. They were too busy running off with handsome, athletic, charming guys who, apparently, wouldn't treat them properly, wouldn't love them like they deserved to be loved, and didn't appreciate them.

Because what woman in their right mind wants to have sex with a fit, handsome man who wines and dines them in fancy restaurants, hotels, and luxury villas, when they could shag a scruffy wanker around the back of KFC after being treated to a Bargain Bucket and a rant about the perils of immigration?

The mess in Neckbeard's apartment wasn't the only reason I decided to kill him, but it played a pivotal role. It was the icing on the cake. Because as bad as his apartment, his personal hygiene, and his sense of style were, I detested his personality even more. He was an overweight, unfit, slob of a man who spent his days trolling young women on social media, calling *them* "fat cows" even though they were a quarter of his size and "sluts" just because they had more sex than him.

His chat-up technique consisted of sending them crude and long-winded messages, followed by an impromptu cybersex session. His prose could make a prostitute blush and an English major despair, but to him it was poetry, and any woman who didn't fall for it was either a prude or a lesbian. When they inevitably rejected him, his pièce de résistance was to insult them repeatedly until they blocked him.

I spent several weeks watching his activity online and studying him through the grime-covered windows in his ground-floor flat. He lived an uneventful life offline, going to work, coming home, eating, masturbating, sleeping, and repeating, with very time for friends or showers in between. Online, however, it was a different story. I struggled to contain myself as I watched him slouched on his sofa, his hand stuffed down his pants, his eyes on a small tablet screen as the TV blared indiscriminately in the background and he pestered some poor, innocent girl whose only mistake was to exist in a place he could find her. Hour after hour, day after day—his life was a perpetual cycle of monotonous misery.

"I want her young, like *very* young, okay?"

Neckbeard liked to mix things up every now and then. He didn't smoke, drink, or go to many parties, but he did have one vice, and like everything else that he did, it came at the expense of someone else.

"Tell her to dress up like a schoolgirl—yes, you heard me."

He ordered escorts like anyone else would order pizza, and he wasn't shy about asking for extras.

"How much would it cost for anal?"

And because he saw it as a paid service, he didn't feel the need to wash before the event. He didn't even change his clothes.

He left reviews for the women he slept with on escort sites, picking apart their performance and their bodies and gloating when he made them climax, refusing to believe that any of them were faking it, even though there was a good chance all of them were.

"What if I wear a condom—oh, okay. Yeah, of course, I knew that."

Everyone leaves a trail online, everyone can be tracked, but Neckbeard was easier than most. He used the same obscene username wherever he went and on everything from his social media likes, which displayed an obvious proclivity for schoolgirls in intentionally (and sometimes accidentally) suggestive poses, to his obsession for *Pokémon* and the comments he left on amateur porn videos asking for the names of unwitting victims of revenge porn.

Among all the insults, negativity, racism, sexism, and xenophobia, there were moments of weakness, moments where Neckbeard lamented on his inability to find Mrs. Right. If only he could find a woman who didn't seek physical perfection; a woman who could see his inner beauty, whatever and wherever that was.

If he knew how obsessed I had been with his online activity, how much attention I had paid to his scattered prose, his insulting comments, and his disgusting home life, he might have been flattered.

7

Abi had never been a good sleeper. She worried too much. She worried about what people thought of her, about where her life was heading. Her grandmother told her that the older you got the less you cared, but to Abi, it was the opposite.

In her childhood, she worried that her parents would die, her friends would reject her, and her favorite band would break up. In her teens, she worried that she wouldn't find a job or a boyfriend and she'd end up penniless and alone. In her twenties, it was all about finding stability. Now, in her thirties, there was very little that Abi Ansell didn't worry about.

At 3 a.m., after an hour of clock-watching and a night of worrying about her neighbor, her age, and whether she was eating enough fiber, she finally climbed out of bed and trudged to the kitchen with phone in hand. She didn't bother to turn the lights on, even when she flicked on the kettle and added a spoonful of powdered stevia into her favorite mug. It was a ritual she had performed many times. She could, and often did, do it with her eyes closed.

With a cup of steaming hot coffee in hand, Abi entered her office, again choosing to leave the lights off. She sat in her swivel chair and leaned back, phone in one hand, coffee in the other, her pale face illuminated like some miserable specter as she swiped through her social media accounts and soaked up whatever meager entertainment they provided.

Abi had accounts on all major networks but rarely used them for personal reasons. They existed either to promote herself as a freelancer or to connect with people she met in real life, as well as a few people from her past. The former she did happily and willingly, the latter was an unfortunate side effect of the former.

She had never been very popular at school. Her childhood best friend was a boy named Simon. He was weird, lonely, and they didn't have much in common, but they lived next door to one another so they were destined to be best friends. In high school, she made friends with a group of mean-spirited, under-achieving girls who never really appreciated her and constantly poked fun at her for being too quiet, too shy, too "weird."

Those same girls had tracked her down just a couple years ago. She used a pseudonym so that she couldn't easily be found, but they had managed to find her, stumbling across her profile after she posted a comment on a friend's profile they were loosely connected with.

They seemed very interested in everything that she said and did, wondering where she had been "all these years," and seemingly mistaking her teenage contempt for friendship as they invited her on journeys down memory lane. Their initial curiosity faded when they learned that Abi lived a life even less exciting than theirs; their nostalgic group chats ended when they realized they hadn't shared many notable experiences.

Their relationship now consisted of swapping occasional likes and comments, which was pretty much the same relationship that Abi had with everyone else in her life.

Abi sighed as she scanned her inactive timeline—the odd comment from a guy she'd met playing a mobile game, an enigmatic post from an old client who wanted the world to know he was angry at someone or something, but didn't want to commit to an actual name, place, or story. She turned off the screen and stood, ready to return to bed, but a light outside her office window caught her attention.

The window wrapped around the front corner of the house, providing a panoramic view of her street. The light in her next-door neighbor's yard had snapped on and had pinned someone in its fluorescent glare. He was standing in the middle of the yard, unmoving. Judging from his stiff and rigid position, Abi reasoned he hadn't seen the light or expected it to turn on.

Abi watched as the man slowly gathered himself and raised a hand to his forehead, shielding the light from his eyes to give himself a better view. He looked to his right, away from Abi and down the street, punctuated by occasional streetlights and a distant bedroom light. He then turned toward Abi and looked directly at her, just as the security light snapped off and bathed him in darkness.

NECKBEARD

Neckbeard waited impatiently for his prostitute as I waited patiently outside. It was a cool night—calm, quiet. The windows were thin, and I could hear every word from the TV inside the room as he watched a succession of YouTube videos, his impatience and appetite growing with each suggested video and skipped commercial.

Every now and then, he would open another tab to browse videos on Pornhub. He had favorited the ones he liked best and clearly knew them all intimately. They all featured young girls and they were all amateur videos, shot by the participants themselves—a young girl masturbating in a tartan skirt, a young couple enjoying a hasty romp on a park bench. He had memorized his favorite timestamps in all the videos and cycled through them with unnerving speed, getting himself prepared for the night ahead by watching the moments of climax in each of his favorite clips, no doubt picturing doing the same thing.

By the time his date arrived, he looked ready to explode and jumped at the sound of the doorbell. I had been so engrossed in his activities and the silence of the successive still-framed climax shots that it also took me by surprise, too. He stood with a noticeable bulge in his pants, made some readjustments, and then hurried to the door, ready to ruin a young girl's life.

The girl the agency sent wore a large black coat with a hood pulled over her head. She looked like the grim reaper as she stood in the doorway, her diminutive stature the only thing that gave her away. I watched through the windows as he helped her with her coat, escorted her to the bedroom, and then unceremoniously dumped her on the bed.

She seemed taken aback, the fear in her eyes evident. I wasn't an expert, but I had seen enough of these encounters on TV to understand that it usually began with a drink and some small talk, a bit of verbal foreplay to ease the tension. The escort site reviews had suggested the same thing, with many men complimenting the girls on how they made them feel at ease and took the time to be accommodating.

Neckbeard wasn't interested in any of that. He wasn't the nervous, anxious sort—he didn't see it as an awkward exchange. She was there to do a duty, to fulfill a need. To him, it was as basic as taking a shit or eating a pizza. He set an alarm on his phone to make sure he got his money's worth and unclipped his belt.

I snuck around to the front of the house, keen to avoid seeing any of the gory details and to make sure I didn't miss my opportunity. In his haste, he had left the door unlocked. The noises from the bedroom—fake moans of pleasure from her; real moans of exasperation from him—drowned out what little sound the door made as I slid inside the house and clicked it shut behind me.

In his reviews, he played the role of a stud. In between comments about how a girl's breasts "could have been bigger" or how he noticed "stretchmarks and cellulite" and would have preferred them with "a little less pubic hair," he boasted about going all night long. But I knew enough about his personality to know that he was lying. I'd also had the misfortune of watching him masturbate, both in person and via the clips he had sent to unfortunate and unsuspecting women.

I didn't have long.

My thoughts were confirmed when I heard him reach a loud climax seconds later. I slipped inside the bathroom, barely suppressing a smile when I heard the escort follow Neckbeard's vociferous climax with a meek attempt of her own. She had clearly seen the reviews and knew that if she wanted a full five-star rating, she either needed to fake it or be the embodiment of perfection.

His need for her to climax was borne not of empathy, but of a desire to be the alpha man, the macho stud who could get the job done and leave any woman quivering in delight. It was the image he portrayed online, the person he pretended to be when professing his frustrations to other sad, lonely Neckbeards.

I heard the bed creak and groan, followed by a loud exhalation and a messy throat-clearance. He had rolled off her and was now seemingly lying beside her, no doubt grinning like a simpleton while she wondered if her work was done and if she could go home for the night.

—

Neckbeard never paid for the night. He didn't even pay for the hour. He talked a good game online, but he knew his own limitations and took the shortest appointment that he could get, which was half an hour. If they had offered him five minutes, he would have accepted and used every single second of it, getting his money's worth before the poor girl even made it through the front door. But they didn't, so he reluctantly paid for the full half hour, blew his load in a few minutes, took a short nap, and then began round two.

Twenty-five minutes into the appointment, with his snoring shaking the foundations of the house like a passing bullet train, Neckbeard's alarm sounded. The snoring broke; he spluttered, coughed, cleared his throat, and then said, "You wanna go again?"

The girl, undoubtedly, did not want to go again. I had spent the previous twenty minutes in the closet, calmly planning my actions, but I could have just as easily been making myself a cup of tea in the kitchen. She wasn't going to move from her position beside him; she spent the entire time just lying there, staring at the ceiling, regretting all of her life decisions and quietly waiting for the half hour to be over. But she felt obligated to accept, her reluctance palpable as she agreed.

He subjected her to another few minutes of rushed, uncomfortable sex, after which he paid her, and she left. She was quick to get out of the house, not even taking the time to freshen up or decontaminate in the bathroom. Neckbeard followed her out, keeping pace with her hurried steps and hinting that she was going to get a good review for her efforts.

He shut the door after her, and I heard the lock followed by a sigh of satisfaction and a declaration, "That was amazing. I loved carving that cunt wide open."

Ironic, I thought. Neckbeard and I shared a common interest after all.

8

The security light clicked on again, and Abi saw that the intruder next door was still staring, his eyes seemingly boring into hers.

Abi knew that he couldn't possibly see her. The office was pitch-black, and she was standing several feet from the window. He wouldn't be able to see more than a reflection from the street, but something deep within her, the same part of her that told her to hasten her steps when walking through a dark alleyway, climbing dimly lit stairs, and sleeping in unfamiliar surroundings, suggested otherwise.

The intruder stared at the office window for what felt like several minutes. Eventually, the security light blinked out, he disappeared, and Abi felt a sense of relief. She grabbed her phone, dialed emergency services, and continued to watch, waiting for the light to detect movement and for the intruder to be visible again.

"Emergency services, how—"

"Police!" Abi hissed. "I think my neighbor's being burgled."

The light snapped on again. Abi saw that he was carrying a large sack in his right hand and heading down the side of her neighbor's house.

There was a pause on the other end of the line, followed by a click, as Abi was transferred.

"Police, can I take your name, please?"

"My name is Abi Ansell," Abi said, her heart feeling like it was going to explode out of her chest as she edged closer to the window.

"How can I help you?"

Her hands were sweaty, the phone felt abnormally hot against her ear. She switched the phone to her left hand, wiped her right hand on her nightdress, and then switched back.

"My neighbor is being burgled!" Abi said, her impatience audible. "There's a man—"

Just as she spoke, the intruder made himself visible again, stepping under the security light for a second time. He paused under the light, looked down the street—

"I think he's already been inside. Oh my God, I hope he hasn't done anything."

—and then back to Abi's office window.

"It's definitely a *he*? Can you see the man now?"

"Yes, I'm looking at him right now. He's—he's—" Abi's heart sank. She stood upright and sighed as the man turned away from her. "He's my neighbor," she finished.

"Excuse me?"

"He's my neighbor," Abi repeated. "Shit. I'm so sorry, I—I—I didn't realize."

There was a pause on the line. Abi could have sworn she heard the operator snigger. "That's okay, ma'am. So, there is no crime taking place?"

"Unless being weird at four in the morning is a crime?"

"Luckily for you, ma'am, it's not. You have a good night now."

The operator hung up, leaving Abi red-faced, shocked, and a little annoyed. The intruder in the spotlight was Robert. He seemingly hadn't realized that the house had a security spotlight, which explained his rigidity and his prolonged stare, but in the heat of the moment that hadn't occurred to her.

It was time to go to bed. The late hour and her sleep deprivation was clearly making her paranoid, but before she retired for the night, she saw the security light snap on again and saw that Robert was carrying yet another bag. She quickly retrieved her phone, opened her camera app, and zoomed in on him.

He had a black trash bag slung over his shoulder. It looked a lot heavier than the first one, his movements slow and steady, his back arched, his steps staggered. Abi also noticed that he was trying to stay out of the glare of the security light as he made his way down the side of the house, all while shooting furtive glances this way and that.

Abi slowly shook her head. "As if you couldn't get weirder," she muttered to herself.

She watched him disappear from view, watched the security light blink out again, and then waited. As she expected, he appeared again moments later, captured by the light as he moved across his yard and into the darkness beyond. There were no streetlights directly outside his house so Abi couldn't see what he was doing as he left the fluorescent glow of the spotlight. But she did hear a car door closing, the muffled click audible above the sound of blood rushing like waterfalls in her ears.

Moments later, she saw him enter the spotlight again, this time edging along its periphery. He was walking backward, hunched over, his steps staggered.

Abi edged closer to the window, keen to see what he was doing. Her attention was fully focused on her strange neighbor when she dropped her phone. The sound was deafening in the small room as the device clattered against the windowsill before resting against the window with an audible *ping*.

She froze, and so did Robert. Unable to move, no matter how much she wanted to, she was forced to watch as Robert dropped whatever he had in his hands, straightened up, and stared right at her. This time Abi was certain that he had seen her.

9

Robert stared at the office window for interminable seconds, before turning his attention to the downstairs window and then giving up entirely. He resumed what he had been doing, much to Abi's relief.

She picked up her phone, making sure she didn't so much as brush the window, and then backed away. Enough was enough. Almost at the exact moment that she had dropped her phone and potentially alerted her neighbor to her presence via what must have sounded like a knock on the window, she had seen what he had been dragging. It was a large black bag, bigger than the others. Potentially big enough to fit a human body.

Abi returned to her bedroom and spent the next half hour staring at her phone and debating whether to call the police or not. Her neighbor was lugging suspicious bags from his car into his home in the early hours of the morning. He clearly didn't want anyone to see what he was doing, which meant he was up to no good. Her early encounters with Robert also fired warning signals in her mind.

He was somewhat of a contradiction. He seemed anxious, weak, pathetic even. He was a bumbling idiot, mixed with a sweaty creep. But that seemed contrived. There was an intelligence behind his eyes, a confidence in his gait. It was like he was trying to be something he was not, trying to hide something that he *was*.

Isn't that what psychopaths and sociopaths do? Abi thought. *Is he trying to play the bumbling Hugh Grant role and failing miserably?*

The idea scared her more than the thought that he was just a weird, awkward, and possibly perverted creep.

She thought back to her phone call with the emergency services. She had made a mistake and had been made to look like a fool. They implied that she was the weird one, not him.

Abi reasoned that if she did contact the police and they did investigate, Robert would know she had phoned them. If it turned out that he wasn't doing anything illegal or that he was really good at hiding it, she would become a target. The idea of living next to one of her failed online dates was terrifying enough without having to worry about being murdered in her driveway.

She told herself that she would sleep on it, although she doubted that she would actually get any sleep.

"The police are fucking useless, dear. My sharts are more useful."

"Well, I don't know about that."

"Trust me, dear. I dated a pig for three years. He was racist, homophobic, sexist. He saw himself as the embodiment of the human race, even though he was built like a Weeble and had a tiny penis. He used to tell me that anything more than a mouthful was a waste."

"Ah, Gran. I don't need that mental image at ten in the morning."

"It was hairy too and covered in spots. It was like a fun-sized Mounds after someone had nibbled the chocolate off."

"I think I'm going to be sick."

"Imagine how I felt," Martha said, the grin on her face belying her words.

"And you dated him for three years?"

Martha shrugged. "It was the eighties. I had nothing better to do."

Abi sighed, deflated, slunk back into her chair, and shrugged her shoulders. "So, what do I do?"

"Stop worrying, that's what you should do," Martha instructed. "He was dragging some heavy bags into his house in the early hours of the morning, so what? This is the twenty-first century, dear, people lead busy lives and do crazy things at all hours of the day. He's also just moved to a new house—maybe he was just unloading some books or clothes. They could have been kinky sex toys for all you know—point is, it's probably nothing illegal. You're only having those thoughts because he was a little weird during a date and then happened to move next door."

"Happened to move next door? Big coincidence."

"Also not something that can be arranged in a few hours, and that's all he had after your date. Think about it, dear."

"Maybe you're right."

Abi had spent most of the night willing herself to sleep—counting her breaths, calming her mind. But every time she felt like she was making progress, every time her mind cleared just enough for her to ignore the rampant thoughts that clawed at her conscience, she found herself being dragged back.

Images of Robert had flashed across her mind, as if seared into her eyelids.

What was he up to?

Had he seen me?

Should I call the police?

One minute she was cursing herself for overreacting, the next she was picturing him standing over her bed, his fingers around her throat, that familiar expression of witless solicitude on his face.

Maybe she had him all wrong. Maybe he was doing something harmless, like moving more possessions into his new house after a busy day at work. He was shy and awkward, that much was obvious, so maybe he just preferred to move possessions when everyone else was asleep. He could even be an insomniac. He could have spent the night tossing and turning, before deciding to run a few errands that he had initially planned for the morning.

Or maybe he really was creepy. Maybe he was up to no good and those bags contained stolen items or body parts. Maybe, just maybe, they were the remains of the last woman who had allowed him to get too close, a woman who had seen all the warning signs but hadn't acted on them quickly enough. Maybe he was bringing her into the house to bury her under his floorboards, turn her flesh into home decor, or knit himself a fleshy tuxedo.

Abi had never been a good sleeper, and thoughts like that didn't help.

As blackness turned to gray and the silence of the night was punctuated by bird song and the distant roar of traffic, Abi gave up and reached for her phone. She had spent the rest of the morning stalking Robert online, delving deeper than she had before their first date, scouring forums, stalking his friends, Googling old usernames.

She expected to encounter deranged rants, the ramblings of an unquiet mind. What she actually found was rather plain, boring, and sparse.

It wasn't political, it wasn't dark. If there was an archetypical serial killer profile, this wasn't it. As she flicked through short, carefully considered posts declaring his love for the latest comedy films, fantasy TV shows, and video games, Abi found herself feeling guilty for suspecting that Robert could do something so horrible.

He was as dull as it was possible for a person to be. It was as if his entire online life had been constructed by an algorithm programmed to "normal" and "boring." There was nothing worrying, nothing scary, nothing exciting.

One of the posts was a meme of Dexter brandishing a knife in the House of Commons and promising to make the country great again as he glared menacingly at the members of parliament. It caused Abi to do a double take, but she knew it was harmless political satire. If you could judge a person's intentions by how much shit they posted on social media, her grandmother would be on the Most Wanted list.

There was something deeply pitiful about Robert's presence online. His profile was not of a socially active, positive, fun-loving thirtysomething, but a recently widowed seventy-something who had just discovered the internet. His Twitter account was populated by people whose sole purpose was to exchange followers and who rarely paid any attention to what any of those followers said; his Facebook friends were private, but judging by the scant activity in the comments of his posts, he had only a few friends and none of them seemed local. No one tagged him in pictures or mentioned him in posts; everything had a lonely vibe—one man's words repeatedly falling on deaf ears.

Abi gave up after an hour or so, feeling a little better about herself and a little less convinced that her neighbor was going to sneak into her bedroom and violently murder her. She eventually drifted off to sleep around seven or eight in the morning, only to be woken up two hours later by a notification on her phone.

"Are you with me, dear?"

Abi realized she had been asleep, her grandmother's words filtering to her as if through water. "Sorry?" she muttered.

"I lost you for a minute there, dear. You're slipping away like a junkie. Maybe you should go back to bed."

Abi shook her head and reached for her coffee cup, taking a long and satisfying gulp, draining what was left in the cup. "I'll be fine. I just need a walk, and some more caffeine. *Lots* more caffeine." She stood, stretched, and then paused, waiting for the stars to stop dancing in front of her eyes and her world to stop spinning.

When her vision cleared, she saw that her grandmother was glaring at her knowingly and gently shaking her head.

"What?" Abi said, half smiling.

"You need to start taking care of yourself, Abi. You don't sleep at the right time; you barely leave the house—"

"I'll be fine."

"—And God knows how long it's been since you last had sex."

"Gran!"

"God gave you a vagina for a reason, Abi, it's about time you showed him some appreciation."

Abi ignored her grandmother's comments and focused her attention on a mirror above the kitchen sink. She was a mess. But she was too tired to do anything about it. She quickly tied her hair back in a ponytail and splashed some water on her face.

"You're not going out looking like that, are you?" Martha commented as her granddaughter left the room.

Abi sighed and quickly grabbed a baseball cap and pair of sunglasses from the bedroom, hearing her gran's muffled words from the kitchen—*"your poor, poor vagina."* She checked her appearance one more time, happy that while she didn't look great, she also didn't look like herself, so it didn't matter. Even if she did, it still wouldn't matter. She could walk down the street naked but for a length of toilet paper nipped between her ass cheeks and no one would care.

Abi planted a kiss on her grandmother's head. "I'm going out for a proper cup of coffee and some fresh air, you want anything?"

"Oh," she beamed, "get me some of those flapjacks, would you? The chocolate chip ones."

"You realize they're basically all butter and sugar, right?"

"Of course, that's why they taste so good. Oh, and pick me up a Mounds."

10

Abi wrestled many fears and anxieties on a daily basis; some big, some small, most illogical. A psychologist had once told her that everyone battled with anxiety and irrational fears. "Confidence," he said, "is just a smokescreen employed by people who have learned to hide, deny, or accept their fear."

Knowing that confidence was an illusion didn't make her feel better. If anything, it made her worry more about the future of humanity. How can we hope to evolve, to grow, and to continue doing amazing things if we're all secretly worrying that we've left the oven on?

The psychologist wasn't acting in a professional context. She had bumped into him at a house party, quite literally, and he'd given her his spiel after listening to her mumble her way through an apology while trying to clean wine from his pants. If she had been an actual patient of his, instead of a random madwoman trying desperately to feign interest while she crossed her legs and internally debated the pros and cons of using a stranger's toilet, she might have pushed him further.

Some of her anxieties could be traced back to actual memories, such as the time her rabbit escaped and was run over on the road, causing her to double-lock and triple-check every pet's cage thereafter. Or the time she became momentarily trapped in a public toilet, causing her to avoid them when possible and leave the door ajar when not.

One of her oldest habits had been formed on Halloween when she was just nine years old. She'd opened the front door to find a tall grim reaper standing before her, his bony face staring back at her, his clawed hand reaching for her. It was one of the neighbor kids trick-or-treating, and she'd opened the door just as he reached for the bell, catching her unaware as she began her own Halloween adventure. In that split second, she thought she had come face-to-face with a monster. She soiled herself, screamed, slammed the door in his face, and spent the rest of the night being consoled by her grandmother.

Since that day, twenty-plus years in the future, she never left the house without checking through the peephole first. It hadn't saved her from any further Halloween incidents, but it had helped her avoid awkward conversations with neighbors and postmen.

It was one of the few irrational fears that served her well, and as she pressed her face to the peephole, she was thankful once more. No grim reapers were waiting ominously for their share of fun-sized Snickers bars, but she did see something that scared her nearly as much.

Robert was walking past her house and looking her way. Abi's heart stopped momentarily, and she felt the same way she had felt last night, knowing that he couldn't possibly see her but feeling like he was looking directly at her.

His gaze lingered in her general direction and then flickered upstairs, to the same room Abi had been in the previous night when she phoned the police. He was still staring at the office when he disappeared out of view, on his way down the street.

Abi retreated from the peephole and waited, her heart still pounding heavily.

He's just an awkward, weird neighbor, she told herself as she pressed her eyes closed and waited for the anxiety to subside. *I'm overreacting. Nothing's going on.*

But what if something is going on?

What if he really is up to something?

She took a deep breath, checked the peephole one more time, and then silently opened the door. He would have made it to the end of the street by now and would have turned a corner out of sight, but she still double-checked to be sure.

The street was empty, with no potential awkward encounters, no small talk to be dragged into, no questions she didn't want to answer. Robert was probably heading into town, which meant she would have to follow him, a prospect she wasn't entirely happy with. There was also a chance he could turn around and head back, in which case she would bump into him and be forced to endure another conversation.

Her feet were rooted, her eyes darting down the street and then to Robert's house. It was empty. Inviting. In a few steps, she would be standing in the same place Robert had stood last night; a few steps more would take her down the side of the house, into the backyard or to the front door. The house beckoned her, practically begging for her to take a peep through the windows—the curtains open, the lights off.

With her head down, she quickly scurried across the lawn to his front door. She paused, composed herself, and then knocked three times. He wasn't going to answer; she knew that much. It was an excuse in case she was being watched or Robert caught her in the act.

I just wanted to welcome you into the neighborhood, that's all.

Her heart rate increased with each passing second, but she fought through it. After the first three knocks, she edged closer to the front window and peeked through, turning her baseball cap around before pressing her hands to the side of her face to block out the sunlight.

I knocked and you didn't answer, so I panicked a little. I got it into my head that something might have happened, and I couldn't live with myself if I didn't do anything. I was just taking a peek to make sure you were okay.

The living room was empty but for a small two-seater sofa, a coffee table, and a laptop. Robert had just moved in, so she didn't expect to see a fully furnished home, but she had expected to see some boxes, bags, or other junk.

When she peeled back, she realized that her sweaty hands and face had left an impression on the window. She used the window's reflection to check behind her and at either ends of the street, keen not to turn around lest she look suspicious to any onlookers. If there had been a sight or sound of anyone else on the street, she would have retreated immediately, no doubt losing her composure at the same time, but there wasn't. It was quiet, unusually so, and that spurred her on.

A small part of her told her to stop, to give up and let things be, but a greater part of her knew that something wasn't right. She wanted answers. After pausing at the front window momentarily, standing with her hands on her hips in a theatrical look of befuddlement, she quickly walked around to the back of the house.

Our house has the same layout and I know it can be hard to hear the front door if you're in the kitchen, so I thought I would try the back, as well.

The side of Robert's house was separated from hers by a stretch of paving slabs bisected by a wooden fence. There were two gates at the front of the fence, the left leading down the side of her house and into her backyard, the right into Robert's. With a glance down the street to check that her creepy neighbor hadn't made a quick return, she opened the gate on the right and quietly closed it behind her.

—

Abi's hand, coated in a thin film of sweat, trembled uncontrollably as she reached for the patio door. Her mind raced with thoughts of what she might find, what might happen to her. The window at the back of the house looked onto the dining room, but the blinds had been closed and she saw nothing but her pale, petrified expression staring back. She had been about to leave, preparing to race down the side of the house and run to the comfort of her home, when she spotted the door.

It was unlocked, the lever stuck in the "open" position, visible through the clear glass surface of the sliding door. The same doors had been fitted on her own house. She'd spent months worrying about the flimsy mechanism, constantly checking and rechecking to make sure it was locked, going so far as to leave via the front door, walk to the back of the house, and check from the other side just to be doubly sure. At first, Martha found it funny and would play tricks on her, cheekily unlocking the doors while she was outside checking them, causing her to repeat her fastidious cycle several times. Eventually, Martha tired of the joke and paid to have new doors fitted, much to Abi's relief.

With her hand gripping the handle, Abi closed her eyes and pulled. There was no relief when she felt the door open and heard the satisfying creak as it slid across its rollers. There was no sense of adventure coursing through her veins as she stepped inside and quietly slid the door shut before her. There was no curiosity eating away at her as she moved quietly through the dining room and entered the living room. There was only fear—a growing, niggling fear that resisted every step she made and told her to flee. She fought through it.

Abi headed straight for the laptop, which sat unopened on the coffee table. Her own laptop had facial recognition software that automatically unlocked every time she opened it, but this machine was old and incapable of advanced security features. It could have been secured with a PIN, but none had been set and Abi was given instant access to the desktop. Despite being an older machine, the desktop looked brand new, clear, empty. Abi reasoned that Robert was either just as fastidious as she was, or he had recently formatted the computer.

In addition to the standard OS icons, there was a folder marked "Current." Abi opened it without hesitation and was greeted with two additional files. The first of these was a Word document fixed with a padlock symbol, suggesting it had been secured with a password. Abi didn't have time to try and guess his password, nor did she need to, because the second folder, marked "Pictures," was unlocked.

She opened the folder after several messy miss-clicks, her fingers quivering madly, her anxiety increasing with each passing second. What she saw inside made her even more anxious and even more determined.

One of the folders was alarmingly named "Victims," but it was the second that drew her attention the most.

"Abi/Martha."

She mouthed the name several times, not quite taking it in, not understanding why her name and her grandmother's name were on Robert's computer. "What the—"

With a little less eagerness and considerably more apprehension, Abi moved to click on the folder, but the laptop trackpad failed to register. Initially, she panicked, believing the computer to have crashed. After dragging her finger quickly across the screen, she realized the inaction was due to the trackpad being coated in a film of her sweat.

She wiped her hands on her jeans, used the cuff of her shirt to clean the trackpad, and then paused to steady herself, squeezing her eyes shut and taking several sharp breaths. There was no telling what she would find, but she knew now that her fears had not been unfounded, her phone call to the police had not been a moment of neurosis from an unstable woman.

"As anxious as I was," she imagined herself saying as she related her story to the police, moments after they apologized profusely for reacting the way they did, "I had never felt more alive." In actual fact, she felt like she was on the brink of death, her heart ready to explode out of her chest, her arms weak, heavy. Adrenaline raced through her body like electricity, and blood rushed so violently in her ears that she worried she wouldn't be able to hear the sound of the door if it opened.

But she did.

The sound, when it came, was just as deafening as the noise in her ears, just as shocking as the adrenaline that coursed through her body.

The front door opened onto a hallway and was just a few steps from the door leading into the living room. Abi quickly rose to her feet, her eyes moving from the living room door to the laptop and then to the sliding doors she had entered through.

The folder on the computer glared at her when her eyes met the laptop—one click from discovering what he was up to, one click from learning whether he was an obsessed lover, a crazy stalker, or an aspiring serial killer. A click from knowing if she was heading for the "Victims" folder, and if the content there chronicled his murder victims or rape victims or if it had something to do with revenge porn, snuff films, BDSM pictures, or just poorly worded sexual conquests.

The keys were pulled out of the lock; the door creaked loudly as it slowly closed.

Abi dived for the laptop. As desperately as she wanted to open the folder, she knew she didn't have time. She closed the folder, slammed the lid down, and then backtracked. That's when she heard the living room door open, stopping her dead in her tracks, rooted to the spot in the middle of the room, in direct sight of her former date and potential killer.

Abi swallowed despite the lump in her throat, stood firm despite feeling like her legs were about to buckle, and regretted every decision she had made over the last ten minutes.

11

The seconds that followed felt like hours. Abi had her back to the open door and her hands raised in submission. She expected to hear Robert's voice—for him to shout, scream, or even just swear at her. When she heard nothing, she gradually turned around.

The door was closed. Robert was nowhere to be seen.

The room filled with the sound of rushing water and the sharp pitch of a tuneless whistle. Abi relaxed, lowered her arms, and breathed a sigh of relief. Her house was built at the same time as Robert's and was all but identical except for two features. The first was the patio doors, which had been changed when Abi's paranoid obsession became too much; the second was the downstairs toilet. An elderly couple had lived in the house before Robert. After the wife fell seriously ill and could no longer climb the stairs, the husband turned the downstairs coat closet into a powder room.

Abi had never much liked her old neighbor Mr. Parker. He was a loud, bigoted creep with an annoying laugh and wandering eyes. He tried his luck with her on more than one occasion, and even got hands-on. When she rejected him, he had called her a prude, then a lesbian, and then a slut, contradicting himself with a flurry of insults that led to her leaving his house and escaping his grubby clutches.

She'd only wanted to borrow a few tea bags.

But despite everything he had said and done before his very timely passing, at that moment she was thankful for the old Nazi bastard and his amateur plumbing.

With another glance at the laptop, more in forlorn hope than anything else, Abi shuffled toward the patio door and beat a silent retreat. The patio door slid shut just as the living room door swung open and Robert made an appearance. Seconds later, as Abi pressed herself tightly to the wall and peeked through the glass doors, she saw him retreat upstairs and then return with a laptop bag. He stuffed the laptop in the bag, checked his watch, and then hurried out the front door.

Abi was relieved, but that relief quickly turned into anger, incredulity.

What's in that folder and why is it named after me?

Who or what are the "victims"?

What is he up to?

The police wouldn't help her, she knew that. Robert was up to something, and his laptop confirmed that. It was obvious, but it was also obvious that they would be even less receptive and more mocking than they had been the night before.

"He has a file named after you and your grandmother on his laptop, you say? What's in this file?"

"I don't know."

"How do you know he has it?"

"I broke into his house and used his laptop."

The idea that he could have been taking pictures of her without her consent infuriated her, as did the idea that the police would deem her concerns to be unfounded at best and neurotic at worst. What worried her most were his intentions, and what it would take for her and her grandmother to be moved into the other folder.

Unless we're already there, she thought suddenly, feeling her heart sink. *Unless his victims are women that fell victim to his stalking, his harassment.*

He could have upskirt pictures, hacked nudes, and sex videos.

He'd have a hard time getting anything like that from me.

But my gran . . .

But as scared as she was, she *had* to find out what he was doing, and with the adrenaline still coursing through her veins and giving her a high she had never felt before, she reasoned that now was the perfect time.

She decided to follow him, to see what he was doing. She looked different enough for him not to recognize her, especially if she kept her distance, and she also knew that if she didn't strike now, when her adrenaline and anger were at their peak, she might let doubt and fear get the better of her.

Abi exited the cul-de-sac that she shared with her grandmother, budding stalker, and neighbors she barely knew. It led to a busy road, flanked on this side by a row of terraced houses and on that side by a large industrial estate. The former traced a path down to the center of town and to a row of shops, pubs, and other failing businesses struggling to stay afloat in the digital age;

the latter spanned a vast chunk of open space, filled with factories, parking lots and garages, and the odd concrete-and-chalk soccer field.

Robert was visible in the far distance, heading toward the center of town. She put her head down and followed him, keeping a brisk pace to ensure she didn't lose him.

Her heart rate had slowed since her close encounter in the house, and she wasn't an anxious mess. She no longer felt like she was doing something wrong, no longer had that niggling sense of criminality in the back of her mind.

Robert turned a corner at the end of the street, and Abi seized the opportunity to increase her pace, taking fast but short strides, smiling at passersby as if to confirm that she wasn't up to anything suspicious. The town was small but dense, with a population of more than fifty thousand. In winter, the streets were empty, with the residents holed up in their homes or local watering holes, but in summer, it was a different story entirely.

"They're like ants," her gran often said. "You don't see them all year but as soon as the sun is out and you're ready to enjoy a nice picnic in the park, the fuckers are everywhere." The park was at the other end of town and would no doubt be filled to the brim with picnicking residents and tourists, all keen to soak up the sunshine. Robert was heading in that direction and Abi was hot on his heels. She didn't know what he had planned, and she certainly didn't expect him to be up to anything suspicious on a summer's afternoon in full view of the entire town, but that didn't stop her. She was drawn to him, knowing that the laptop bag he carried over his shoulder contained something that she needed to see.

A family of four turned the corner just as Abi raced toward it. They startled her and she nearly ran into them. The man, wearing a tank top and shorts—tufts of hair poking out of every crevice and a strong smell of cheap deodorant wafting from every pore—held up his arms to steady her.

"Watch yourself, love."

Flustered and breathless, Abi quickly apologized.

"It's a lovely day!" He grinned from ear to ear as he spoke, a faint whiff of beer on his breath. "It's too nice to be rushing anywhere, take it easy!"

The family brushed past her. The sun-kissed wife left her with a bright, tanned smile; her spirited children exploded into energetic conversation.

Abi didn't share her grandmother's disdain for the season and the people it attracted. She didn't consider herself a people person, but she liked the heat and the way people responded to it. Rain and cold made people miserable, angry, and petulant; sunshine brought out their cheer.

She wore a smile as large as the hairy man and his happy family, but it quickly faded when she turned the corner and realized that Robert had stopped a few feet ahead of her, ducking into the shade of a pub doorway to chat animatedly on his phone.

He sounded angry, although Abi couldn't hear what he was saying, and while she could only see his profile, she guessed that he looked angry, as well. She was about to take a step back and duck out of view when Robert stared right at her. A young couple had exited the pub, and as Robert stepped aside to let them by, his gaze fell upon her.

Abi froze, her mind racing as she prepared to talk herself out of what could be a very embarrassing situation.

Hello, imagine seeing you here!

So, what are you doing here?

Should we get a drink?

But before she surrendered to her own awkwardness and began a conversation with her wannabe murderer, Robert turned the other way and continued his phone call, his words still out of earshot. There was no recognition in his eyes, nothing to suggest he identified her underneath the hat and behind the glasses. He hadn't even given her a second glance.

You may be obsessed with me, Abi thought to herself. *You may have a bunch of creepy little photos on that machine of yours, but you're clearly not smart enough to know when I'm standing right in front of you.*

Abi pulled out her phone and rested against the wall, lest she look as odd and as out of place as she felt. She strained herself to hear what he was saying, but only caught a few stray words above the chattering noises from the pub on her left and the traffic on her right. He said no a lot and also blurted out "I'm working on it." It wasn't enough for Abi to deduce who he was speaking to or what he was speaking about, but she doubted it was relevant.

Stalkers and serial killers work alone, she told herself. *He's probably just having an argument with his boss.*

12

The searing sunshine didn't last long. A heavy rain cloud shuffled in front of the sun and cast its dark and miserable aura on what had been a bright and wonderful afternoon. The skies turned gray, the heavens opened, and the citizens of Abi's small town scarpered like the ants her grandmother believed them to be.

"The British summertime is like losing your virginity," Martha once told her. 'You get excited. You throw on your best skimpy clothes, let your hair down and prepare for a day to remember, only to end up disappointed, wet, and annoyed thirty seconds later.'

Abi recalled those lewd but accurate words as she followed Robert down the street. Her first time had been just as miserable and short-lived as her grandmother had suggested. The old woman had been told nothing about it, of course—Abi kept all the gory and depressing details to herself—but she had a way of knowing regardless. Call it intuition, call it experience, whatever it was, she could read Abi like a book.

Robert still had the phone pressed to his ear, but he was moving with a little more urgency now, his feet treading freshly fallen rain as he hurried down the street and slalomed the retreating sunseekers. Abi hurried past a man wrestling with a T-shirt in the doorway of a hairdresser's, his flabby torso seared an uncomfortable shade of pink and glistening with moist sunscreen. She sidestepped a panicked woman pushing a stroller, the laughing baby enjoying the unexpected shower and reveling in the high-speed retreat, his dimpled cheeks set into a wide grin, his bright blue eyes fixed ahead, his chubby face bobbing from side to side as if on a rollercoaster.

Robert eventually ducked into a large coffee shop, followed by two giggling teenagers, keen to get out of the rain. Abi went in after them, instantly irritated by their high-pitched chatter but glad for the distraction. She watched as Robert wiped his phone on the seat of his jeans, checked the board above the counter, and then stepped into the queue. Abi and the girls ahead followed suit.

This time she was close enough to hear what Robert was saying, but every time he spoke, the two girls ahead of her, both wearing bikini tops and low-cut denim shorts, drowned him out.

"I know what I'm doing—" she heard Robert say, followed by, "Oh my God! That was insane. Did you see that?"

"It was out of nowhere! We should totally sue the makers of that app. Sunny all day, my ass."

"Totally."

Abi groaned, and one of the two girls turned to look at her, her features set into a scowl. If she had her grandmother's bravado, she would have responded with a short, snappy remark, instantly putting the two girls down and silencing them. But Abi wasn't her grandmother. She replied with a warm smile and the girl turned away, continuing her conversation.

Abi waited for her turn in the queue, growing increasingly frustrated by the inane and high-pitched chatter of the two girls but knowing that she couldn't make a scene. Not only was she scared of confrontation, but she didn't want to draw too much attention to herself when she was just a few steps from Robert.

She told herself not to get stressed out, not to worry. Robert was in the coffee shop because he wanted to work, she reasoned. His laptop was slung over his shoulder, and he probably had very little food or drink at home. There was no furniture, either. He was there to work, she knew it, and she would watch him work and see what he was up to.

Robert finished his phone call when he reached the counter, placing his order and then dropping the phone into his pocket. He shared a laugh and a joke with the server, collected his coffee, and then sat down next to the door, brushing past Abi without so much as a glance.

The girls were next, hemming and hawing as they debated over whether to opt for hot or iced coffee, the hot and wet day seemingly confusing their usual ritual. All the while, Abi watched Robert through the mirror behind the server. He had plonked his laptop bag on the table and sat hunched over it, his coffee in one hand and his phone in the other. If he had gone there to work, he wasn't in a hurry to get started.

The more she watched him, the more she worried. There was a table next to him, and he had his back to it, making it the perfect spot for her, but it would mean sitting within a few inches of him. She would also have to walk past him to get there, and if he looked up, her face would be just a couple feet from his.

If he recognizes me now, she thought to herself, *what can I say?*

Oh yes, that was me back there at the pub and I did follow you in here, but I'm not stalking you, I swear.

He's the one that's supposed to be stalking me, she thought, her anxiety turning into temporary amusement, *and yet here I am decked out in sunglasses and a hat looking like Inspector Clouseau.*

And for what? So, I can watch him work or hear him on the phone with his boss?

She laughed softly and shook her head, suddenly realizing how crazy she had been and thinking about what her grandmother would say when she told her.

"When you're ready."

Abi snapped out of her daydream to see that the two girls ahead of her had been served and the server was now waiting impatiently for her.

"Sorry?"

"Do you want to buy something or are you just here for the view?"

"I—I—" Abi hesitated and then stepped forward, closing the gap between her and the counter, clearing her throat. "Yes, I would like something." She smiled warmly, but it wasn't reciprocated.

The server looked no older than twenty. Her long blonde hair had been tied into a ponytail, pulled so tight that it fixed her with a permanent resting bitch face. Her lips taut, her eyebrows narrowed. Her arms were folded across her chest, where a low-cut top partially covered a striped apron that bore the name "Lisa."

"Do I have to guess or are you going to tell me?" Lisa asked bitterly.

Abi felt her face getting redder and redder. It didn't take much to fluster her, but the young, impatient server was ticking all the boxes.

"There's a queue, miss," Lisa said, emphasizing the word *miss* to sound like the hiss of a venomous snake.

Abi began fumbling around in her bag, not entirely sure what she was looking for. "I—I—"

Lisa sighed and rolled her eyes. She turned to the young male server behind her, currently frothing foam for a tall latte, and shook her head, a gesture that he returned with an eyeroll. As Abi scanned the board above the counter, she saw Lisa make a point of checking her watch before looking beyond Abi's shoulder at the gathering queue. Abi turned herself to look and there were only two people there, both of whom didn't seem to care about the wait and seemed more embarrassed than angry.

There was a slyness in the young girl's eyes. She was enjoying it. Abi guessed that the story would find its way onto Instagram or TikTok by the end of the day. Abi would be transformed into a boomer or a Karen; the story told via a series of poorly spelled and massively exaggerated captions while the girl performed an irrelevant dance.

She'd flash some flesh, pout some more, and probably gain a few hundred new followers while Abi retreated to her home and proceeded to regret and overthink every aspect of the encounter.

The thought alone made her angry and embarrassed. The first caption hadn't been typed, the idea merely a hint behind Lisa's wry smile, but already Abi felt her skin flushing and her heart rate quickening.

"I'll have a coffee," Abi said eventually, composing herself just enough to avoid stumbling over her words. Lisa rolled her eyes and opened her mouth to offer another snide remark, but Abi got there before her. "Large. Black. Thank you."

The young girl turned away, barely acknowledging the order. She whispered something to the male server and they both looked at Abi before turning back to one another and sniggering like schoolchildren.

Abi had never been bullied at school. She had never fit in, as she didn't have many friends and didn't feel like she belonged, but she hadn't been targeted in any physical or emotional way. During moments like this, she often wished that she *had* been bullied, as that way she would have some experience, she would have toughened up, and she would be able to bite back instead of just standing there and waiting for the ground to swallow her up.

As she watched the young girl brew the coffee she had ordered, Abi caught sight of herself in the mirror and saw how red and flustered she looked. Moments earlier, she had been proud of herself for doing something daring, something that she would have typically avoided at all costs, but she had been brought back down to earth with a big wet slap on the face.

To make matters worse, she saw that the two young girls were now sitting where Robert had sat and he was nowhere to be seen.

"Three-fifty," Lisa said abruptly, thrusting out her hand, her beady eyes, plastered with an excessive amount of blue eyeshadow, glaring at Abi.

Abi handed the girl a five, calmly took her coffee, and then left the shop with her head held low. She didn't tell the girl to keep the change, and she certainly didn't deserve a tip, but she wanted to get out of there as soon as possible.

Outside the shop, she looked around for Robert, but he was nowhere to be seen. Laughter from inside caught her attention, and she looked through the window to see that Lisa was now serving someone else and was enjoying a laugh and a joke with them, as if she was the friendliest, sweetest person in the world.

"Bitch," Abi muttered under her breath, feeling her anger return.

13

The rain poured relentlessly from the heavens, soaking Abi from head to toe, her shirt and trousers plastered to her skin. The excitement and the adventure from earlier in the day had quickly turned to a disappointing mess. She was wet, tired, and annoyed. She was also still clueless as to what Robert was doing, but the more she thought about it, the more she doubted herself and questioned everything she had done and had allowed herself to believe.

Robert could have just been keeping track of his dates. Maybe, she thought, that was his little black book, details of his sexual conquests and failings. She imagined herself opening the file marked "Victims" and seeing a portfolio of extreme rape porn alongside some perverted checklist. Her own file was likely filled with pictures from her dating profile and downloads from her grandmother's social media account.

It was perverted. Maybe even a little sick and twisted. But it wasn't illegal. It wasn't life-threatening, and it didn't warrant wasting an entire morning pissing about in the pouring rain, dealing with stuck-up teenagers and drinking terrible coffee.

Abi had left the house that morning feeling happy, inspired almost; she had walked into town with an air of confidence. Her day-to-day generally consisted of sitting behind a desk, staring at a migraine-inducing blue screen and sending dozens of emails. She had relished the opportunity to do something different, but it had ended in abject misery.

She gripped the coffee cup tightly in her palm as she remembered the smug expression on the young barista's face. If she was anything like her gran, and at moments like that she dearly wished she were, she would have slapped the smug grin off her face and delivered soul-crushing rhetoric that would have made her the praise of the town.

If only.

Instead, Abi had been the one humiliated, she had been the one to walk away embarrassed and red-faced. She wasn't like her gran; she couldn't bite back, and she definitely couldn't fight back. A small part of her also knew that if she *had* been her gran, she wouldn't have been placed in that position. The young girl wouldn't have zeroed in on her if she thought there was a chance of her fighting back.

Abi had all but forgotten about Robert when she made it back home, barely offering a glance in the direction of his home. The rain stopped as soon as she approached her house, a crack of sunshine breaking through the concrete clouds and returning some light to the miserable day.

"Typical," Abi said, feeling the sunshine on her face as she dug around in her pocket for her keys.

"Holy shit, dear," Martha blurted as Abi walked through the front door and found her grandmother relaxing on the sofa, tablet in hand, the Twitterverse at her mercy. "You look like hell."

"Thanks."

Martha knew Abi well enough to sense when something was wrong. The irreverent septuagenarian immediately rose to meet her, leaving her callous quips for another time. Martha removed her granddaughter's hat, stroked wet strands of hair from her face, and then helped her to the sofa.

"Sit down, love," she said, taking the time to retrieve her tablet lest her granddaughter spy on her online exploits. "Let me get you a nice cup of coffee. Here, I'll take this—" She retrieved the coffee cup from Abi's palm and paused. "It's full."

"Like I said, I went to grab a cup of coffee."

"But it's black, dear. You hate black coffee. You like white coffee, remember?" she added, as if Abi had gone senile. "Very white. I've seen less milk in a cow's tit."

"Maybe it's for you."

"Maybe?"

"You like black coffee, right?"

"I also like hot coffee, dear."

Abi shrugged.

Martha regarded her granddaughter's meek reaction and left the room, taking the cold coffee with her. Moments later, she returned with a blanket, a hairdryer, and a hot cup of coffee loaded with milk and sweetener. "There you go. Get that down you and you'll warm up in no time."

"Thanks, Gran."

"Then maybe you can tell me all about it?"

Abi shrugged, immediately bringing the coffee to her face and relishing in its warmth. “There isn’t much to tell.”

“At the very least you can tell me where my fucking flapjack is.”

Abi laughed, immediately feeling a little better. She watched passively, her mind on other things, as her gran carefully helped her out of her wet clothes, peeling them off like sticky plasters and then quickly drying them with the hairdryer and a towel.

A few minutes later, she was naked but for her underwear and a towel wrapped around her head, her body temperature cooling as quickly as the drink in her hands.

“I should just go to bed,” Abi said, defeated by the day.

“It’s barely midafternoon! Sleep now and you won’t get any sleep tonight.”

“I didn’t get any sleep *last* night,” Abi reminded her grandmother. “I need to sleep at some point.”

Martha shook her head. “My mother always used to say you should never go to sleep angry, sad, or horny.”

“I’m a thirty-four-year-old woman who lives alone with her grandmother and has no friends. If I lived by that rule, I wouldn’t sleep.”

Martha brightened, her finger thrust in the air, a smile on her face.

Abi sighed. “You’ve either had a eureka moment or you’re about to ask me to pull your finger. If it’s the latter, now’s not the time.”

“Why don’t you run a nice hot bath and use those things that I bought you from that fancy shop in town? You know, the one that smells like a brothel. Bath—bath—bath salts, that’s the one.”

“Bath salts?”

“Yeah, everyone’s going crazy for them apparently. The kids love them.”

Abi suppressed a smile. Her grandmother was more experienced than most women her age when it came to the internet and social media, but she was clueless with everything else. “I think you mean bath bombs.”

“Bath bombs, bath salts—whatever. The point is, they’ll make the bathwater look like a rainbow and your ass crack smell like Christmas. That’ll cheer you up and calm you down and if you’re feeling up to it you can always—”

“—Please don’t say masturbate.”

“That wasn’t the word I was going to use, but okay.”

THE QUEEN OF INSTAGRAM

Fame goes to everyone's head. It's human nature.

We're social creatures. We crave attention and praise, from the crappy crayon drawings our parents hang proudly on the fridge, to the medals we covet and the success we desire—life is a constant battle for attention. We want to be the best sibling; the best pupil; the best employee. We want to be of the few, not the many. And when we get the attention, when that spotlight shines down upon us and bathes us in the masturbatory glow of self-satisfaction, we stop trying. We stop pandering to the needs of others because we no longer need them to get where we want to be.

Some see themselves as godlike figures, above everyone else, to be revered and respected; others shirk from the spotlight, realizing that the dream is better than the reality. In the end, they all end up the same way—their brains disconnected from reality by way of extreme narcissism, dissociation, or double-barrel shotgun blast.

The Queen of Instagram had all the hallmarks of a narcissistic diva. She saw herself as more important than others; spent her days appealing to her fanbase and her nights proclaiming her greatness to whoever would listen. In her mind, she was a superstar, the most famous person to come out of her small and insignificant town since Scott Johnson, a notorious local pervert caught with his dick in Mrs. White's Jack Russell. The deeply disturbed individual's exploits were the stuff of urban legend, even though he was very much real and very much alive.

Unlike Mrs. White's dog.

She referred to herself as the Queen of Instagram, a title she had given herself after her very first post—a blurry selfie taken in her parents' bathroom, her pouty lips and glossy skin doing little to detract from the grime-covered walls or the hair-matted soap on the sink—had attracted modest attention from local perverts.

It wasn't very regal, but it was enough to launch her mediocre career. In two years, she gained over five thousand followers, at which point she celebrated with a professional photo shoot and turned her delusions of grandeur up to eleven. Months later, she was into double figures—her ego growing along with her follower count.

A product of the Instagram generation, as well as the public-school system; drinking vodka and sucking off local drug dealers around the back of the local co-op, before being promoted to local royalty when she discovered the combined virtues of a front-facing camera, duck-face, and a push-up bra. She spent all her free time on her phone, her eyes glued to the screen at every opportunity, obsessing over how many likes she was getting, how many comments she had received, and whether any actual celebrities were responding to her messages.

The Queen of Instagram was hunched over her phone when she left her place of work, her eyes fixed on the screen even before the glass door swung shut behind her. The heat of the morning had been cleansed by a heavy storm, the streets rich with the fragrance of ozone, the pavements slick with rainwater. She wore a sleeveless top and a short skirt that exposed her tanned legs and arms to the elements, but she didn't seem to mind. Her steps were brisk, as if on autopilot, going about her usual daily activities while still absorbed in her social media exploits.

I followed close behind, close enough to smell her—coconut-scented shampoo, cheap perfume, stale coffee, cigarettes—and close enough to arouse suspicion if she saw me. But she wasn't turning around, didn't care what other people were doing unless they were doing it on Instagram, and unless it benefited or entertained her in some way.

The streets began to steadily empty, the afternoon turning into evening as I tracked her hasty, robotic steps. She passed at least half a dozen people on her way through the winding streets, over the boundary of the park and through a small clearing, but she didn't acknowledge any of them. She stopped momentarily to snap a quick selfie, putting two fingers up to the camera in a meaningless gesture she no doubt thought was cute, but she barely broke stride and remained oblivious of my presence.

The walk from her place of work to her home took just over twenty-five minutes. It was longer than I had expected, but I was relieved to see that the evening had set in fully, the last dregs of sunshine drained from the skies, the streetlights firing sporadically, illuminating our journey and giving her just enough light for a couple more selfies.

The Queen of Instagram didn't live in a palace. It wasn't even a house. She lived on the ground floor flat of a converted terrace, accessed via an alleyway that ran down the side of the flat and wrapped around the back—tucked away, out of sight.

I waited until I heard the door close and then entered the alleyway, moving into the shadows and out of sight. The alleyway was littered with cigarette butts, broken glass, and the remnants of a homemade pipe. It stank like a public toilet and was likely being used as one.

The Queen of Instagram had only been home for a few minutes, but already she was talking to her subjects, telling them how stressful her day had been before announcing she was going to take a hot bath. She finished with a few product plugs, a kiss, a wink, and a wave.

As one of her newest followers, subject number 10,052, I was able to watch every second on my phone. She invited me into her life and I gladly obliged, making my way into her home and preparing for the VIP treatment.

The Queen of Instagram lived in a home fit for a servant. The back door opened into her kitchen; a cramped musty hovel tucked away at the back of the house. Unlike Neckbeard, who had been one of her followers, the Queen could and did cook. There were sauce-stained pans in the sink, a dusting of flour on the countertop.

A light from the connected dining room lit my way as I glanced over the pictures on her fridge. Unlike the images on her Instagram account, these hadn't been carefully curated, but just like those Instagram snaps, her half-naked form and duck-faced pout was the focal point in all of them. She had a way of drawing your eye, even when she was with friends, from the muscled-torsos of ex-boyfriends and one-night stands to a leggy brunette who appeared in most of the images.

One photo depicted her poolside next to half a dozen girls, all stacked in a neat, orchestrated line, like a synchronized swimming team preparing for a performance. There were girls taller than her and fitter than her, but she still stood out.

The Queen turned on the hot water in the upstairs bathroom, the pipes grumbling like some massive, motorized stomach. The house seemed to shudder momentarily, as if waking from a long slumber before its mechanical machinations were drowned out by the sound of pop music blasting in all directions and from all rooms.

One of the speakers was in the living room, just a few steps away from me. Its size belied its power as the noise reverberated throughout the first floor and carried upstairs, where it joined at least one other speaker.

I hurried through the dining room, where a small wooden table rested unused against the outside wall, and into the open-plan living room, where she kept her computer and spent most of her time.

The computer was tucked away in the corner, placed in a way that prevented any webcam watchers from seeing the living room or the rest of the house. The machine had been left on; its secrets hidden by a screensaver. A collage of visual effects danced from edge to edge on the flat-screen monitor as the annoyingly addictive melodies of Katy Perry echoed throughout.

I turned from the computer to the stairs, eager to see what she had been doing, to hack into her virtual life as I had hacked into her real one, but the music drowned out her approach and dampened my confidence.

The first song stopped and the noise transitioned to a deathly silence. I waited, still, in the open, and listened for any signs of life. Initially, my own heartbeat was the only sound that greeted me, but interminable moments later, the noise of the running water filtered through, accompanied by the sound of angelic humming.

Another song began, the noise returned, and I ran to the kitchen to prepare. The second song was much shorter, but I had everything that I needed. I was breathless when it droned into its final chorus, but I was also excited. I was eager.

The second song finished, fading to silence once more. I waited at the foot of the stairs. My eyes and ears focused on the speaker, waiting for the silence to end and the noise to commence, praying that it wasn't a ballad.

Seconds passed without a sound before a bass guitar eased its way slowly in. I turned back to the stairs, ready to ascend, knowing that my approach would be drowned out by the sound of the music. Then I saw her. She was standing at the top of the stairs, naked from head to toe, her hair tied behind her head, a look of horror on her face. In one hand, she held a fluffy white towel, in the other a bottle of shampoo.

In any other circumstance, I might have admired her figure. I had seen hundreds of pictures of her in a bikini and tight-fitting clothing, and all had stirred the same reaction in me. Her beauty and her body were the things that earned her fame, mainly from perverted old men who wanted to fuck her and desperate young girls who wanted to be her. In that moment, I was in a position that only a handful of her followers—and no doubt half the male population of the town—had been in.

But this wasn't the time for admiration.

I reacted before she did, taking advantage of the fear that seemed to freeze her to the spot. I cleared four or five steps before she threw the bottle and the towel at me, the first missing my head by an inch, the second landing at my feet and causing me to stumble. She yelled something and then ran in the opposite direction, her words drowned out by the music as the bass gave way to electronic beats and the house filled with noise once more.

The Queen sprinted into the bathroom just as I stumbled to the top of the stairs and grabbed the banister to steady myself. The water was still running, the music still playing—both noises interspersed by screams from the town's biggest Instagram whore.

She made it into the bathroom and shut the door behind her, but I was close, knowing she was only a few steps from her phone. I threw myself at the door, my shoulder clattering into the hardwood, cracking the lock and forcing it open. The Queen rebounded under the force, her head bouncing back off the tiled floor, her body skidding clumsily on the slick surface.

Even in her weakened state, her head no doubt spinning, a trickle of blood tracing a line from her skull to her buttocks, she reached for her phone. She was quick, acting on instinct, and in a split second she had activated the device and loaded an app.

I jumped to my feet and dove for her, prying it out of her weakening grasp.

"Please don't hurt me," she said, dragging herself backward to rest against the bathtub, now close to overfilling.

"Bit late for that, isn't it?" I laughed. Her eyes locked onto mine, forcing me to turn my attention away from her questioning stare and onto the phone.

I assumed that she would have tried to phone the police or, at the very least, a friend she kept on speed dial. Instead, she had opened one of her favorite apps and was in the process of doing something she did every day.

"You tried to Livestream me?" I asked, baffled. "You get attacked by a crazy person in your own home and your first response is to Livestream me to your followers?"

She didn't answer, she just stared, her breathing labored and heavy, her eyes focused, unblinking. I didn't know if she was dead, dying, or brain-damaged, but it didn't matter—she had given me an idea that would make my night complete, an idea that excited me even more than ripping her limb from limb.

"I think you may be onto something." I grinned, dropped to my haunches to meet her at eye level. "After all, you always wanted to be a star, didn't you?"

I met her stare for several moments, and just as I prepared to tease her some more, to suggest that her dead-eye stare meant her brain had already departed this world, her expression changed. A realization slowly dawned on her; a quizzical look filled her eyes. There was even a smile curling the corners of her lips.

"Don't I know you?" she asked.

14

Abi didn't need bath salts or bath bombs to relax, but she did get some assistance from a tumbler of whiskey. After a hectic day, one in which she went from being a brave detective on the path of a strange mystery, to a scared woman humiliated by a barista, she was glad to curl up in bed and get some sleep.

She was out before it was dark and didn't surface until seven the following morning, at which point she awoke to the sounds of a noisy garbage truck squeaking and rattling its way down the street. After making a cup of coffee and grabbing a bite to eat, she sat in silence and skimmed through her phone, first checking for client emails and dealing with whatever she could while in an un-caffeinated state, then moving onto her personal emails.

She was delighted to discover that someone had messaged her from one of the dating apps she used, one where she had been honest with her profile description but vague with her image, her face half-covered by a glass and her features obscured by sunlight streaming in from behind.

"StevieBoy83," she said aloud. "Doesn't sound very promising, but . . ." she made an appreciative face. "Not bad."

His profile picture depicted a man in his mid to late thirties with graying hair and an immaculate smile. He wore a blue cardigan and had his arms wrapped around a large collie. On flicking through his other pictures, Abi didn't find any of him with his shirt off, standing in front of a bathroom mirror, making a pouty face, or downing a bottle of beer in a busy pub, all common photos that men posted, all photos she hated.

She didn't want a child trapped in a man's body, and she didn't want a "lad." StevieBoy83 seemed mature, friendly, likable—a rare triple threat. The longer she spent on his profile, the more anxious she felt about opening his message.

What if he's a creep sending me a dick pic, like the weirdos my gran keeps attracting?

What if he's got the wrong person?

What if he's a scammer?

Her heart was beating fast when she finally clicked the message, but she instantly settled down, a wave of relief washing over her when she saw the message was as polite, friendly, and normal as his profile had been:

I've written and rewritten this message a dozen times and still don't know what to say. So, I'm just going to keep this simple—my name is Steven, I really like your profile, and I hope we can chat. I like to read and write, although I'm nowhere near as talented and experienced as you in that department, and I also have family issues—although, don't we all!

She read and reread his message, at first smiling, then grinning, then laughing softly, her face flushed. She hovered the cursor over the *reply* button as her mind raced a mile a minute.

Of course! How could I refuse a message like that? It beats most of the other messages I get on here. At least you're honest! I'm Abi. Nice to virtually meet you. So, what do you do, Steven, and who is that beautiful dog in your picture?

She scanned her message several times, checking she hadn't made an embarrassing mistake, and then hit Send. For the first time in weeks, she felt excited, giddy almost. Men were a dime a dozen on dating sites, but good men were hard to find. In the beginning, she'd received dozens of messages a week and had been thankful for them. They stroked her ego, made her feel good about herself, even though the majority of them amounted to little more than monosyllabic grunts and unsolicited dick pics. But then she realized that the same messages were being sent to countless other women.

Contrary to what the bottom-shelf women's mags suggest, men are complicated creatures. They are still human, even if their actions don't always corroborate that, but once you take away their ability to approach face-to-face, to talk, to smile, and generally to show off their assets like a peacock spreading its wings, they are all very similar. Online dating strips them back to the bare bones, and once you do that then everyone begins to look alike.

Experience taught her that there were only four kinds of men on online dating sites.

The first kind was the most detestable, the Dick Pic brigade. The incels, the perverts, the creeps. They believed that the entire female species was secretly just as desperate and primal as they were and that all it took to win their affections was an unprompted and unsolicited picture of their genitals. They were clearly proud of what God had given them and believed it was enough to replace small talk, dinner dates, and foreplay. They believed their penis was a magic wand that could expedite them straight to the fun stuff.

The second group spoke in monosyllables, often approaching women with a simple "Hey," followed by a "What's up?" upon realizing they had their attention. This group, although harmless at first, could quickly transition into group 1 if the conditions (a little alcohol, a flirtatious comment) were ripe.

Then there were the copy-pasters. Initially, Abi had been very impressed by their eloquence and wit. They wrote long messages. They were funny, well-spoken, kind. But she later discovered that they were simply copy-pasting the same messages to hundreds of girls, and in many instances, they weren't even writing the message themselves. This realization dawned on her when she replied to one such message and the eloquent, well-spoken gentleman turned into a complete numbskull who suddenly lost the ability to use vowels.

The final group were the serious ones, the ones that took the time to read her profile and send her a message to prove it. They were everything that the third group was, only genuine, and they were fun to talk to. They weren't always perfect, of course, Robert had been a part of that group after all, but it was the best that online dating had to offer.

Abi watched her inbox for five minutes, waiting and hoping for a reply, but not expecting it. She was eager, but nervous; keen but shy. *What if he turned out to be just as crazy as Robert? What if his next message was a picture of his erect penis followed by a suggestive smiley face, what if—*

Her chaotic thought patterns were cut short when a reply landed in her inbox.

Her heart sunk when she saw that it was indeed a picture with the words *"What do you think?"* written above.

In that moment, she questioned everything she thought she knew about online dating, but then the picture loaded, and she saw an image of a dog staring back at her.

She had never been happier not to see a penis.

Abi prepared a response, but a notification on her phone changed her mind and her mood, drawing her attention away from the messages and towards the local news app.

The headline read, "Local Girl Massacred in Own Home."

Abi recognized the girl—short, blonde, slim. Their relationship was minimal, passing—she lived and worked in town and Abi had bumped into her on occasion. The girl was young, fit, and very pretty. If the headline was to be believed, she was also dead.

Abi clicked the image of the girl and loaded the video. An apartment came onto the screen, and Abi recognized it as one of the old tenement blocks on the edge of town. They had been built for the town's workers, before being converted into student flats. They were tightly packed—facing each other like lost guests at a wedding—separated by thin stretches of alleyways and tiny backyards.

The house at the front of the awkwardly stacked cluster was alive with activity—law enforcement, forensics, men in suits. Members of the public and press stood on this side of the camera, the hustle and bustle captured by unseen microphones as a reporter spoke over them.

"This morning police found the body of a young woman, Lisa Farrell." An image of the girl flashed on the screen. She was wearing a bikini and pouting, looking like a model as she posed for the camera in front of a gorgeous Mediterranean beach. The image faded and returned to the scene; a reporter stood before the camera as the chaos continued around her.

"Police were responding to online reports about a viral video," the reporter continued, her expression stern and unblinking, "one that depicted the apparent torture and murder of the young girl. The video, filmed by her murderer, was uploaded to Instagram and Facebook using the victim's phone and account. It was seen by most of her followers within the first few hours, after which it spread far and wide. The video was eventually taken down, but it appeared on countless other social networks and file-sharing sites and is believed to have been seen in excess of five million times overnight."

She paused for effect. "The details of the video are too graphic for us to go into here, but it's believed that the killer spent time torturing her before killing her on camera. The young victim was gagged and tied throughout the ordeal and was unable to shout, scream, ask for help, or fight back."

The video ended. Abi turned off her phone and slowly lowered it to the table.

"You okay, dear?" Her gran was standing in the entrance to the kitchen, concern on her wrinkled face. "You look like shit."

"Did you hear the news?"

"About the young lassie?" Martha nodded and entered the kitchen, flipping on the kettle before resting against the counter and facing her granddaughter. "Tragic, isn't it?"

"Tortured and butchered, they said. They posted the video online. Said it was too graphic to even mention."

Martha sucked in a breath through her teeth. "They posted it online? Sick bastards." She shook her head. "Poor lass. But, you know, these things happen. Probably pissed off the wrong person or shagged around too many times. Nothing for you to worry about, dear."

Abi didn't share the same sentiment as her grandmother. She didn't believe that anyone deserved something so horrific, and she didn't believe there was nothing to worry about. A voice in the back of her head told her that she should be worried, she should be terrified, because that voice was trying to convince her that Robert had something to do with it.

Was she one of the Victims?

She had to be. What were the odds of two killers living in one small town?

But if he did kill her, then why?

Did she get in his way, did she know something that she wasn't supposed to know?

Did he get a kick out of it?

Am I next?

"Do you want a cuppa, love? I can put a nip of brandy in there, return some color to those cheeks. You're never going to find a man if you look like a bulimic on Thanksgiving."

"Gran!" Abi snapped.

Martha shrugged. "Suit yourself."

The old lady poured herself a cup of sweet, black coffee, cupped it in her hands, and remained standing at the counter, her eyes staring absently through the steam that rose from the cup. "This video," she said slowly. "You said they posted it online. . . ."

"You must be kidding me, Gran."

"Nothing wrong with a bit of curiosity, dear. You watch horror films, don't you?"

Abi shook her head in disbelief, staring daggers at her grandmother. "A young woman was butchered in her own home by a *real* killer. This wasn't Freddy Krueger. She wasn't Jamie Lee Curtis. It was real."

"You're mixing your horror films, dear."

"That's not the point!" Abi said, throwing her hands up. "It's a fucking snuff film, not a horror film."

"You're right, you're right." Martha sipped her coffee, watched closely by her granddaughter. She made a move to look at her watch, then at the clock on the wall, then at the counter. She began to whistle, stopped, put her cup down and picked it up again. "I just remembered that I have to—" she turned her attention to her granddaughter, surprised to find that she was already staring at her.

"You have to what?"

"I have to meet my latest online friend for a short conversation."

Abi didn't respond, she just stared, shaking her head.

"If you'll excuse me, I'll be in my room talking to a handsome young man from Berlin, and definitely not watching a snuff film."

PART 2

HER

The Queen of Instagram had abdicated, her story making its way around the world. The front pages and newsreels showed her at her best—pouty lips, enigmatic smile, sultry pose—but the internet opted for something a little less glamorous and much more befitting.

She had spent two years carefully crafting her online persona, showing the world a glamourous girl who spent her days relaxing, her nights partying, and her weekends vacationing. She didn't show them the truth—the hours she spent serving customers and dealing with complaints. The makeup and Photoshop tricks. The credit card debt. But it didn't matter. They followed her because of the glamour shots, the nightclubs, the dresses, and the bikini pictures; they followed her because she was beautiful, aspirational, perfect.

In their eyes, thanks to her careful manipulation, she was everything they wanted to be, everything they wanted to be with. And now, in one night, the truth had been revealed, the green curtain yanked open.

She was no queen, and she wasn't perfect. She died in a damp-ridden flat, lying in a pool of piss and blood. A fitting end for a fucking fraud.

Everyone in town had learned of the Queen's demise, including the woman who found a way into my every thought and played a part in every fantasy. As a bright morning gave way to a soulless afternoon, I watched her through Her living room window, Her eyes glued to her phone, Her weary features gradually turning from delight—a joke from a friend, a funny news story, a Facebook meme—to absolute horror. I witnessed the moment that the news broke, the moment that she realized a girl she probably knew, had maybe even bumped into, had been butchered in her own home.

The veil of stability and security had been lifted—the sweetness of her precious little life had soured. I watched the entire spectrum of negative human emotions fill Her features. Horror became anger became sorrow became fear.

She reminded me of one of my very first kills, an older gentleman and his wife. He returned home unexpectedly to find me standing alongside his bedridden wife, looking down at her lifeless form. Initially, he had been smiling, ready to greet his wife and gift her the flowers he had just bought. It was their anniversary. They had been together for just under half a century, a lifetime, but one that had been cut short in an instant.

The smile turned into confusion when he saw me. He was old, possibly a little senile. It took him several seconds to react, seconds in which I saw his features change as his mind processed what was happening. At first the confusion became contentment when he assumed I was a home nurse. This quickly turned to shock when he saw his wife's face. He cycled through sorrow, depression, and panic before he got to anger; the thing that surprised me the most was that he didn't seem to be panicking about his own fate. His attention was on her, not me, not himself. There was panic in his eyes, because in that moment, he realized that he had lost the woman he loved. He'd been abandoned, alone in the world without the partner who had been by his side throughout, the guardian angel who had been there when his family and his friends died; the companion who stayed with him when he lost his job, suffered a mental breakdown.

Killing him had been easier than killing the woman. He didn't put up as much of a fight, despite being stronger, fitter, and healthier than her. The sorrow, pain, anger, and confusion had faded by the time he took his last breath. There was something else there, something unexpected. It could have been relief, it could have been contentment, it could have been a result of his brain shutting down—whatever it was, it was an image that stuck with me.

She didn't process quite as many expressions or as much ambiguity, but as with the old man who died at the foot of his wife's bed, she was shocked, appalled and, eventually, possibly when she convinced herself that it was a one-off, the result of an angry ex and not an indiscriminate killer, she was relieved.

15

"So, Abi, how have your experiences been so far with all this online dating business?"

"Okay, I suppose."

"Met any nice men? Other than me, of course."

"Nice? Sure, I suppose you could say that. Just . . . not for me."

"Good answer. Very diplomatic."

"What about you, what have your experiences been like so far?"

"Absolutely fucking terrible." Steven laughed. Abi joined in, feeling at ease in the company of her date. He sipped his Double Jack, sighed audibly, and smacked his lips. "No disrespect to my dates, of course. I'm sure they said the same things about me."

"Ah, surely not. What's not to like?"

"You're too kind, Abi Ansell." He beamed a wide smile that Abi couldn't help but reciprocate. He had thin lips and a weak, stubbled chin, but when he smiled, his face came to life—dimples popping on his cheeks, his eyes bright. He had been waiting for her outside the restaurant and greeted her with a smile as soon as she stepped out of the Uber, right before he closed the door for her, kissed her on the cheek, and ushered her inside.

Abi instantly felt at ease, like she had known him for years. She hadn't felt that way with any of the others. Most of the time she was anxious, nervous, and that made her feel uncomfortable and do stupid things. She often spent the night speed-eating, clock-watching, and desperately trying to fill awkward silences with everything from mouthfuls of complimentary bread to small talk about the weather.

Steven was different. Relaxed, confident, charming—all traits that made her feel comfortable in her own skin.

"I have to say, though," he added, "I'm not usually this forward. I have never gone on a date with someone this quickly after meeting them. Hand on heart." He placed his hand on his chest, his wide-childish grin still beaming.

"Me neither," Abi said, placing her hand on her chest and laughing along with him. "And don't worry, sometimes it's good to be forward. Life's too short to mess around. As my grandmother says, 'Embarrassment is better than regret; if you want to do something, do it.'"

"Sounds like a smart woman."

"Smart, maybe. Insane and obscene, definitely. She always says that if you're not fucking, sleeping, dancing, or drinking, you're just wasting time." Abi paused and flushed a little, adding, "Pardon my French."

"Not exactly the sort of inspirational quote you'll see on your auntie's Facebook timeline, but I can't disagree. I like the sound of your grandmother. If this doesn't work out between us, you'll have to hook me up with her," he winked. Abi laughed.

"But seriously," Steven continued. "Moving this quickly is very unusual for me. I just—I don't know. The last girl I spoke to—" he paused to check himself, leaning close, "—you don't mind me talking about previous dates, do you? That's not uncouth, is it?"

"No, no, of course not. Go for it."

He leaned back, smiled, and took another sip of his drink. "Okay then. Sometimes I get ahead of myself—do you want another drink?"

"No, no, I'm fine."

He smiled again. "Anyway, so what was I saying—ah yes, my date. She was great, or at least she seemed great when we spoke online. We sent messages back and forth for weeks, maybe even months. We spent a lot of time asking each other questions, learning about one another, and so on. When we finally arranged to meet . . ." He raised his eyebrows and shrugged. "We had nothing to say to one another. Like, at all."

"Really?"

Steven nodded. "Barely spoke a word. Turns out, there was no chemistry there. We'd both spent weeks sending occasional messages to each other, going through the usual questions—jobs, aspirations, education, family, political preferences. It was like we were just checking them off as we went, never realizing that there wasn't any kind of spark and overlooking the fact we didn't really have anything in common."

"That must have been a painful night."

"Oh yes. I ate so fast I had the hiccups for a week."

"Well, let's hope that's not an issue tonight." Abi reached for her glass of red wine. The waiter had brought their drinks as soon as they'd sat down, right after Steven took her coat, placed it on the back of the chair, and then waited for her to sit. Abi wasn't big on chivalry—it made her feel awkward and she didn't know where to put herself—but there was something about Steven's charm that put her at ease. They had spoken very briefly through instant messages earlier in the day, getting to know each other with a two-hour chat that took place when Abi should have been working. They spoke about random things, pointless things, funny things, but throughout their conversation, he had surreptitiously pillaged her for information, learning what she liked to drink, where she liked to eat, when she was free.

"Forgive me if this sounds forward," he had said to her eventually, interrupting a conversation about a recent meme that they both found humorous, "but would you like to come to dinner with me tonight?"

As soon as she agreed, surprising herself with her own willingness, he informed her that he had already booked a restaurant. He found one that served pad thai, her favorite dish, and he also booked a table that was tucked away at the back of the restaurant. Either he wanted some privacy, or he had picked up on her social anxiety and had done it for her benefit. In any case, she was delighted.

She raised her glass toward him. "Here's to a night free of hiccups and banal banter."

He lifted his glass. "To being hiccup-free," he echoed. "Cheers."

They clinked glasses, locked stares, and Abi felt an immediate warmth rush through her body.

"So, tell me, Abi, what's the worst date that you've had?" Steven sipped his drink and stopped, glass still raised. "And please don't say this one. I don't know if you've ever seen a grown man cry but . . ."

Abi giggled, an instinctive reaction that surprised her. She wasn't a giggler. She didn't even know she was capable of giggling.

"No, definitely not this one," she reassured him. "I don't know . . ." Her eyes looked off into the distance. There was only one date, one story, that she could tell. She'd been on bad dates, there was no doubt about that, but nothing compared to her date with Robert and nothing she could say would top the things that had happened since that awkward night.

"Well, there is one."

Steven opened his hands expressively, "Hit me with it. Let's see if I can top it."

"It's a bit of a strange one."

"Don't worry, I'm sure I've heard worse."

She shook her head, a deadpan expression on her face.

"That bad, huh?"

"You have no idea."

His gleaming demeanor shifted somewhat when he noted her stern expression. He clearly thought that he had spoken out of turn, touched on a traumatic event and triggered her in some way. Abi broke into a smile to put him at ease, "It's not tragic or anything like that," she told him. "It's just very weird and creepy. You might think I'm insane if I tell you."

He raised a curious eyebrow and joked, "Who's to say I don't already think that?"

"Tofu and peanut pad thai?" Abi's laughter was cut short by the waiter, who stood over the table with a plate of food in each hand. She held up her hand and moved back, watching with delight as he put the plate of steaming food down in front of her. She had barely eaten all day. The breaking news that interrupted her mid-morning conversation with Steven had killed her appetite.

After that, she had been so preoccupied with their conversation—not to mention the preparation that followed as she put on her makeup, fixed her hair, and spent over an hour finding the perfect outfit—that food had been an afterthought. Only when she saw the food in front of her and felt her stomach contract as if grasping for the plate did she realize how hungry she was.

"And yours, sir." The waiter placed the second plate in front of Steven, said, "Enjoy your meal," and then left.

"Saved by the bell," Steven said, holding out his glass again. "Cheers—here's to a delicious meal with great company."

They clinked glasses again and Abi delighted in sharing another smile with him.

"And to hearing all about your creepy date another time."

"Definitely," Abi said, with a firm nod. "Be best if you get to know me first, though, otherwise you may run away."

He had a mouthful of food, his eyes wide as he stared at her, chomping hungrily and shaking his head to suggest that he wouldn't run. Abi giggled, again, only this time she didn't feel embarrassed.

16

Abi had one of the best nights of her life. She felt comfortable, laughed throughout, and there were no awkward silences or embarrassing moments. Nor did she feel self-conscious or bored. It was how she always envisaged the perfect date would go and how none of her dates had ever gone.

But despite being at ease, she felt the pang of anxiety when they stepped outside and headed for the Uber. She recalled her encounter with Robert—the awkward kiss that had turned into an even more awkward handshake, the resulting chase through the park. She wanted to kiss Steven, but she didn't want to make the first move; she didn't want the night to end, but she also didn't want to be the one proposing they extend it.

"It's still early. Do you want a nightcap?"

When Steven spoke those words, Abi immediately relaxed, her mind going back to where it had been throughout the night. "I'd love to."

They had already arranged for the Uber to take them both home. The plan was for it to drop her off first, during which she envisaged an awkward backseat goodbye with a fumbled kiss and a mumbled agreement to meet again. It would then drop him off at his house, ending the night for both of them. She was so happy they had agreed to extend the night, so lost in conversing with Steven on the backseat, that she didn't realize the car was still going to her house until it pulled up outside.

Steven thanked the driver, and before she could think of an excuse, he was out of the car and holding the door open for her.

"My lady," he said, making a swooning gesture.

Abi clambered out silently, laughing but trying to keep her voice down.

The Uber drove off and left them both in the driveway, looking up at her house. One of the upstairs lights was still on, but it was pitch-black downstairs.

Steven hooked Abi's arm through his and then made a move to walk down the driveway. She resisted, halted. "Do you mind if we don't go inside?"

Steven looked a little confused. "If you're worried about it being a mess, don't be. Trust me, mine's a lot worse."

She laughed. "No, it's fine. It's not a mess."

"Oh, okay. Then . . . neither is mine."

"I just—I just—" she sighed. "Okay, so I probably should have told you this, but you know the grandmother that I mentioned?"

"The amazing and obscene old lady? How could I forget?"

"Well, I live with her."

"Oh."

"I know, it's weird."

"What? Don't be stupid. I lived with my parents until I was twenty-seven. Now *that's* weird. If anyone asks, I was just looking after them in their old age. But between me and you, I was a lazy slob who had it easy and didn't want to let go."

"At least you're honest."

"Yes, although sometimes I wonder why." He looked up at the bedroom windows and then the front door. "Do you have a backyard?" he wondered, eyes still on the door.

"Yes."

"Are there any lights?"

"A spotlight and a bunch of little solar lights."

"Chairs?"

"Four."

"Then what are we waiting for? It's a warm night, the moon's out, your X-rated granny is asleep. I'll book myself an Uber for a couple hours, you grab some booze and blankets, and we'll reconvene in the yard. Deal?"

"Deal."

Abi opened the front door quietly, shutting it and locking it behind her. She hadn't been that embarrassed about living with her grandmother. It wasn't something she was ashamed of, so it wasn't something she felt the need to hide. Martha was an amazing person and a joy to live with. But despite her love for her grandmother, Abi didn't want the old lady to meet Steven.

She imagined Martha greeting him in her nightdress, her suggestive smile giving away even more than the thin, almost-transparent silk. Within seconds of introducing them to one another, her grandmother would swear and say something incredibly inappropriate, leaving Steven shocked and not sure what to do with himself. Then, as he wondered whether she was unwell, insane, or just uncivilized, she would ask probing questions and leave no stone unturned as she quizzed him on everything from his marital status to his STD history.

Abi stood in complete darkness, not even willing to turn on the light lest her grandmother sense the activity and the opportunity that it brought. She looked to the top of the stairs and the faint light that emanated from her grandmother's room and she waited, listening for any sound of movement. Martha didn't snore—she barely made a noise. But if she was awake, she would be tapping on the keyboard, sending messages to unsuspecting young men and looking for mischief at every turn.

Abi couldn't hear any sound except for the forceful beating of her own heart. Relieved, she grabbed a couple glasses and a bottle of wine from the kitchen and then slipped outside. Her first instinct was to study Robert's house, directly adjacent to hers and separated by a tall wooden fence, but the garden chairs were set back and, from where they sat, they would only be able to see the second story of his house. If he were inside, hiding in the darkness behind the second-story windows, he would be able to see them.

The thought sent a chill down her spine and raised goose-pimples on her flesh.

She sat down next to Steven and poured them both a glass of wine, shooting occasional glances at Robert's house as she did so.

Was that movement? Did I just see someone?

Don't be stupid. Probably just a reflection.

"Cheers." Abi raised her glass and ignored her fears. "To a wonderful night."

"Cheers," he echoed. "To a great night indeed." He drank and then added, "And to your gran, who sounds like a great woman. Shame I can't meet her."

"Trust me, it's not a shame."

"Ah, come on, she can't be that bad."

Abi tucked her legs underneath her body and pulled her sleeves down over the hands, keeping the brisk night at bay. "You'd think that," she said, smiling, "But . . . put it this way. Have you heard of Nasty Gran?"

Steven returned her question with an intrigued shake of his head.

"It's her Twitter handle."

"Your gran uses Twitter?"

"Oh, yes."

"My gran barely knows how to work the toaster. I set up an email account for her a few years ago and had to delete it when I discovered she had been responding to spam. Every time she received spam, she would respond to politely decline and thank them for thinking of her."

"That's sweet."

"It's insane is what it is. It's a good thing she didn't have any offers from Nigerian princes, God knows how that would have turned out."

"Think yourself lucky," Abi said. "My gran has argued with everyone in town. She had a dig at the mayor last month, calling him an 'over-fed, undereducated swine' because he rejected plans for a supermarket."

Steven shrugged. "I'm still liking her."

"She gets . . . *dirty* pictures from young men—"

"*Dirty* pictures? You can say the word, you know," Steven teased.

Abi dismissed him with a wave of her hand. "You know what I mean. She gets those pictures and instead of ignoring them or reporting them, she files them away on her computer and then sends the men a detailed critique."

Steven laughed, nearly spilling his wine. He slapped a hand to his mouth, aware that he might wake the woman in question. "I'm sorry, but that's hilarious."

Abi nodded. "I suppose, but she can also be a nightmare. She got into this feud with a local troll recently. A real waster. He would post all kinds of horrible stuff and when she called him out, he focused his attentions on her, doing everything he could to try and expose her, embarrass her, belittle her."

"Sounds like a prick."

"One hundred percent. But she got her way in the end. Gran has a razor-sharp wit."

Steven used his sleeve to wipe the remnants of spilled wine from his chin before blotting it against the seat of his pants. "Does she usually meet your boyfriends?" he asked, his eyes on the task at hand.

"Not if I can help it."

He finished and turned to her, an expectant look in his eyes. "What about your most recent adventure?" he quizzed. "If I remember rightly, you owe me a story."

"I was hoping you'd forget about that."

"I'm like an elephant," Steven said. "And not just because I have a great memory." He winked.

Abi shook her head, unable to suppress a smile. "That was pathetic, but I'll let it slide seeing as you've been doing so well so far."

"Come on then." He shifted in his seat to face her directly, the glass of wine cradled in his hands. "Tell me all about this guy. Warts and all. And by that, I don't mean literally. Unlike your gran, I won't judge, but I'd prefer not to hear about another man's warty junk."

"There was no warty junk," Abi said. "At least, not that I know of." She poured herself another drink, topping up her date's glass as she did so. "Okay," she said eventually, after much stalling. "But promise you won't think less of me."

"I can't promise that, but I promise that I'll *pretend* not to think less of you."

Abi told him everything. She was anxious at first, unsure how she would come across, but the more she spoke, the more she realized how sane her situation was. Yes, she had made a fool of herself in front of the police and yes, she didn't have a lot of proof, but she was within her rights to be paranoid and to suspect her neighbor of foul play. These thoughts were confirmed by Steven, who was hooked on her every word and seemed desperate for the details.

"This is like one of those late-night crime and investigation documentaries," he said at one point, "you know, the ones that end with you being murdered in your sleep."

"That's comforting."

"I'm sure it won't happen to you," he assured. "But just in case, maybe sleep with the light on."

Abi told him about sneaking into Robert's house and following him into the town—she didn't leave anything out. All the while, the two of them shot furtive glances toward Robert's house—still bathed in blackness with no sign of activity behind any of the windows.

"If all this is true, then who was the girl? We're assuming he killed her, as well, right?" Steven asked. "But why did he kill her? Was she an ex of his or was it completely random?"

Abi shook her head. She had asked herself the same question. "More likely to be someone that rejected him. Or—" She shrugged. "Maybe that's just what he's into. I mean, she was pretty popular online, she lived and worked in the area. Maybe he just saw her around and thought . . ."

"I'll kill her?"

Abi shrugged. "Sadists don't need a reason to be sadistic."

"Good point."

Abi watched as Steven drained his glass, his eyes on Robert's house. As he finished the last dregs, he brought the glass down slowly, seemingly confused. It was one of the few times she hadn't seen him smiling all night and the expression concerned her.

"I don't mean to alarm you," he said. "But I'm pretty sure I just saw a flash."

Abi followed his gaze immediately. "Are you sure?" she asked. "Maybe it was a reflection of headlights. There's a road over in that distance—"

"Not only that . . ." Steven pushed. "And now, correct me if I'm wrong, but I'm fairly certain that window wasn't open before."

Abi had enjoyed one of the best nights of her life, had felt more comfortable, more at ease than she had ever been, and for the first time she hadn't worried about work or making a fool of herself. But the moment she saw the open window and confirmed Steven's suspicions, all that disappeared.

The anxiety, the paranoia, the dread—everything returned, rushing through her like a cold wind.

He's been watching us.

He opened the window so he could hear.

How loudly had we been speaking?

Loud enough?

"Shit," she hissed under her breath, taking a leaf out of her grandmother's phrasebook.

He could have heard everything.

17

"They think it's the work of a serial killer." Steven sighed, his breath clipped with static as it filtered down the phone line.

"They?"

"Just gossip right now. The police are refusing to confirm it, but that's two murders."

"But the young girl was just murdered," Abi reminded him. "Did he rush off and kill someone else straight away? Did *he* do it? Maybe it was like a murder-suicide thing."

"That's one of the rumors. But the word on the street is that he was killed first."

"The word on the street?"

"Okay, you got me, I mean Facebook. I just wanted to sound like less of a boomer." Abi could practically hear Steven smiling through the phone, and the image brought a smile to her own face. "He was found by a neighbor this morning. Could have been killed a day or two earlier."

"Jesus," Abi said. "But it could still be a coincidence."

"Massive coincidence for a small town."

"But a coincidence just the same. This is a crappy town full of crappy people."

"Weren't you born and raised here?"

Abi laughed. "Maybe I'm the exception."

"Fair enough," Steven said. "The simple fact is, and I don't mean to make you paranoid here, but you could be living next to Ted Bundy."

"Nah," Abi said, dismissively. "Robert's not attractive or charming enough to be Ted Bundy."

"Controversial statement, but I see where you're coming from. In any case, you should keep an eye out for him."

"You think I should phone the police?" Abi wondered. "I just—I don't think they'll listen, not after last time."

"I don't think so either. You don't really have anything to go off. There is a tip line and you could probably give his name, but so what? A friend of mine used to work in law enforcement. He told me that whenever a case gets lots of media attention, everyone and their dog calls to offer their support and none of them have anything helpful to say." He paused, seemingly deep in thought. "I have a better idea."

"What's that?"

"I think we should go out for lunch and talk it over. Do some sleuthing. Preferably over a coffee and a slice of cake."

Abi smiled. Despite everything that had happened over the last few days, despite fearing that her conversation last night had been overhead by her next-door neighbor, she had slept well for the first time in weeks. She went to bed with a smile on her face and awoke in great spirits. Steven had sent her a message to tell her how great the night had been, how much fun he'd had, and how he wanted to see her again. As soon as she confirmed, he phoned her. His voice had done more to lift her mood than her morning dose of caffeine.

"It's a deal."

Martha was waiting for her when she hung up the phone, a stern look in her aging eyes, her arms folded across her chest.

"Who are you talking to?"

"A friend," Abi said, taken aback by her grandmother's quizzical stare. "What's the problem?"

"Did you bring him here last night?"

Abi nodded, suddenly realizing what the issue was and predicting exactly what was to come.

"And why didn't you introduce us?" Martha unfolded her arms, pulled out a chair at the breakfast table, and sat down, her eyes fixed on the granddaughter. "I would have liked to meet him. Size him up. See if he's good enough for you; if he's funny, charming, handsome. If he has a nice ass."

"That's why," Abi said. "Because I don't want you grabbing my boyfriend's ass."

Martha's jaw dropped open; Abi immediately realized her mistake.

"Your boyfriend?" Martha had an unmistakable glint in her eye. "Well, that's unexpected. This relationship's moving faster than my bowels after a curry. Let's hope it's not—"

"—Just as messy," Abi finished. "Yes, let's not. And what did I tell you about scat imagery at the breakfast table?" She shook her head. "Firstly, you were asleep. Secondly, I only met the guy yesterday. I didn't want you scaring him away with your suggestive questions and talk of penises, asses, and bowels."

"You only met him yesterday and already he's your boyfriend?" Martha wondered, eyebrows raised. "And he came around to the house? Where did you meet him and where can I sign up?"

Abi refused to answer her gran's questions. She got out of the chair, planted a kiss on her forehead, and made for the bathroom. "I have to leave. I'm meeting . . . *someone* for coffee and I need to get ready."

"Someone? It's him, right? Is it him? Where are you going—is it a sex thing? Can I come?"

"Gran!"

"Sorry."

Abi's morning improved with every passing moment. After checking her messages, she discovered she had been paid and didn't have a lot of work. As a freelancer, a lack of work was usually a bad sign, but she was welcome for the break and knew the work would come when she needed it. She also felt bright and refreshed, despite waking with a mild hangover.

The night had ended with a kiss and a hug from Steven, followed by her gushing over how much fun she'd had and how she wanted to do it again. Initially, it felt like she'd ruined the night and had been too clingy and too forward, but those feelings disappeared when he reciprocated and expressed even more delight and willingness.

The shower invigorated her and there was a song on her lips as she changed into a fresh set of clothes, kissed her grandmother, and then left the house. She was in her own world, her bright smile a facade that hid a feeling of pure ecstasy, a feeling she wasn't accustomed to. She was in such a good mood, so blinded by her happiness, that she didn't check the peephole before she left the house. If she had, she would have seen Robert standing at the end of her driveway, waiting expectantly for her.

Abi's bright morning quickly darkened.

"Oh, hello Abi," Robert said. A smile slithered onto his face; it looked fake, ominous, evil. He was standing just a few feet in front of her. "Fancy seeing you here. We should stop meeting like this!" he snorted and then fell silent, seemingly embarrassed by the outburst.

Abi offered a meek smile in reply, her hands on her phone, ready to be used as a weapon or a warning. She briefly thought about pretending that it had rung and pressing it to her ear, but she doubted she could pull it off and her fear kept her rigid and unable to think on her feet.

"I've been hoping to run into you, actually," Robert said. His face hardened, the fake smile faded. The veil was ripped away. "I think we need to have a chat."

Abi's heart was racing. Her body didn't feel like her own; her ears rang. She was on the brink of a panic attack. "Re-really?"

He nodded, looked down at his feet and then slowly brought his attention back to her. "I know what you're doing."

Abi instinctively looked at her phone and quickly opened the phone book before turning back to Robert. She visualized the app, dialed 999 without looking, and then waited, her thumb hovering over the call button. "Wh-what do you mean?"

Robert seemed confused initially, his gaze locked on hers. Then he looked away again and began twiddling his thumbs like a scolded schoolboy. "I know you're avoiding me," he explained. "I know you're not really interested."

The words didn't filter through initially. Abi was a split second from hitting the call button when she realized what he was saying.

"And I'm okay with that, I really am." His eyes met hers again. Abi realized that what she had assumed to be a fake deceptive smile was actually anxiety. He was just as scared, just as anxious as she was. "I mean, I like you. I thought we had a good time. I know it wasn't the best first date and I'm okay with that. But . . . you don't have to avoid me."

"I wasn't—"

"It's okay," he said. "I would have probably done the same. It's fine, honestly. But maybe we can be friends?"

She didn't answer him straight away because she still didn't believe him, didn't trust everything that he said. He had spied on her and had possibly taken pictures of her. He wasn't the innocent, harmless gentleman he portrayed. But at that moment, she felt like there was a chance she had made a mistake, that he was just a helpful, hopeless guy who felt embarrassed by their awkward first date.

"Of course." She wore her best smile and slipped her phone into her pocket. "I'd like that."

"Great." He seemed genuinely pleased.

She peeled back her sleeve and gave a cursory glance at the bangles on her arm, hoping he wouldn't notice she wasn't wearing a watch. "But I really have to be somewhere."

"Of course, no problem. Another time maybe."

They exchanged a muted smile before Robert headed back toward his house. Abi moved slowly, waiting until he was well out of reach before setting off in the opposite direction.

"Oh!" Robert called to her when he was halfway down his driveway. "You should check me out on Instagram. I love it—I'm kinda addicted. I spend way more time on there than I should, trying to be the next viral sensation like every other mug out there! You know how it is."

—

"He said what!?" Steven was shocked, just as shocked as Abi had been and for the same reason.

Abi nodded. "*Check me out on Instagram*," she mimicked. "I mean, in any other circumstance, it's harmless. But he never mentioned it to me on the date and he brings it up after everything that happened with that young girl, after he knows I think he's the killer? That's messed up."

"He definitely knows you think that?"

Abi wrapped her hand tightly around her coffee cup, sighing as the heat burned through the thin cardboard exterior and seared her hand. "He has to." Her voice trembled. "That window wasn't open initially. He was spying on us, and he opened it so he could hear us better."

"Scary, isn't it?" Steven said somberly, taking a long and slow drink of his coffee as he stared out of the window.

For the briefest moments, Abi considered that she may have been overreacting and that Robert wasn't the person she suspected him to be. But that comment, and the smug, knowing expression on his face when he said it, instantly confirmed her suspicions.

She had arranged to meet Steven in a small café, away from the main street where camera crews still gathered and locals tried their best to get their faces on TV. Steven had been waiting for her with a comforting embrace and a hot cup of coffee—again, he ordered for her, and again, she didn't mind.

A young man was on his own behind the counter, a gaunt and solemn expression on his face as he watched a TV fixed to a bracket in the corner of the room and aimlessly wiped the counter with a dry rag. The TV was tuned into a local news program where an equally solemn-faced reporter calmly retraced the steps of the young girl who had been butchered only a couple days earlier.

The reporter reviewed the steps that the young girl had taken on the night of her death. The piece had been filmed at night and was overlaid with voyeuristic imagery to give the viewers the impression that the cameraman was stalking her. His lens fixed on her bare legs as she walked, the sounds of her footsteps amplified. At one point she turned to look over her shoulder and the camera focused on her face and froze while the reporter narrated her own dramatized doom: "If only she knew that the man following her, the seemingly innocuous man who probably looked just like everyone else she had seen on that day, would be her killer."

The local news networks and websites had been running around-the-clock coverage of the murder, uncovering every detail and doing all they could to prolong the report and squeeze as much news out of it as possible. They had spoken with family members and friends, had interviewed employers; they had even tracked down some of the people who followed her on social media, one of which gladly gave an hour-long interview, even though he had never met her and lived a hundred miles away.

Once they had covered everything there was to cover, they began dramatizing it, adding their own spin, reaching their own conclusions, and treating law enforcement's ambiguity as a license to bullshit.

As the makeshift-victim returned home and opened the door, the cameraman caught up with her. The camera was thrust in her face, capturing her in close-up as her mouth opened wide to scream. The image froze again, and the local reporter playing the role of the victim spoke: "She posted an update to her followers and then began her night of terror. She was mocked, tortured, terrorized, and eventually died in the apparent safety of her own home."

Two teen girls watched the news piece closely, absolute horror in their eyes. They struggled to even break a smile and their red, puffy eyes indicated they had spent the better part of the morning in tears. They clearly knew or knew of her, but in a small town like this, and with the media going crazy, everyone would be claiming to have some connection to the girl or the all-but-forgotten man—the newly discovered murder victim—who wasn't attractive, young, or newsworthy enough to warrant as much attention.

The town hadn't experienced anything worse than occasional antisocial behavior and idle gossip, but it was now in the grip of what the media were convinced was a serial killer.

Abi swallowed thickly at the thought, pulling her attention away from the two girls, whose eyes were still fixed to the screen, and back to the TV. As if to confirm her thoughts, the focus had now switched to the other murder. The reporter was standing outside a dilapidated apartment on the edge of town, an area popular with drug addicts.

Abi watched intently as the reporter spoke. "A haven for addicts and criminals. Home to the hopeless, the helpless, and the most depraved." The ground floor flat behind her had been sealed with police tape. The doors and windows had been sealed up.

The reporter continued to layer the drama on thick. The area was indeed one of the worst in town, but it was a victim of extreme poverty and bad luck and wasn't the portal to hell that she made it out to be. It wasn't an unruly ghetto in the middle of war-torn Somalia. At best, it was PG-13 depravity, a far cry from the worst neighborhoods in the biggest cities; it was home to graffiti, antisocial behavior, and underage drinking, not shootings, drug running, and gang rape.

"Crazy, isn't it?" Steven said, his eyes also on the TV. "This used to be a quiet town."

"It still is," Abi said. "Just because we have a crazy bastard on the loose doesn't change that."

Steven cleared his throat and fell silent. When Abi turned to him, she saw that his eyebrows were raised and there was a shocked expression on his face.

"What?"

"Did you just swear, Abi Ansell?"

"Did I? It must have slipped out."

"Well, I mean—I don't know what to think. I thought I was spending time with a sweet, wholesome, innocent young woman and now . . . my mother was right, you don't know who you're meeting on these online dating sites."

Abi sniggered. "Sorry."

He waved his hand dismissively, grinning. "Don't worry, I think I actually like this side of you. And if what you've said about your grandmother is true, it only makes sense. It has to rub off on you."

"I suppose."

"And if you one day turn into an old, bitter, angry lady who swears a lot and has a catalog of catchphrases, I won't mind. In fact, it kinda turns me on."

"The idea of me turning into my grandmother turns you on?"

"Yes . . . I see how that might have sounded."

They both laughed. For a moment, their eyes locked, but Abi quickly pulled her gaze away, feeling an unexpected twinge of embarrassment. "So, your mother doesn't like online dating sites?" she said.

"God no."

"Is she still alive, if you don't mind me asking?"

"No," Steven replied. "She was murdered by a guy she met on Plenty of Fish."

Abi's jaw dropped open, but Steven quickly jumped in—

"Only joking. It was cancer. Much less funny, and not much of a punchline."

It was his time to break eye contact. He turned his attention to the window as an elderly couple walked by, arm in arm, each supported by a cane, stuttering methodically as one.

"Way to lower the tone," Abi said eventually.

The comment seemed to bring Steven back into the conversation, he offered a short, sharp laugh, shrugged, and then focused his attention back on her, his elbows resting on the table, his right hand supporting his head. "So, tell me, what do you think about this serial killer business? If it is Robert, what's his game?"

Abi shrugged. "I don't know. I mean, killing the girl makes sense. I mean, it's not *normal*, and it's definitely not justified. Unless she was a bitch—" She laughed and then stopped herself. "I'm sorry, that was in bad taste."

Steven's eyebrows raised again, a look of surprise, shock, and one that he expressed often. It was an expression that Abi liked—it animated his entire face, adding wrinkles to his forehead, life to his eyes.

"Forget I said that," Abi said, eliciting a smile from Steven. "What I mean is, men like Robert, assuming he is the killer, target women like that all the time, right?"

"Of course."

"I'm no expert, but I'm a writer, and I think we're all secretly a little obsessed with serial killers."

"Not just writers. I've gone down many Wikipedia serial killer rabbit holes. I don't mean to sound creepy, but a couple years ago, I discovered a page that listed all historic serial killers by their victim counts and notoriety, with individual pages on each. That was like the holy grail for me and pretty much kept me occupied for weeks."

"Really?"

Steven nodded. "And don't look so surprised, you started it."

"Yes, but I'm a mild-mannered, innately anxious woman. You're a charming, handsome, thirtysomething man. Throw some childhood abuse into the mix and you're the prime candidate."

"Little harsh, but you called me handsome and charming, so I'm going to let that one slide." He grinned from ear to ear and Abi found herself admiring his expression once more, from the way his smile exposed his gleaming white teeth, to his unblinking, trusting stare.

"So, the girl makes sense, right?" Abi said. "I mean, they didn't say anything about sexual assault, but even if that didn't happen, he still humiliated her. He recorded her murder, posted it to everyone, and no doubt rejoiced in watching as her once-gleaming reputation was steadily ruined and her legacy went from a drop-dead gorgeous supermodel to . . . well, to a corpse."

"Shit, when you put it like that."

"The man—the other victim—doesn't make sense."

"Maybe he's bisexual, gets a kick out of humiliating both sexes."

"I saw images of the guy. I read the stories on news sites. They weren't as sympathetic to him as they have been to this girl. Trust me, if it was only a sexual thing then he has zero taste and was scraping the bottom of the barrel."

Steven shrugged, his attention back on the window as a couple of teenagers rode by on bicycles, their laughter cutting through the relative silence of the café. "You don't think it is a serial killer, then?"

"I don't know."

"They both lived alone. They both died in their own homes. It's a very small town. Apparently, the methods were a little different, but it has to be, right?"

Abi shrugged, not wanting or willing to face the truth.

"From what you told me about Robert," Steven continued. "He sounds a little awkward. Weird. Maybe . . . maybe . . ." He seemed to temporarily disappear in thought, staring absently into the middle distance. "Maybe he's humiliating people who humiliated him. Maybe it has nothing to do with sex or pleasure, maybe he's not a sexual sadist and just wants to hurt those who hurt him."

"That's a lot of maybes."

Steven nodded but looked very serious, very concerned. "You know what that means if it's true, right?"

Abi mirrored his concerned. “I humiliated him by rejecting him and now he wants to kill me?”

“Pretty much.”

“If you’re trying to make me feel better, you’ve failed.”

18

The thumping bass, the crunching guitars, the wailing singer—every sound cut through Abi like a knife. There was a sickness rising in her, emanating from the pit of her stomach, clawing at her throat and infecting her mind.

It began, like it always began, with the sense that she was drifting away from the world, as if she were behind herself, her eyes a video camera, her world unreal. In an instant, the happiness, the calm, the normality—it all came crashing down. Her heart quickened, her palms became sweaty, the sickness rose, and she felt like she was ready to pass out.

"It's just a panic attack," her gran told her once, "It'll pass. Calm down. Buckle up. Ride it out." But knowing it was just a panic attack didn't make it any better; knowing that she wasn't going to die didn't make her less sick or woozy.

Death wasn't the problem. If she dropped dead, at least she wouldn't have to face the embarrassment of being roused by a bartender while everyone gathered around her, fretted over her, and then treated her like some invalid. No, death wasn't the issue, passing out was. If she passed out, she would have to face the indignity of exposing her flaws to strangers, of bringing everyone's fun to a standstill and attracting the entire attention of the room.

That's what made her sick, that's what made her feel ill at ease, and the more she thought about it, the worse she became.

"Is everything okay?" Steven's voice filtered through as if underwater. He didn't look worried, not yet, but he could see that she was uncomfortable. His words should have spurred her into action, they should have dragged her out of the panic and into the real world, but they made her worse.

Why's he asking that?

Am I pale?

Is my nose bleeding?

Do I look like I'm going to pass out? Because I certainly feel like it and if I look like it as well, maybe it's really going to happen, maybe—

She felt his hand on her shoulder, a gentle squeeze, a comforting smile. He guided her to her feet. "Let's step outside," he offered. "Get some fresh air."

Abi felt herself walking after him and felt her feet carrying her. It was as if she were walking on air, pushed by the force of the music and the chatter in the bar.

Seconds later, they were outside, and just as quickly the sickness faded, forced back down from whence it came. Reality snapped back, the panic dissipated, and when she turned to Steven, glad for his company and delighted she hadn't passed out or thrown up in front of him, she noted that he was smiling at her.

"You good?" he asked.

She nodded. "Sorry, not sure what came over me there."

"One minute we were chatting, then the band started doing their thing and then . . ." He shrugged, uncertain. "You looked like you'd seen a ghost."

She smiled meekly, unable to explain herself.

"You know the band or something?"

"Actually, yes," Abi said with a laugh, before shaking her head. "But that's not why. Sometimes I just . . . panic, I suppose. Weird, I know, but—"

"Not at all," Steven interjected, eliciting a grateful smile from his date.

"It's the noise, the chaos, the people—and as soon as the panic sets in . . ."

"You start to worry yourself even more," he finished with a knowing smile. "I've been there. Panic begets panic."

He wrapped his arm around her, and she moved in close, feeling safe and warm under his towering stature.

"I used to be the same," he said, his voice heavy with bass, almost palpable as she rested her head against his chest. "It wouldn't take much. A little too much caffeine, not enough sugar—I'd feel different, unwell, and if I was in a place I wasn't entirely comfortable in, that would be enough to kick-start the panic."

Abi nodded. There was a chance she had also consumed too much caffeine or too few calories. They had remained in the café for several hours, drinking cup after cup. In the early afternoon, they'd avoided an exodus of news crews and the trail of locals that fled in their wake to visit a food stand. Abi had eaten a small portion of fries, despite the gnawing hunger that grabbed and pulled at her stomach. She didn't want to look greedy, and she didn't want kebab-breath on a date.

They ate their food on a bench outside the stand, watching passersby and making a game out of it. They began by guessing whether couples were related or dating, before moving onto a game where they guessed what people were doing on their phones—was the man in the suit texting with a business partner or a mistress; was the kid in the baseball cap stalking his best friend's girlfriend or sexting his ex?

There was an air of excitement in the town. More chatter, more groups, more drama. You'd expect the murders to create fear and a sense of panic, but it just seemed to give everyone something to talk about. They all wanted to voice their theories and state what they knew, even when what they knew was the same as the next person.

Abi hadn't intended to spend the day with Steven, but the longer they spent together, the harder it was to walk away. So, when he asked if she wanted to go to a local pub, she didn't think anything of it.

"What do you think of the band?" Steven asked, apparently feeling a need to change the subject.

Abi grumbled an indifferent reply.

"Yeah, not great, are they?" Steven said. "Singer is a bit annoying and the bassist seems to think he's some kind of rock god, throwing his guitar around like he's swinging his dick."

Abi peeled away from his chest. "He *wishes* his dick was that big."

Steven laughed. "There's your grandmother coming through again. And I thought I was dating a prude!"

Abi stepped back, a look of fake indignation on her face. "Firstly," she said, aiming a finger to the sky. "I'm not a prude, I'm just polite, that's it. Secondly," she edged in closer again, her face just inches from his. "If we're officially dating, does that make you my boyfriend?"

Steven seemed surprised and Abi instantly worried that she'd jumped the gun and spoken out of turn.

Was it too early?

Are second-date declarations just for rom-coms with limited running times and stories to tell?

Have I blown it?

Her fears were dispelled when he nodded, sporting a grin he wore from ear to ear.

Abi kissed him, instantly feeling the remnants of her anxiety and everything else that had boiled up inside of her just fade away, out into the still night. He pressed his hands to her face, and she flinched, surprised at how cold they were. He pulled back, ready to apologize, but she dove in again, kissing him harder, pressing herself tightly to him.

They kissed as the music played and, only when the song ended, when the noisy, poorly played cover gave way to a round of unenthusiastic clapping, did she peel away.

"You're right," she said, "the music is shit. But the company is fantastic."

She noted an element of surprise in his eyes and his rigid stance. He was shocked, as if in a temporary trance, his gaze locked onto hers. Eventually, he pulled away, freed himself, and asked, "Should we go back to yours?" There was a hunger in his voice, a desperation that she hadn't heard before, and one she felt rising in herself, as well.

"It's early," she said. "My gran . . ."

"She can join us," he paused and then quickly corrected himself. "For a drink. She can join us for a drink, I mean."

Abi laughed. "It's a good thing she didn't hear you say that. Her knickers would have been around her ankles before you grabbed the wine." She tapped him on the shoulder jovially, noting the shock in his raised eyebrows. "Why don't you call an Uber and I'll just nip inside to use the toilet?"

"Okay, deal."

Abi slipped back into the pub, and as soon as he was out of sight, she pulled out her phone, eager to check on the whereabouts of her gran. They didn't have a landline number, and while Martha did have a smartphone, she didn't use it to receive calls. It was a Twitter machine, something she could use to access the internet, troll people on social media, and receive a deluge of sexts from unsuspecting men who didn't know a septuagenarian catfish when they spoke to one.

Martha refused to give out the number, insisting that people would only use it to bug her, make demands, and tell her that yet another friend had died.

Abi was on her gran's Twitter page when she bumped into the bassist from the band, causing her to nearly drop the device.

"Excuse me," he said dismissively, his attention focused on a young blonde girl who clearly wasn't interested. Steven had been right; the bassist did swing around his instrument like it was his penis, and as soon as he finished his set, he put the guitar away and tried to do it with the real thing, latching on to any vagina that seemed the least bit interested.

"It's okay," Abi said, moving out of the way. Their eyes locked and he paused, staring at her for an uncomfortable length of time.

"Don't I know you?"

Abi shook her head. She did know him, and she hated him. In a town this small, everyone knew everyone, and even Abi, who had lived a relatively sheltered life, had encountered her fair share of assholes, friends, and acquaintances over the years.

"You look familiar," he pushed. "Did we fuck?"

Her jaw nearly hit the floor. The blonde girl standing next to him recoiled somewhat, but also seemed amused by the question and keen to hear an answer. Everything that Abi had felt before leaving the bar came rushing back to her—the panic, the fear, the sickness. She felt like she was going to pass out again, like the entire bar was staring at her.

In reality, she knew that there were only a few people there. The rest of the band were in the process of leaving when she returned to the pub, the barman was on his own behind the bar and there were only a handful of customers, but in that moment, it felt like she was on stage and being judged by thousands.

"I have to go." Abi pushed past the self-assured musician and headed for the bathrooms. He shouted after her. There was a note of recognition and it was followed by a snigger, laughter she could have sworn was coming from everyone in the bar.

She shut the bathroom door behind her, entered one of the stalls, locked the door, and sat down on the toilet, breathing deeply, her eyes closed. It didn't take long for her moments of panic to pass, but Abi hated herself for feeling this way. She hated herself for letting her paranoia get the better of her and for believing things that she knew, deep down, simply weren't true.

Her phone rang and without even looking Abi knew it was her grandmother. As crazy as the old woman was, she had a sixth sense for knowing when something wasn't right. At age fifteen, Abi suffered the sort of unbearable trauma that no child should ever suffer when she watched her childhood home burn to the ground with her parents inside.

It broke her, changed her, and alienated her—she became angry, bitter, and rejected every friend, family member, and social worker that tried to help. Her grandmother was the only one who understood, the only one who stood by her throughout those dark times and the lonely years that followed. The night her parents died and her life changed forever, Martha sat Abi down for a heart to heart, one in which Abi expected to hear the same old cliched nonsense she'd heard spouted on countless TV shows and in many films.

Instead, Martha told her, "Nothing happens for a reason. Nobody goes to a better place, and life is meaningless."

When the words eventually sank in, Abi had asked, "So, what's the point?"

"Think of it like a video game. If you have an end goal, a reason for playing, you do your best to stay alive, to accumulate points, to get as far as you can and do as much as you can. You get angry when you lose, upset when things don't go your way. It's fun, for the most part, but there are times when that happiness is offset by the grind, the repetitive missions, the fact that you get lost or keep failing." Abi hadn't questioned why her grandmother knew so much about video games, as she had always seemed more technically adept than she was. "But if there's no purpose, no end goal, no fear of losing, failing, or getting lost, no missions or targets, what do you do?"

"Run around like an idiot trying to have as much fun as possible before I get bored and quit?"

Martha had nodded assuredly. "There you go, dear—the meaning of life. Now, why don't you put the kettle on and make us both a cuppa?"

The phone continued to ring, the noise echoing throughout the empty bathroom. Abi answered it after a minute or so, but she didn't wait for her grandmother to speak, didn't give her a chance to worry. "Hey Gran, sorry, I can't speak right now, but don't worry, I'm doing fine and will be back soon." She hung up without waiting for a response, smiling as she recalled the words her beloved guardian had said to her many years ago.

After several minutes that felt like hours, she pulled herself together, checked her reflection in the mirror—her eyes wide, her mascara smeared, her hair ruffled—and left. Her head was held high as she walked out of the bathroom, her grandmother's words replaying in her head.

The bar seemed empty—without the thousands of staring eyes she had envisioned before, without the shouting or the laughing. Steven was waiting outside with the Uber, his phone in one hand, the open door in the other.

"You're here at last," he said. "I thought you'd climbed out the bathroom window and done a runner." He pointed to the door. "Your carriage awaits, my lady."

She smiled, curtsied, and then slipped inside.

19

"It's very unusual for her to be out at this time," Abi noted. "I mean, don't get me wrong, my gran is not one of those knit-all-night old ladies who want to be home by 6 and in bed by 8." Abi shrugged. "In fact, that sounds more like me than her."

Steven found that amusing, but quickly hid his laugh and held up a hand to apologize.

"She likes getting out there. Spending time with men, drinking, partying—"

"I need to meet this woman."

"But . . ." Abi continued, confusion etched her face as she gestured around the living room and shrugged, "not at this time and not without telling me."

Steven shifted on the couch, throwing one arm over the back while cradling his wineglass in the other, his legs folded, his posture relaxed. "You were out all day," he noted. "Maybe something came up. You said she doesn't have a phone—"

"She has one, she just doesn't give out the number. In fact, she called me before."

Steven paused, the lip of the wineglass inches from his mouth, expectation on his face as he looked at Abi. "And? What did she say?"

"I didn't give her a chance to speak."

"Oh."

"Maybe I missed something important."

"She's probably out there having fun and you're getting worried for nothing." Steven leaned forward, holding out his free hand and gesturing for her to sit down next to him.

Abi nodded, relented. "Maybe you're right."

"Sounds like a tough woman," he said as Abi settled down next to him, instantly feeling at ease as she sank into the soft material, the natural groove in the old sofa pushing them together like magnets. "What could have possibly happened to her?"

"Good point. There isn't a mugger in the world that could get the best of Martha Ansell."

"There you go, that's the spirit. He moved his wineglass from one hand to the other and then wrapped his free arm around the back of the sofa, his hand coming to rest on Abi's arm, applying gentle pressure to encourage her to move closer.

There was a break in the conversation as they both sat in silence, listening to the sound of one another's breathing, contemplating the day behind them and the night ahead. Steven eventually broke the silence, seemingly compelled to keep the conversation going. "My gran was nowhere near as adept," he said. "I mean, she was a great woman, and she had her own skills. She played the piano in her youth, and she was as sharp as a tack until the day she died, but she was useless with technology. She once called the phone company to say she needed a new phone line installed, and when they went to her house, she gave them an old iPhone."

"Gran basically raised me," Abi said. "In fact, she's the reason I got into freelancing. She was my motivation, my drive. It was thanks to her that I got a computer and the internet before anyone else in my class. Back in the days when it took several minutes to connect, and everything shut down whenever someone called you." Abi laughed. "I was shy at school so the internet, and my Gran, made me the person that I am." She arched her neck to look at Steven's face. "I'm not sure if that's a good thing or a bad thing, but it's definitely something."

"It's a good thing," Steven exclaimed, "of course it's a good thing. You're smart, creative, fun—I mean, I've only known you a couple days, but I'd say your gran and your crappy old dial-up modem did a pretty good job."

"Thanks."

Steven leaned over, kissed her on the top of the head, and then slowly stood. "Anytime." He groaned as he rose to his feet. "Now, if you'll point me in the right direction and excuse me for a moment, I need to use your toilet." He beamed at her as he placed his wineglass down on the coffee table and then straightened some creases out of his trousers.

"Upstairs, first door on the left."

"I'm not going to discover anything untoward, am I? Maybe find your collection of BDSM magazines or discover you have a secret addiction to painkillers."

"No chance," Abi retorted as Steven wandered off in search of the toilet. "I keep my drugs and porn mags in the garage."

Abi searched frantically on her phone while Steven was in the toilet, checking Facebook, Twitter—hoping her grandmother was safe and well, but also hoping that she wouldn't appear just as things were getting heated with Steven.

Martha never approved of Abi's boyfriends, but neither did Abi. Her last few relationships had been a product of circumstance and boredom. She had grown tired of being alone, weary of sleeping by herself night after night. She worked too much, socialized too little, and simply didn't have time to date, so she often settled for men she didn't like, men that were dull, arrogant, annoying; men who didn't have the best personal hygiene, were sexist pigs, or, in some cases, blatantly cheated on her.

The relationships never lasted and, in most cases, Abi found herself introducing the men to her grandmother simply because she knew that Martha would give her the confidence that she lacked to end the relationship. Martha was Abi's catalyst for change, the kick up the ass that she often needed but always avoided.

Steven was different. He was kind, sweet, caring, handsome; he seemed to genuinely care for her, and while it was impossible to know what the future held. he also didn't seem like the cheating sort.

Although, as her gran had said numerous times in the past, "Most men are cheating bastards, the rest are just bastards." The words, and the cheeky, sardonic way that her grandmother expressed them, made Abi snigger. She was still sniggering when Steven returned.

"You've either just found some funny cat pictures on Facebook, or there is something hilarious about the way I pee. Please tell me it's the former."

"It is, of course it is."

"Phew," he said, wiping an imaginary line of sweat from his forehead. "I have this niggling fear that I'm doing something wrong, only everyone is either too polite or oblivious to tell me."

Abi met his comment with a blank stare, an eyebrow raised.

"I should explain," he added, "before you call the men in white. When I was younger, I used to wipe my backside standing up." He held up a hand, silencing Abi before she spoke. "I know, weird. But, apparently, like a quarter of the population do that. The other three-quarters do it sitting down, which is what I do now. But because no one speaks about it, these two groups never meet, everyone assumes that their way is the right way, or the *normal* way, and they get on with their lives."

"That can't be right,"

"I shit you not," Steven said with a firm nod, before adding, "pardon the pun. And the imagery in general, I know this is not a great topic for a second date."

"It's interesting, interesting is *always* good."

He shuffled next to her on the couch, picked up his wine. "Also, I was in my twenties before I realized that the way I put on a sweater is weird. I sort of like ball it up and then throw it over my head."

"That does sound weird."

"I would give you an example, but I don't want you swooning when I take my top off. I could lose you for the night."

Abi laughed and shoved him lightly on the arm, shaking the wineglass in his hand. "Good call. We wouldn't want that."

"So, now I have this fear that someone is going to come up to me and tell me that I'm peeing wrong, or I'm eating wrong, or sleeping wrong." He drained the wine in his glass. "Imagine being—told at thirty-seven that you're basically not . . . *humaning* properly."

"Good word."

"Thank you. Feel free to use that one with your clients. Do you not have that?"

"Not really. I mean, I'm an anxious person, I'm worried of a lot of things, but . . ." She shook her head, still grinning. Her eyes were fixed on his face, but he was staring out into the yard, his mind seemingly elsewhere.

"I'm weird, I know," he said, distantly.

"Not weird. *Quirky*, I think is a better word. At least that's what people tell me." She laughed, but he didn't reciprocate. "Everything okay? I haven't embarrassed you, have I?"

Steven turned to her. "No, no. If anyone has embarrassed me, it's me. I just . . ." His eyes returned to the patio door and the yard beyond it.

It was dark outside, the thick grass that covered the garden and the swaying trees that stood near the perimeter fence were only just visible, black silhouettes caught in the silvery glow of the moonlight. Everything else was just a reflection of the light inside the living room, emitted by a lamp beside the couch and the flickering flames of candles on the coffee table.

Abi watched the dark trees dance, her blurred reflection staring back at her. "What is it?" she asked, feeling the warmth of the evening immediately drain out of her.

"I don't mean to scare you or anything." His eyes were fixed on the patio door still. "I just—I could have sworn I saw someone in your yard."

Abi's heart dropped to the pit of her stomach; her body tensed. Her hand gripped the wineglass so tightly that she felt it flex in her palm.

"Maybe I'm just being paranoid. It might have been my reflection or just a tree. But—" He turned to her and seemed to note the horror on her face. "I should check it out."

WANNABE

"I'm in a band," he said, a broad grin on his face. "We play progressive metal, sorta like Tool, only with more—I don't know—meat, more—" He clenched his fists and made a throwing motion followed by an impassioned grunt. "You know what I mean?"

Absolutely fucking not.

I shook my head in disbelief, barely able to suppress a grin as I hunched over my Red Bull and listened to the aspiring rock star chat up an impressionable, vacuous redhead behind me.

"Totally," Red replied eventually, giving him the answer he had hoped for.

"So, this band of yours, Tool, are you in town right now?" she asked, completely missing the point.

I had underestimated the extent of her stupidity.

"I'm not—"Wannabe began, before pausing and adding, "yeah, we're playing across town tomorrow night. Big show. Thousands watching."

I watched his reflection through a mirror behind the bar, his lips curled like the sadistic smile of The Joker as he realized he'd just convinced an attractive young girl that he was a legendary rock star.

If I wasn't so desperate not to draw attention to myself, I would have vomited on the bar. He was the epitome of sleaze, the master of cringe. She was the third girl to have entered the bar since I had been there, and he had tried the same trick on every one of them. I stayed at the back, collar up, hat down, sunglasses on—trying to avoid giving anyone a description they could relay to the police. I watched him cycle through the same bullshit with all of them.

"That's so cool."

"Yeah, but I'm kinda used to it by now. Just one of those things."

Red's mouth was agape, a simple look for a simple woman. "So, what do you do?"

"I play a little, I sing a little. And I write all our songs. Maybe I could even dedicate one to you?"

He didn't sing and the songs he wrote were barely worthy of a campfire singalong, let alone a chart-topping success. He played the bass in a local cover band, one made up of high-school dropouts and unemployed rejects. The closest any of them had gotten to rock superstardom was beating Beginner level on *Guitar Hero*.

He worked part-time behind the bar and spent his days cleaning tables, scrubbing toilets, and begging the bar manager to let him busk on the weekends. Whenever he was on his break, he would let his long hair down, roll up his sleeves to expose his tattoos, and then perve on every newcomer with long legs and a vagina.

Wannabe was used to failure. His life had been a procession of misery and rejection. His mother walked out on him when he was ten and both his education and his aspirations had failed him. He hadn't paid attention at school and spent most of his time snorting speed and smoking dope. All sense had been willingly emptied out of his head, only for the education system to unleash him on the world at seventeen with barely a brain cell worth salvaging. Wannabe seemed to embrace failure and take rejection in his stride.. When the women rejected him and his lies, knocking him off his high horse, he just jumped right back on and humped it until it gave in.

"What's your most famous song? I can put it on my phone."

"You can't," he said quickly. "We're having issues with copyrights—agents, managers, record companies, you know how it is. It's only available on CD."

Smooth. Sickeningly so.

Red clearly wasn't interested in whether he was telling the truth or not, nor was she smart enough to read him. If she had been, she would have Googled the name of the band and wondered why the real leader single of Tool was twenty years older, significantly balder, and American.

"I have all the CDs at my place if you want to listen?" Wannabe pushed. "It'll be good to relax before the big gig tomorrow."

"I'd love to."

Wannabe gave a signal to the bar manager and then turned to leave, his arm around the red head's shoulders. The bar manager shook his head in disbelief and grumbled angrily to himself. I finished my drink, checked my watch, and then followed.

Wannabe was right about one thing. There was going to be a big show and he was the leading man. But he didn't have to wait until tomorrow.

20

Abi sat, rooted to the couch, the tips of her fingers pale from gripping the wineglass as she watched Robert edge closer to the patio door. He hovered one hand over the handle, the other over a switch for the outside light. With one last glance at Abi, he yanked opened the door and snapped on the light.

Abi sprang to her feet and skipped after Steven as he jumped into the yard, his senses on high alert. The muscles under his T-shirt were noticeably rigid, tense; the vein in his neck pounding rapidly.

The sound of the sliding door rattling in its housing reverberated throughout the house as Abi yanked it shut and was immediately followed by another noise, one that drew both Abi and Steven's attention. It came from Robert's side of the fence—a clattering, banging. Steven immediately took out his phone, opened turned on its flashlight, and then pointed the glaring light at the fence.

Abi remained inside the house, watching Steven from the threshold. She was reluctant to step outside, but she had an inkling as to what the sound was. Judging by the way Steven glared at the fence, the way his eyes opened wide, his jaw set rigid by clenched teeth, she could also imagine what he had seen.

"What the fuck are you doing!?" Steven barked, his attention on the fence, holding his subject in place with the beam of his makeshift spotlight. He advanced, shuffling baby steps, his gaze never leaving his target.

"I—I—I—"

Abi's heart sank when she heard the mumbled reply. She hadn't known her neighbor long, but she recognized his anxious utterances. She knew it was Robert. And in the time it took Steven to move across the garden, to edge closer to the fence and force his intimidating posture on her neighbor, she also understood exactly what had happened.

"You were spying on us," Steven yelled, echoing Abi's thoughts.

"No—No, I swear—"

"We're going to call the police—" For the first time in the confrontation, Steven turned to Abi, his gaze softening. "Call the police, Abi. Tell them your creepy neighbor was spying on you."

Abi nodded quickly as Steven spoke to her, desperate for him to finish and to focus back on Robert, worried that every second he was distracted was a second that he was at risk. If a lifetime of horror films had taught her anything it was that you never turned your back on a crazy person.

Steven turned away from Abi, back to Robert, whose flustered, heavy breathing she could hear from inside the house.

"Please don't phone the police," Robert said. "You don't need to do that. I wasn't doing anything, I swear."

"Yes, you fucking were," Steven barked. The anger in his voice made Abi flinch, but she didn't move. She wanted to head back inside, grab her phone, and call the police; she wanted to run to the kitchen and get a weapon just in case. But she did none of those things and remained where she was, frozen, uncertain.

"I wasn't, I—"

"I saw you," Steven reaffirmed. "What's your game, eh?" He was close to the fence now, just several feet from Abi. A few more steps and he would be out of her eye line and within inches of her neighbor.

Abi closed her eyes tightly, breathed deeply. A dizziness came over her. Her blood raced through her body, creating a waterfall of chaos inside her head, making her legs weak, her stance unsteady. She placed her hand on the wall and leaned against it, taking some of the weight and strain off her weakening legs.

Come on, Abi, now's not the time.

"We know what you're up to," Steven said, now fully out of Abi's line of vision.

There was a moment of hesitation and defiance. When Robert replied, the fear and shock in his voice had been replaced by uncertainty, bordering on bemusement. "What do you mean?"

Be strong, Abi.

"You've been spying on her. Watching her. Stalking her. And that's not all, is it?"

"Isn't it?"

Steven's tone changed, it became lower, softer, his words carried on a wave of disgust: "We know it was you."

"Do you? Because I don't, I don't even know what the fuck you're talking about."

What would Gran do?

Abi opened her eyes, feeling anger rising, hatred growing. She forced the anxiety aside, took another deep breath, and finally stepped over the threshold and into the yard. The cool night air greeted her immediately, as did the bickering rivals who stood on either side of her fence.

"Hello, Abi," Robert said in a tone that neither she nor Steven appreciated.

Abi remained still, standing several feet behind Steven, her eyes fixed on her neighbor.

"You better watch yourself," Steven barked, turning back to Robert, thrusting his finger at him.

"Okay, but can you put your light down now?" Robert said, his tone growing more confident and carefree by the minute. "You're going to give me a headache."

"Good!" Steven barked, maintaining his threatening posture but looking visibly perturbed by Robert's sudden personality shift. He lowered the phone and was about to turn off the app when he noticed something. The beam focused back on Robert, this time on his hands.

"You were taking pictures," Steven accused.

"What? Don't be—"

"Why else would you have your phone out?"

"None of your business."

"You're right, it's not. But I bet the police will be interested. Did you phone them, Abi?" Steven asked, the light glaring into Robert's face, forcing him to shield it with his hand.

Abi shook her head. "No, I-I don't think—I mean—"

"You made the right choice, Abi," Robert said smugly.

Steven glared at both of them in turn, a low, grumbled grunt of exasperation escaping his lips. "You keep your eyes off her," he warned.

It wasn't the right choice; it was the only one. Abi knew that, and underneath the anger, she knew that Steven did, as well. He hadn't committed a crime, not that they could prove, and while he had been incredibly creepy, they had no way to prove that he had been in the yard. Pictures could be deleted; lies could be told. It had been a good day, and Abi didn't want the police to spoil that any more than Robert already had.

"You're lucky we're in a forgiving mood." Steven closed the flashlight app and put his phone away.

Abi noted a look of smug satisfaction on Robert's face as he removed his hand from his eyes and tucked it into his pocket.

"What is your game here?" Steven pushed.

"What do you mean?"

"You know what I mean. First, you go on a date, then the next thing you move into the house next door, you follow her around, hide in her yard—"

"Allegedly."

"Excuse me?"

"Allegedly, I hid in her yard. I'm not admitting to anything."

Steven paused, his mouth agape as he processed the conversation and the blank expression on Robert's face. "You're messed up."

"*Allegedly*."

Steven shook his head in disbelief. "Tell me, what is it you're up to?"

Robert shrugged. "Just enjoying the night."

"Really? In that case, where have you been tonight?"

"I don't need to answer your questions."

"You fucking better answer my questions," Steven barked. "Otherwise I'll scale this fence and—"

He stopped when Abi rested a reassuring hand on his shoulder. "It's okay," she said. "Just forget about him."

She could feel the tension in his shoulders, could sense the anger that coursed through him. But when he looked at her and noted how anxious she was, how uncomfortable she was with the situation and how clearly desperate she was for it to be over, he relaxed.

"You better stay away," Steven told Robert, his words softer, his tone still threatening. "If I see you anywhere near this house again, I will break your fucking face." He held his stare for interminable seconds and then pulled away, following Abi as she beat a retreat into the house.

"Good advice," Robert said as the two departed, "I have some advice for you—"

Steven stopped just short of the patio door. Abi slid inside, eager to away from the confrontation.

She watched Steven's face as Robert continued, "Be careful with that one, she's not the little angel that you think she is."

"What did he mean by that?" Abi was angry. The tension, the anxiety, and the worry had wrestled for control inside her head over the last couple of hours before giving way to indignation. "I'm not the angel you think I am?"

Steven shrugged, somewhat amused by Abi's anger. "Firstly, I don't think you are a little angel. I knew you had a fire in you—anyone with a gran like yours can't be wholly innocent. Secondly, so what? He's just a creepy little incel who pins the blame on you because you refused to date him, sleep with him, and succumb to his every bizarre whim."

"Bastard," Abi spat, draining the last of her red wine.

"You have a face like thunder," Steven noted. "And it suits you. You need to get angry more often."

"For as long as that prick is around, I will."

"Keep talking dirty to me, you're turning me on."

Abi laughed and shoved him hard, sending him into a panic as he desperately tried to stop himself from spilling his wine.

"I think I'm a little drunk," Abi said after watching him struggle and then diverting her attention to her empty glass and the bottle next to it.

"You're not alone." Steven put his glass down on the table. "Maybe we should call it a night."

As soon as he spoke those words, Abi's attention went to the back door. They had turned the outside light on and drawn the curtains, but the commotion still unsettled her. She had panicked after walking in the kitchen and seeing her own reflection in the window; had hurried during three visits to the bathroom, craning her neck to see the small window behind her, fearing that his smug face was on the other side of the frosted glass.

If her gran was there, she wouldn't have felt the same level of paranoia. Martha was strong. Nothing fazed her. But the old woman hadn't shown her face.

"Maybe I should sleep here tonight." Steven seemingly read Abi's mind.

Abi wanted him to stay. She dreaded to think what would happen if she was forced to spend the night alone—she was tired, tipsy, anxious. The night would be spent pacing the floor and peeking through the curtains. Eventually, she would drive herself insane and would be found either curled in a ball in the corner of the room or chasing her neighbor around the yard with a machete and a mouthful of obscenities.

"Okay." Abi nodded, a smile on her face as she pictured herself naked, machete in hand, and in hot pursuit of her perverted neighbor. It certainly wouldn't be the worst outcome, but with Steven there, it was one she didn't need to worry about. "But I can't be bothered dealing with my gran's crude questions right now, so you're going to have to keep quiet."

He held up his hands, palms open, before squeezing his lips shut tight and drawing a finger across them.

"Assuming she actually returns," Abi added, another concern jostling its way to the front of her busy mind. "God knows where she is or what she's up to, but she'll probably wander back in the early hours, drunk as a skunk, stinking of kebab meat and beer and singing."

"Your gran eats kebabs and drinks beer?"

"Yes, amazing, isn't it?"

"It really is. I mean, I haven't even seen this woman, and already I think I'm in love."

"Fuck off," Abi hissed jokingly under her breath, shoving him on the arm again.

"Abi Ansell," he retorted in reply, shaking his head in feigned displeasure. "You're not the sweet, innocent girl I fell for. In fact, you're a kebab, a wig, and a few beers away from turning into your gran."

Abi glared at him, an eyebrow raised. "Does that turn you on?" she winked.

He looked appalled at first, but then he nodded. "A little bit."

WANNABE

Wannabe lived in rented accommodation above a butcher's shop. By agreeing to take Red back to his house, he was showing her how little he respected her intelligence. Here he was, an apparent millionaire rock star preparing to play to thousands, and yet he had chosen to spend the night in a dingy second-floor flat as opposed to a five-star hotel.

I couldn't hear their conversation, but I knew what men like Wannabe were like, I knew how their minds worked, and I had a fairly good idea of what he had told her. As I followed behind, far enough not to arouse suspicion, close enough to see where they were headed, I pictured him telling her that he had borrowed the apartment from a friend.

I like to live rough when I'm on tour, I imagined him saying. *It keeps me connected to my roots and means I can put in a more meaningful performance.*

If I didn't find him so repulsive and didn't believe that Red would have believed anything anyone told her, I would have been impressed.

Wannabe reminded me of Neckbeard. He wasn't as physically repulsive. He was cleaner, fitter, moderately more attractive, charming, albeit intermittently. There was no sadism there, either. Manipulation and deception were used for sexual advancement, not for the sheer hell of it. But he was still despicable, selfish, and narcissistic.

I found myself gaining on them with every step I took. I kept my movements slow, methodical, but their steps were staggered and interrupted by groping, kissing, and shrill laughter that echoed throughout the empty streets like banshee screams. They were clearly having a lot of fun, even though they'd only known each other for a few minutes.

They began looking over their shoulders at me, firing furtive glances. I knew they weren't smart enough to realize I was following them. They didn't have anything to fear or anyone to suspect, but they seemed unsettled by the fact that I was there. I retrieved my phone from my pocket and began fiddling on the screen, using the opportunity to significantly slow my steps and make it clear that I wasn't following them.

When I looked up again, they had vanished.

Shit.

The streets were empty, devoid of life and movement, the silence broken only by the sound of distant cars and monotonous music thumping from a nearby house. The promiscuous imbeciles were nowhere to be seen.

There was a chance they were hiding and watching me, a chance they had seen me, anticipated my intentions and turned the tables. A chance, but not a likely one. Muffled laughter and hasty footsteps quelled my doubts and settled my anxiety. The sound came from an alleyway ahead and to the right. It was Red—I would recognize that shrill voice and vacuous tone anywhere. Wannabe was trying his best to silence her, but his hushed warnings were just as loud as her laughter.

They were hiding, and they hadn't spotted me.

Wannabe had surprised me. He hadn't lied to his provisional partner about his home. He hadn't even intended to take her back. Either he had decided that she wasn't worth the time and effort, or he was just so horny that he couldn't wait.

The alleyway wrapped around the back of an abandoned pub and came to a dead-end behind a boarded-up apartment block. It was here that the young and stupid lovers decided to share their first kiss, hungrily swapping saliva and the remnants of everything they'd kissed, sucked, and swallowed over the last few days—a prelude to their first fuck, in which they would share other bodily fluids and a plethora of STDs.

From behind a dumpster, nestled in the shadow of an overhanging roof, I watched them grasp and pull their way through an awkward and hurried sexual encounter, their actions highlighted under the white glow of a nearby florescent. They kissed, long and impassioned. Wannabe pressed her against the wall, kissing her neck, groping her breasts, and then pulling down her pants.

He turned her around and thrust his face between her exposed cheeks as she squirmed and giggled. Seconds later his pants were around his ankles, his fly ripped open, his erect penis exposed to the unseasonably cool air. The sex was quick, hard, cold, and confusing. Wannabe came after a few thrusts and pulled out; she had barely gotten started, seemingly believing that this was still foreplay and the best was yet to come.

Pants up, hands around her waist, Wannabe leaned in close, whispering in her ear and kissing her neck. She seemed happy with the act, but his goal wasn't to placate her after a hurried and disappointing encounter; he wasn't intent on giving her the same pleasure that she had given him. He simply wanted to surreptitiously wipe his penis on the seat of her pants.

"I'm sorry," he said when she turned around.

"It's okay," she said quickly. "It happens to everyone."

The pause suggested he hadn't expected that. "No," he said slowly. "I was going to say that I'm sorry I just remembered that I have to meet my bandmates at the venue."

"Oh, okay."

Maybe he expected her to be more disappointed, maybe he expected her to put up a fight, call him a liar, and even demand that he take her with him. But she did none of those things. Red might have been stupid and gullible, but she also knew what was good for her, and a five-second fumble that made her feel uncomfortable, cold, and unsatisfied definitely wasn't it.

Her footsteps echoed a hasty retreat on the concrete as she walked through the shadows and out of the alleyway without saying another word and without catching a glimpse of the voyeur hiding behind the dumpster.

Wannabe was in no rush to follow and was already preparing to gloat about his experience, phone in hand, a wide grin on his face. There was no shame, no embarrassment, no sense that he had just given an attractive young girl the most uncomfortable sexual encounter of her young life, not to mention an awkward encounter at the sexual health clinic a couple weeks from now.

He snapped a picture of himself to capture his stupid grin for posterity before taking another while standing in front of the scene of the crime, giving the camera a thumbs-up. If his friends had been there with him, he would be high-fiving them and telling them how amazing it had been and how he'd rocked her world.

As if confirming my suspicions, he pressed the phone to his ear and spoke excitedly to his equally dim-witted friends. "Did you see them?" he asked, "it's not random, and it's not a mistake. That's where I am right now, and I just fucked a gorgeous hot girl here. My dick is still hard, man. And, better yet, she pissed off after!"

Clearly, he wasn't the only asshole in his band. Tool had a lot of explaining to do.

I slipped out from behind the dumpster and made my move. I was bathed in darkness; he was standing under a light. The advantage was mine.

"It's behind the old Queen's Head—"

I removed a large blade from its sheath around my waist and edged closer, knowing his excited words would drown out my approach.

"No, seriously. And it was her idea! . . . No, honestly, look!"

He turned the phone toward me, pointed it directly at me, and snapped another picture.

I froze, locked in place by the Medusa-like flash.

The smile still beamed on his face as he pulled the phone back to his ear and stared absently into the darkness. "See, you get it? I told you, man, it's an alleyway, next to—"

Shit. Shit. Shit.

His smile slowly faded, turning first to confusion and then to horror. "What do you mean?" he asked. "What person? There's no one else here. She left." He tried to laugh it off. "You're tripping, man. Stop trying to scare me and ruin my buzz."

I moved quickly, blinking away the stars from the corner of my ears, heading straight for the idiot sheathed in the glow of the streetlight.

"Mate, you're scaring me—"

I was just five or six feet away when he saw me—too close for him to react. If his brain hadn't been tainted by years of drug use, he might have reacted quicker, he might have heeded his friend's warning and run, shouted, screamed, or come out fighting. But he did none of those things.

Wannabe barely lifted a finger as the knife came down, first near his shoulder, then his upper chest, then his neck. I stabbed him six times before he finally began to fight back, but by that point, it was too late: the aspiring rock star played his last note with a strangled cry that bubbled out through the viscous blood pooling in his mouth.

There was no fight. No resistance. No chance. I treated him to the same experience that he had given so many slow-minded, promiscuous women over the years—it happened so quickly and so brutally that he barely had time to react, let alone acknowledge he'd just been fucked.

He dropped to his knees, his simpleton grin now a picture of horror; his eyes imploring.

There was a glimmer of recognition when he saw me, but it was soon replaced by confusion, desperation, and then fear.

"Hello? Hello!?"

Wannabe rapidly bled out while his dimwitted friend failed to grasp the seriousness of the situation on the other end of the phone.

"Damn it! My bloody phone is playing up again."

I ended the call and checked the image he had snapped. My outline was visible—a black silhouette, the glint of a knife—but there were no discernible features and it was all wrapped in motion blur, with the hood covering my face like the shroud of the grim reaper. I deleted the photograph from his phone. I couldn't do anything about the image on his friend's phone, but I didn't need to. It didn't show anything. I wiped the device with my sleeve and dropped it on the bleeding, gurgling body at my feet.

21

"Steven, Steven!"

He grumbled a lethargic reply, rolled over, and took most of the duvet with him.

"You have to wake up!"

He stirred, lifted his head, stared directly at her, and then flopped back onto the pillow. "Five more minutes."

"Now!"

He groaned again. "What's wrong?" His eyes were squeezed shut, blocking out the morning light that poured through the window and threatened his hangover.

"My gran's home!" The angst was evident on Abi's face.

Steven opened his eyes, blinked away the light. "So what?"

Abi jumped out of bed. A thin gleam of sweat coated her naked back and chest. The thick duvet had trapped the intense heat from their bodies, retaining the moisture and saturating the sheet underneath them. The air was thick, humid. Abi pushed open a window and welcomed the resulting breeze.

They'd had sex, that much she knew, but she could only recall glimpses of it—his hands on her breasts, his head between her legs. The memories stirred something inside of her, made her yearn for a repeat of the experience. She pressed her hands to her thighs, drew them upwards, over the soft, clammy flesh, into the warmth between her legs.

She turned to look at him, eager for more, the excitement growing. The matted hair between his shoulder blades stared back at her and the excitement instantly faded, her hands back by her side.

They had drunk a couple bottles of wine, she had kissed him, and the next thing she remembered, they were in bed. She didn't think she'd been that drunk. She remembered most of the night adding up to getting into bed, but beyond that it was just an excitable blur. He brought her to climax with his mouth. She had held him there, begged him to finish, and he did. Then he kissed her—

She wiped her mouth, twisted her faced. A musty taste lingered on her tongue—she may have been imagining it, but she was sure she was tasting herself. It hadn't bothered her at the time, but she retched a little at the thought.

Her heart sunk when she remembered something else. He had stopped, rolled out of the bed. Desperate for him to finish, she had questioned him, breathless, frustrated; he had a condom in his back pocket, he told her, his jeans were on the floor.

"Don't bother," she had told him. "Just come back and finish. Quickly."

Shit.

She swallowed thickly. Now she definitely could taste herself—musty, unpalatable. Her stomach turned, partly from the alcohol, partly from the memory. Good memories turned to bad, exhilaration to anger.

Stupid girl.

But when she looked at him, noted the compassion in his eyes, the love on his face as he studied her features and beamed brightly, those thoughts and that anger dissipated. There wasn't so much as a glimmer of regret on his face, and knowing that was enough to bring a smile to hers.

A bra had been discarded on the dresser; a pair of panties sprawled next to them. "You have to go," she ordered calmly, slinging the bra over her shoulders. "My gran's home and you need to be away before she wakes up."

Steven sat upright. "I don't mind meeting her."

"But I do."

There was no further dissent. Steven sensed the discomfort behind her eyes. He clearly didn't want to ruin their morning, to spoil the memories of their night together. He sprang out of bed, and she averted her eyes like a schoolgirl on seeing that he was also naked but for a pair of thin black socks.

"You saw it all last night," he said.

"I know, but . . . now's not the time."

"You're worried that my naked body will turn you on, aren't you? You're worried that you'll be forced to throw yourself at me if you spend even just a split second staring at my . . . my—"

"Don't say it."

"Manhood."

"Oh God, you said it." She made a point to look at his penis. "Now I can look, because I know, in my heart of hearts, that I simply cannot sleep with a man who refers to his penis as his *manhood*."

Steven slipped on his boxer shorts, struggling to remain upright as he hopped on one leg and then the other. "What else am I supposed to call it?" He picked up his sweater from the other side of the room, a look of mild bemusement on his face as he tried to recall how it got there. "My member?"

"Your member? You're not an erotica writer from the 1990s."

"My dick?"

Abi was fully dressed now; her clothes scrunched, wrinkled, her hair like an untamed chia pet. "How about you don't refer to it at all? There's more to your body than your penis, you know. Us girls don't treat penises like you treat tits and ass. We don't walk around looking at men's junk and proclaiming, 'Look at the girth on that.'"

Steven halted in the middle of putting on his jeans, wearing a bewildered expression. "I'm not sure if I'm disgusted or turned on."

"We don't have time for either, just hurry up and get ready."

Abi's eyes shifted from the door to Steven and back again. She checked her phone, noted the time, and then prepared to bark another order when his kind words instantly softened her anxiety.

"Last night was amazing." He zipped and then buttoned his jeans. "I just wanted to put that out there before you hurried me out the door."

There was a desperate look in his eyes. "It really was," she reciprocated, keen not to hurt his feelings. He hurried to her and she grabbed him, wrapping her arms around his head, planting a firm kiss on his lips. They remained in that embrace, that kiss, for several seconds, before she felt his hand slide over the arch of her back, rest on the curve of her buttocks, and squeeze. At that point, she broke away. "Not now. You have to go."

"What time is it, anyway?"

"Just past six."

"In the morning!"

She shut the door and glared at him.

"Six?" he whispered, almost hissing.

"I know, and I'm sorry, but she wakes up early."

"I heard her coming back last night," he told her. "Sound of the front door woke me up. You must have been in the bathroom. Good thing it wasn't me, eh? If what you've told me about your gran is true, she would have probably tried to hump me in the hallway."

Abi offered him a strained smile, but he could see that she was in a hurry.

"Okay, sorry, let's go."

Abi opened the door again and stepped outside, gesturing for Steven to follow her. They both crept along the carpeted hallway, Abi stopping at the top of the stairs, Steven halting before one of the closed doors.

He pointed to the door and mouthed the words, *"Is this her room?"*

Abi, horrified, stepped forward and waved frantically at him.

Steven repeated his gesture.

Abi nodded, rolled her eyes, and grabbed him by the arm. She practically yanked him across the hallway and then pointed down the stairs. He held up his hands, signaling that he wasn't going to resist, and when she released him, he began a slow and careful descent.

"You're really worried about this gran business," Steven whispered when they were outside. "Is there something you're not telling me?"

"Like what?"

He shrugged. "I don't know. Is she secretly a pimp? A prostitute? A serial killer? A drug baron? An evil, maniacal overlord hellbent on destroying the world?"

"No. No. No. And—" Abi tipped her head this way and that. "Maybe."

"Maybe? Which one?"

"Does it have to be just one?"

"Cool. So—" Steven stuffed his hands in his pockets and looked both ways down the street. "Now what?"

Abi hadn't thought that far ahead.

"You never thought about learning to drive?" Steven wondered as Abi retrieved her phone from her pocket.

"I can drive. I just don't have a car."

"That's like learning Spanish and never going to Spain."

"Which makes perfect sense if you can't afford plane tickets."

Steven's face twisted. "I'm lost."

Abi groaned. "It's an expensive and unnecessary expense for a writer who works from home and never goes anywhere." Her eyes were on her phone as she spoke. "Although, if I had a dollar every time someone raised that point, I could have bought a Ferrari and had driving lessons from Damon Hill."

"Damon Hill? You know this is 2023, right?"

"And?" she snapped.

"Nothing."

"I just ordered you an Uber, it'll be here in—"

"What is it with you?"

Abi's words were cut short by a raspy, angry shout, and they both instinctively looked to Robert's house, even though they knew the voice wasn't his.

22

Robert's house sat in silence—the curtain's drawn, the car idle in the driveway.

"You're just a troublemaker, is what you are," the voice spoke again.

The two lovers realized it was coming from the house across the street. They saw an elderly, hunchbacked woman staring back at them, the cane in her right hand thrust at them like an accusatory finger.

"Excuse me?" Abi uttered, baffled by the comments, a fear rising deep within her.

"You heard me," the old woman persisted as she scuttled forward like a wounded crab, using the cane to aid her movements before thrusting it back at her victims when she spoke, *"troublemakers!"*

Steven calmly turned to Abi, his hands still stuffed in his pockets, his expression still hazy and half asleep. "Who is this crazy old woman and what is she talking about?"

"You want to watch yourself, young man." The old lady was now just half a dozen feet away, having shuffled her way from the end of her drive to the middle of the road. She wore slippers that had seen better days and were probably older than Abi was, but despite that, and her clear mobility issues, she didn't have a problem traversing the tarmac to make her point known.

"Are you talking to me?" Steven asked, his voice low.

"Yes. She's not right. Watch what you're getting yourself into."

"I don't think—"

"She's a wrong'un," the old lady continued, cutting Steven short, the cane still raised. "Get out while you can. Wrong in the head, if you ask me."

The fear that Abi felt was ushered to one side, her hatred of confrontation kicked to the touch by a raging anger that activated her darkest side. "What the fuck are you talking about?" she yelled, seeing both the old woman and Steven flinch.

"You—you heard me," the elderly woman replied. "I've been around long enough to tell good from bad, young lady, and I know you're tainted. I know who you are, I've heard the—"

"Watch your fucking mouth!" Abi took a step forward and felt Steven's hand clamp onto her arm, holding her back. She resisted, showing the old lady her anger and her purpose and causing her to take a cautious step backward. "Or you will regret it."

The old lady looked shocked—stuck rigid in the middle of the road. "It's true. You are crazy," she said eventually, biting back. The cane came out again, thrusting at Abi, wobbling frantically in her fragile grasp. "I've been watching you. I've heard you. I've seen you. In and out at ungodly hours, doing God knows what."

Steven shrugged. "I've been called worse."

"I know what you're up to," the old woman continued.

"I'm glad you do," Steven said, loosening his grip on Abi's arm as the situation turned from confrontational to absurd. "Because we don't have a fucking clue." Steven looked to Abi as if to confirm and she shook her head in reply.

"Last night," the old lady replied. "I heard you in the yard. Shouting, raving, arguing."

"*My* yard," Abi reminded her. "I was in *my* yard."

"Late at night, when everyone was trying to get some sleep!"

Abi shrugged and shook her head in disbelief.

"I heard you . . ." She looked up and down the street. "*Having coitus.*"

Steven laughed. Abi's jaw hung open.

"Only hussies and hobos have sex in the open like that."

Abi exchanged a glance with Steven, who seemed highly amused by the situation. Over his shoulder, she could see that Robert was also watching, standing brazenly by the window, the curtains now pulled apart to expose him and the room beyond.

This time the sight of him didn't send Abi's heart racing, it didn't make her legs feel weak, because his attention was fixed on the old lady, not her. He was glaring at her, a deadpan, clinical expression on his face.

"I think this one may have lost her mind," Steven told Abi. "We should call the men in white."

Abi ignored him. "We didn't have sex in the yard," she said plainly. "You should get your hearing checked. Or learn the difference between a quiet conversation and full-blown fucking."

"How dare you!" she snapped in reply, darting her head this way, and then, "there are children on this street!"

Abi rolled her eyes. As far as she knew, there was only one, and he was in his mid-teens.

"And I know what I heard," the old lady continued.

Abi turned back to Steven, who merely shrugged. She fired another cursory glance at Robert and saw that he had barely moved—his posture still rigid, his attention still focused on the mad old lady.

"And he's not the first, is he?"

"Excuse me?" Abi asked.

The old lady nodded vigorously, looking like a nodding dog ornament caught in gale-force winds. "That nice man who moved next door. He told me you went on a date with him. Polite, he was, very nice. Didn't say a lot, but I could see it in his eyes. I've been on this earth a long time—"

"No one's disputing that," Steven interjected calmly.

"—and I know what you're like, I know people like you. You led him on, made him believe that you had something, and then shacked up with someone else only a day later. Isn't that right?"

"I don't—"

"You're all the same," the bitter woman pushed, finally lowering her cane. "And knowing your family . . ." She shook her head and spat on the ground, a dry ejaculation that exposed her fake teeth and bitterness "It doesn't surprise me."

The old lady turned around and slowly staggered across the road, down her driveway, and into her home. She never looked back, and Abi watched her methodical movements with anger that bordered on disbelief. It was hard to accept that the woman who took several seconds and several attempts to climb a second concrete step outside her front door, a woman who was even older than her gran and just as rigid as the knobby cane she thrust so menacingly, could spout so much hate.

"Well . . ." Steven turned to Abi when the old lady's front door silently clicked shut and the street fell silent. "That was . . ."

"Unexpected?" Abi offered.

He shook his head. "*Weird* is the word I'm looking for. Let me guess, prudish old lady encounters your mad grandmother, takes an immediate disliking to her, and tars her granddaughter with the same brush."

Abi nodded, her unblinking gaze still fixed on the house opposite, her jaw set rigid.

"I'm surprised she didn't wake your gran up."

"Surprised and lucky. She would have been out here in an instant, ready for war. It wouldn't have been pleasant."

"Two old ladies beating each other with canes while arguing about coitus and trying not to wake the neighborhood children? Pleasant is an understatement; it would have been fucking epic."

Abi managed a forced smile in reply.

"Don't worry," Steven assured her, "I'm met her type before. Don't let her get to you. After all, a big, strong, mature, handsome hussy like you doesn't have anything to fear from a frail old lady."

Abi pulled her gaze away from the old lady's house, her expression softening. "You're a dick, you know that?"

"Very much so. Now—" He threw his arm around her, checked his watch. "We have a few minutes left. Should we wait here for the Uber or should we nip inside for some more coitus?"

Abi laughed. "Maybe just a hug, for now. Wouldn't want to give the crazy old bat any more ammunition."

The two embraced and Abi shifted her attention to Robert's house. The curtains were drawn, the occupant nowhere to be seen. It was like he had never been there, but Abi knew otherwise, and the image of him standing there, glaring at the old woman, his expression still, his eyes alight, would remain in her mind all morning.

23

Martha was waiting for Abi when she returned to the house—her sweater sleeves rolled up past her elbows, her hands pressed to her hips. "Well, well, well," she said, exaggerating each syllable. "The prodigal plonker returns."

"I wondered when you would turn up," Abi said, brushing past her grandmother on her way into the kitchen. She flicked the kettle on and dropped into a chair, cringing as the wooden legs screeched on the laminate flooring. "Let's not beat around the bush, what did you hear, what do you want to know—" She paused, shooting an inquisitive stare at her grandmother as she leaned against the counter. "And what's that old woman's problem? I don't even know the crazy old fucker."

Martha's chuckled. "Ah, yes, Mrs. Hunt the neighborhood cunt. Then again, a cunt is useful. It has a purpose. It makes people happy. Mine has made me *very* happy, in fact—"

"Let's stick with the topic at hand."

"Mrs. Hunt has lived here most of her life. Her family is from the area. Her family's family is from the area. I'm sure she can trace most of her lineage back to an area of just a few square miles."

"Nothing wrong with that."

"Yes, there is, my dear," Martha said, retrieving two cups from the cupboard and assuming the tea-making duties. "It's called inbreeding. It was all the rage in the old days. Even the royal family got involved. But if left unchecked, it creates monsters like Mrs. Hunt."

Abi sighed. "I don't think she's inbred."

"You never met her family."

"Come on, Gran, what's really going on here?"

Martha dropped a cup of steaming tea in front of her granddaughter and took another for herself. She sat on a chair opposite, took a long sip, and then shrugged her shoulders. "As I said, she's just a cunt who can't mind her own business. She's also a prude. As far as she's concerned, you can't even think about sex until you're married. If you're fingering yourself, you better make sure there's a ring on that finger."

Abi wrapped her hands around the cup, took a sip. Her throat was dry, her mouth practically putrid. She could still taste the wine, sweat, saliva and other bodily fluids from last night.

"So, what happened with your little friend?" Martha asked, as if reading her granddaughter's mind. "You had quite the night last night, didn't you?"

Abi nodded, unable to hide a smile as she thought about the night they had spent together, or what she could remember of it.

"Was he good?"

"I'm not telling you that."

"Come on, dear, that's what I'm here for."

"To discuss my sex life in graphic detail? I don't think so. That's not how this grandchild-grandparent relationship is supposed to work."

"But our relationship is different, so tell me, did he have a big cock?"

Abi nearly choked on her tea, but she also grinned and then immediately tried to disguise it.

"That means yes," Martha said, nodding assuredly. "Good for you. It's been a while. You needed a good shag to blow those cobwebs away."

"Gran, can we not do this now?" Abi checked her phone. "It's still very early. I'm hungover. I need a shower, some food. I haven't even checked my emails yet."

Martha held up her hands. "Fair enough. I'll make you a big greasy fry-up. That'll fill you." She stood and headed for the fridge. "Any plans for today?"

Abi shook her head, distracted. She had received a message from Steven, her heart beating heavily when it popped up. She half expected him to be apologetic, to tell her that he had enjoyed the time they spent together but that it simply wasn't working out. In the time it took for the message to load, everything that had happened over the last few days, from the run-ins with Robert and the old lady, to the unprotected sex and the haste with which they had departed, came flooding into her mind.

His first words immediately allayed those fears and put Abi at ease. "Thanks for a wonderful night," they said. "Let's do it again. The sooner the better."

He signed off with a multitude of kisses.

"Don't you have work to do?" Martha pushed.

"Yes. Maybe. I'll check. But I'm tired, so there's a good chance I'll be sleeping all day." She closed the phone and looked at her gran, who was unloading an armful of food from the fridge. "What are you up to?"

"Fuck knows," she replied merrily. "First, we feast, I can worry about everything else later."

—

"What's the kid's name again?" Martha asked, finger on her chin, her eyes staring into the middle distance. "Something New Agey, something poncey—Yolo or Hashtag, or some shit like that."

"Nothing like that," Abi replied. "It was Nivea."

"Nivea? She called her kid Nivea?"

Abi nodded.

"She must have amazing skin."

"I think she just saw the name, liked it, and didn't pay attention to where it came from."

"Not a great way to pick a child's name, is it? You can't just walk around the house pointing at shit and saying, 'That'll do.' Poor sod could have been called Vaseline, or Bud Lite."

"I think you're exaggerating."

"I think you're underestimating her stupidity."

Abi stood, stretched, yawned, and pulled out her phone. "Anyway, enough of this nonsense. I have to try and do some work and then go to sleep. I have a big deadline for tomorrow night and need to do the bulk of the work now if I'm going to finish."

Martha checked her watch. "It's barely seven."

Abi shrugged.

"I'm the one in her seventies, not you," Martha reminded her.

"I'm also tired. I didn't get much sleep and I'm still hungover."

"Lightweight."

Abi shrugged off the comment. "I'm going to take my laptop into the bedroom, do some work in there. You're not going anywhere, are you?"

"Maybe."

Abi retrieved her laptop from the dining room table, leaving a cursory, heart-stopping glance at the patio doors as she did so. The silent, graying night beyond doing little to settle her nerves and calm her tired mind. "What do you mean, '*maybe*'?"

"I mean, *maybe* I have a house party or a rave to go to. *Maybe* I have a life that doesn't revolve around watching soap operas all night."

"Do you?"

Martha shrugged, a smile breaking through her stern expression. "Like I said, *maybe*."

"Okay then. But if you do go raving until the early hours, or you join an orgy or something, try not to disturb me."

"Oh, an orgy, now there's an idea."

"Goodnight, Gran," Abi called as she left the room.

SUNSHINE

"Now you listen here," the old lady, a veritable ray of sunshine, barked down the phone. "I know what you're doing. I may be old, but I'm not stupid."

There was some truth to her words. She was *very* old.

"I know what you're doing. I know your game," Sunshine repeated, the phone cradled tightly to her ear, her free hand waving menacingly at the mouthpiece, as if chastising it. "You're trying to scam me, aren't you?"

Even from my position in the backyard, hiding behind a rabbit hutch, I could hear the person on the other end of the phone, his words filtering through the kitchen and out the open back door in a garbled mess of static. Sunshine had turned the volume up all the way, but the phone was still jammed tight to her ear, and it was clear she still couldn't understand everything he said.

"I told you, I'm not paying another penny," she said defiantly. "You have to fix it for free. . . . But it's your responsibility!" she continued, her tone harsh, her words breaking.

It was a warm night, barely a breeze to disturb it, but the street was quiet. A faint whiff of barbecue hung in the air and a few houses over I could see the remnants of a garden party—chairs scattered, disposable plates, platters and beer bottles littering the grass—under the stark glow of a white fluorescent security light. The light had flickered on and off several times already, catching the movement of some persistent nocturnal critter looking for scraps of food.

"But it's your responsibility. You fixed it for me. You said it was fine. Now it's not fine. What does that tell you?"

The other yards were quiet, still, dark, as if the entire neighborhood had paused to listen in to their crazy neighbor's conversation as she berated a poor IT technician and tried to force him to fix her failing computer, seemingly just as old as she was.

"I don't care if it was three years ago. It's the same computer, isn't it? It should work, shouldn't it?"

If the Karens of the world had a hierarchy, Sunshine would be at the top, waving her cane around and telling everyone that things were better in her day when women were compliant, men wore suits, and everyone was racist.

"Well, if it's got a virus then it must be your fault. It didn't have a virus before you touched it, did it? Listen here, young man." She said those words a lot, demanding a person's attention so she could talk down to them. "I may seem like a sweet old lady, but trust me, you do not want to get on my bad side. If you don't fix my computer for free, I'll be talking to your manager and I'll let him know how you treated a sweet, kindly old lady."

She was built of sinew, bile, and xenophobia—she definitely wasn't sweet or kindly.

"Uh-huh, I thought you would change your tune when I said that."

The smell of urine and straw invaded my nostrils as I edged around the hutch. The rabbit stirred immediately and ran to the mesh, its whiskers poking through, its little nose sniffing.

"Hey, little dude," I whispered, poking my finger through and stroking its nose. "You going to be quiet for me?"

In response, the rabbit seemed to settle, retreating from the wire. It moved to the back of the cage, sat on its hind legs, shifted as if to get comfortable, and then unleashed a mighty thump, its back legs kicking hard against the floor and shaking the cage.

Fuck.

"Shh," I said, placing my finger through.

It kicked again. And again.

"Thank you for finally—" the old woman stopped short.

I rattled the cage slightly, trying to draw the rabbit's attention. It didn't work. It thumped again, even louder this time.

"Hold on a minute."

Sunshine's footsteps shuffled toward the kitchen door; the kitchen light cast shadows on the patio when she stepped in front of it.

Moments later, Sunshine popped her head out, looked left, away from the hutch, and then right, straight at me. The kitchen beamed a halo of orange around the short concrete steps. There was enough residual light for her to make out my silhouette, for her to realize that she had an intruder and to call for help.

After interminable seconds, her eyes squinting, her face squirming, she retreated. "Just the bloody rabbit," she told the technician, her sight seemingly as limited as her hearing. "I tell you, don't ever get grandchildren. You'll end up broke with a house full of toys, a yard full of pets, and a fat little ankle-biter who thinks you're fucking Willy Wonka. Anyway, enough of that nonsense. When are you coming to fix my computer?"

The kitchen door slammed shut, draping the patio in darkness, silencing the rabbit's complaints and giving me time to compose myself.

Despite living alone and having a deep-seated fear of being scammed, Sunshine was very lax about her home security. There were no security lights, no cameras, and while she had locked the front and back doors, she hadn't secured the patio doors.

I knew there was no risk of bumping into anyone as I slipped inside. There were no dogs or cats—nothing beyond a severely neglected and paranoid rabbit. She had one daughter, who lived several miles away and used her as a free babysitter, and a son, who lived on the other side of the country and used her as an ATM.

Sunshine was surprisingly nice to both of them and extended the same respect to her close friends. The few that she had. Everyone else, however, was fair game—the archetypal bitter old woman, a sadistic septuagenarian who turned her anger outward and unleashed it on everyone from the postman to the poor sap who once agreed to fix her computer and then never heard the end of it.

Sunshine was bitter and angry at the world, and that bitterness, that anger, had to be snuffed out.

The house stank of stale piss, of neglected nursing homes, mold, and lily of the valley. The carpets were worn thin by years of shuffling and neglect. A path had been ground into the living room carpet, tracing a line from the kitchen, across the living room, and to the bottom of the stairs—years of practiced movements, of taking the same rehearsed route from one end of the house to the other.

Sunshine shuffled across this line as she finished her conversation. The technician had relented; she was getting what she wanted. But she wasn't happy, and she wasn't thankful.

"What do you mean, goodwill gesture?" she groaned as she scampered across the carpet, pausing to gesture threateningly with her cane. "You messed up my computer and now you're fixing it. That's not a goodwill gesture, is it?"

She smiled, her features cracking like plaster in the sun as they formed an unfamiliar expression.

"I should think so, as well," she said, nodding her head firmly and continuing to traverse the worn path. "I'll see you tomorrow then. Eight a.m. sharp. Don't be late."

She hung up the handset, dropped it on a coffee table, and then entered the hallway. I listened to her mumble and groan, curse and shout, and then heard the familiar sound of a stairlift kicking into action. It was a sound that brought a smile to my face, a sound that signaled the end for this sadistic little sociopath.

I was at the bottom of the stairs when she eventually saw me, the smug smile on her face instantly exchanged for one of shock, then horror, then panic. But she had already buckled herself into the chair lift and it had a long way to go.

"No—No—" she spat, her wide eyes turning from me to the top of the stairs, her little legs kicking madly, as if willing the stairlift to move faster.

The stairlift had climbed just three or four steps. I climbed the first, then the second, my eyes locked on hers.

"What do you want?" she asked.

I shrugged, taking another step, keeping pace with the stairlift. "I hadn't really thought that far ahead," I lied.

"You're not getting my money," she said, "so keep your filthy thieving hands away."

I laughed. I had expected panic and she hadn't let me down. Even sadists panicked when faced with the unexpected. I had also expected her to plead with me, to beg me, maybe even to try and shout for help, but even in the grip of fear, she wasn't letting the tough facade drop.

"I'm not here for money." I took another two steps, the stairlift now past halfway. It chugged slowly and painfully, crawling at a snail's pace. Like everything else in the house, the occupant included, it was old, worn-out, and on its last legs.

Sunshine eyed me curiously, a disgusted glint in her eye. "If you're here to do unholy things to me, I won't let you."

"You mean rape you?" I shook my head. "Now, come on, what do you take me for?"

"Do you want my jewelry?"

I shook my head and noted, with great amusement, that she had slowly unbuckled the seat belt. She knew she was just a few seconds from the top, had glimpsed the wooden cane that she kept against the banister.

"Good, because you're not getting it."

I climbed another step, two from the stairlift, five from the landing.

Her eyes flickered to the cane and then to the bedroom door on the other end of the hallway. I could almost read her thoughts as she contemplated making a run for it, using the cane to keep me at bay as she dived for the phone.

But she was old, unfit, unwell. In her mind, she could move quickly, might be strong enough to knock me out and quick enough to make it to the phone. But in reality, she was none of those things.

Another step, edging ever closer.

"Well," she said, "whatever you have planned—"

Sunshine sprang from the chair, one hand slamming down forcefully on the emergency stop, the other grabbing for the cane. Her reactions took me by surprise. By the time I reacted, it was already too late. She grabbed the rubberized end of the cane and swung; I moved my hands to block my face just as the solid wooden handle came hurtling toward me.

My left wrist took the brunt of the impact as the handle crushed cartilage and cut skin. Something broke and I yelped in pain, clasping the injured appendage with my other hand.

The action threw me off balance, and I fell against the banister and then rocked backward, my leg giving way underneath me. I grabbed onto the banister with both hands, holding on despite the pain that raced through my body. Sunshine didn't wait to admire her work. She ran away—heading for the bedroom, cane in hand, staggering like a frantic turtle.

"Bitch," I hissed through gritted teeth.

I ran after her, squeezing past the stairlift and charging through the open door. I tackled her just as she reached for a phone on her bedside table, dragging her limp and frail form to the thinly carpeted floor.

Another bolt of pain through my wrist, another impact, more agony; I grabbed the back of her head with my free hand, her gray hair like a wire brush beneath my fingers. But she wasn't giving up that easily. She bucked with an unexpected force, knocking me off balance, turning underneath my grasp and forcing me off.

She moved quicker than anticipated and was on her knees soon after shaking me off, the cane swinging madly once more, aiming for my head. I rolled away from the forceful swing and watched as the momentum knocked her over, her eyes wide as she realized her fate and toppled over like some ancient statue. I heard the squishy, crunching sound of bone, cartilage, and flesh meeting a solid surface, but she was ready again just as quickly as I was, pushing herself back onto her knees, her face now bloodied, her breathing heavy.

Another swing of the cane, just as wild, but much less coordinated. It disrupted her balance again, but this time she corrected herself, planted her feet like a boxer preparing for a finish, and swung again, and again—each swing more chaotic, more desperate, none of them connecting.

"You fucking bastard!" she screamed. "I'll kill you!"

She swung again, still on her knees, still putting all her upper body into the action.

I calmly stood, staying out of the reach of the cane and her furious but fatigued swings.

"I'll kill you!" she repeated.

The sweeping, violent movements continued, but were several feet from their intended target. I stood back—hands on hips, breath short and raspy—and watched her fail. She wasn't even looking at me anymore—her eyes were wild, raging, flickering from left to right. It was as if she couldn't see me.

The swinging stopped, the cane limp in front of her, grasped in both hands. She was breathless, panting like a dog, a pained expression on her bloody face. She took a deep breath and then whined as she exhaled; another breath, another whine. "I'll. Kill. You." She lifted the cane above her head, set her eyes in my general direction and then brought it down in one fell swoop, her face and torso crashing down with it.

The cane hit the floor, and she followed it, her bloodied face meeting the worn carpet for the second and last time. I remained standing, contemplating, preparing; as my breathing slowed, hers stopped altogether.

In her efforts to try and kill me, a person who had dared to break into her house and attack her, she'd had a heart attack and done my job for me.

"Fucking hell." I suddenly felt some respect and admiration for the woman.

24

Abi woke to the sound of sirens, a screeching, wailing, wall of noise that assaulted her senses. She had been dreaming. In her dream she was in bed, slamming her hand repeatedly against her phone, trying to turn off what she believed to be her alarm. The more she hit, the louder the noise became, and the more her hand hurt. When she woke, she was confused to discover that the noise was still there, but it was coming from outside her window, not from her phone.

Clambering out of bed, groaning wearily with each movement, she dressed into the clothes she had worn the night before and stumbled to her window. There were two police cars outside her house and another one pulling into view—their blue lights spinning and dancing. Abi's first thought was that they were there to arrest her. Maybe, she thought, they had come about the phone call she made a few nights ago, the one in which she accused her neighbor of robbing his own house; maybe they were there about the confrontation in the yard or the alleged exhibitionism.

When the haze cleared, she determined they were there to arrest Robert. The idea delighted her, kicking her heart into gear more effectively than a shot of caffeine ever could. But then she saw the white forensics tent and the police tape wrapped around the house opposite.

It wasn't Robert. It was her neighbor. Ms. Hunt. The crazy old lady who had led yesterday's verbal assault against Abi.

Abi slipped into a pair of sandals and braced the cold of the morning and the chaos on the street. Her neighbors were out in full force—a crowd of faces that Abi barely recognized. They acknowledged her, some smiled, most didn't; one, a young woman with a baby in her arms, sidled up to her as Abi approached the police tape.

"Tragic, isn't it?" the woman said as she gently rocked the baby in her arms. They were both wearing their pajamas, the child had a dummy stuffed in its mouth and had fallen asleep on its mother's shoulders. The mother looked half asleep. "Poor woman."

"What happened?" Abi asked.

"Murdered, apparently."

"Murdered? But—but—"

She wanted to say that she had just spoken with the woman yesterday, to say that she couldn't possibly have been murdered, that it was too unreal. But she couldn't get the words out. Partly because she was shocked, partly because the argument made her a prime suspect.

"Terrible, isn't it?" the young mother said. "It's like living in LA."

The confusion must have been evident on Abi's face.

"Because of the murders, I mean. And not, well, everything else."

Abi nodded.

"It's like one of those crime shows. Murder, violence. Police everywhere. You can't trust anyone. Can't even walk outside by yourself." She slowly shook her head. Abi felt like the woman was a few breaths from telling her that it was better when she was a kid, when everyone left their doors unlocked, neighbors spoke to one another, and murder hadn't been invented. But her mind was on other things. "They could be shooting a documentary about us before long," she said. "We could be famous."

Abi sighed inwardly but tried not to let her contempt show. "Who did it?" she asked.

"No one knows. Looks like they got away." She paused to adjust the baby and then added, "Again."

Abi instinctively turned around and looked at Robert's house, remembering the way he had looked at the decrepit old woman, the unrelenting, unnerving stare he had given her. She half expected him to be staring back at her, a smug expression on his face, a wink, a knowing look. But the curtains were drawn, there was no sign of movement.

"Tracy found her this morning," the woman continued as two officers began taking notes from onlookers, moving quickly from one to the other, a procession of potential witnesses. "She feeds her little bunny rabbit every morning and then pops in for a chat and a cuppa. A pair of gossips, if you ask me, but that's by the by. Seems unfair to judge them on it now."

No shit.

"She found the body and phoned the police. By the time they got here, she'd already announced it on Facebook and woke half the street up to tell them." The woman laughed, shook her head slowly, and then continued her hypnotic rocking. "Crazy, but she was probably in shock."

"How long have you been out here?" Abi wondered.

The young mother made eye contact for the first time. "An hour or two," she stated. "Why?"

"You didn't happen to see my next-door neighbor out here, did you?" Abi asked, hooking a thumb over her shoulder to gesture to Robert's house.

"Average height, dark hair, quiet, bit weird?"

"That's the one."

"No. He's probably the only one not here." She laughed. "Lucky bugger probably slept through it all, just like my little Tyrone here."

Abi offered a fake smile in reply, glancing at the baby, who seemed at peace on his mother's shoulder.

"Good morning, ladies." A deputy had made his way around to Abi and her neighbor, pen and notebook in hand, quizzical expression on his face. He looked young, much younger than Abi. "Can I ask you a couple quick questions?"

They both nodded and the young officer turned to Abi. "I'll start with you first, ma'am, if you don't mind."

When prompted, Abi gave the officer her name and her address, before telling him that she didn't know the woman. "In fact, I don't really know any of my neighbors," she admitted.

"I can vouch for that," the woman with the baby said. "I've been here four years and I think this is the first time we've met. Seen you around a few times, but didn't want to impose. You seem like a private person. I get that." She shrugged. "Same goes for everyone else around here. Everyone keeps to themselves, apart from the older folk."

Abi was embarrassed by the admission, but the young officer accepted her answer. She told him that she had spent the night working and had then slept.

"Does anyone else live with you?" he asked.

"Yes, my gran."

The woman with the baby flashed Abi a confused stare, suggesting that she knew even less about her neighbors than she thought.

"But we were together last night, we didn't hear anything."

He nodded, scribbled something down on his notebook and then asked, "Have you seen anything suspicious lately? Anything at all?"

Thoughts of Robert raced through her mind. She thought about the strange way he had acted on their date and in the days afterward, the files she had found on his computer. She thought about the time she had spent with Steven, and how she suspected Robert of watching them, first out back then in the house.

Every thought that entered her mind was dismissed.

"Nothing," she said, shaking her head and emptying all those suspicions out of it. As much as she suspected that Robert was up to something, as much as her instinct told her that it was him, she didn't have proof. She had nothing more than paranoid allegations the police would see right through. Telling them could also risk diverting Robert's attention—and possibly his anger—to her. "Nothing at all."

"Well, if you think of anything, give us a call." He left her with a smile and then moved on to the woman with the baby. Abi heard her give her name as Michelle and realized that she had no idea who she was, had never heard her name before, and didn't even know that there were young children on the street.

The thought depressed her, and the old lady's death depressed her even more. Dying alone had always been one of Abi's biggest fears. She had no friends, few surviving family members, and no stable relationship. There would be no one there to mourn for her, no one to say, "I knew her, she was an amazing woman."

She retrieved her phone from her pocket, wincing as a bolt of pain ran from her wrist to her shoulder, her REM exploits leaving their mark. Steven didn't answer on the first ring, or the second. She double-checked the time, couldn't remember whether he was supposed to be at work or not, and on the third ring she left him a voicemail, putting some distance between herself and the deputy as she did so.

"Steven, I need to talk to you," she said. "Nothing serious, well, not for me anyway. Okay, that sounded mean. I'm just really bad with voicemail." She sighed deeply and moved even further out of earshot of the questioning deputy. "The old lady across the road was murdered last night. I think it might have been Robert. I mean, I don't know, but . . . can you please call me or come around when you see this? I want to speak—" The phone beeped, the voicemail cut off, and Abi hung up.

Another bolt of pain, another wince, as she dropped the phone in her pocket and returned home while bemoaning her problematic start to the day.

PART 3

25

T*all, dark, has a knife. Not much to go on,* Steven thought to himself. *Although it is creepy.*

He looked up from his phone. The soccer match was nearing its conclusion—twenty-two kids chasing after a ball with no semblance of order while their coaches yelled meaningless instructions and ordered them back into position. He saw one of the young girls chase after a loose pass, showing an impressive turn of pace to backtrack and reach the ball before it went for a throw-in. She tried to volley the ball downfield, but it sliced off the outside of her foot and smashed into the face of an unsuspecting soccer mom.

Steven grinned and lit another cigarette, watching as a crowd gathered around the red-haired and now red-faced spectator, treating her minor injury and moderate embarrassment with the care reserved for an injured soldier on the battlefield.

A notification drew his attention back to his phone. He saw a voicemail notification appear, sighed, and then ignored it, telling himself that he would deal with it later.

His attention switched back to the image on his phone—the specter of death, as one commentor called it.

It had been taken by a friend of Matthew Graves, a local musician murdered in an alleyway less than a mile from the field where Steven stood. Graves had been speaking to the friend seconds before his murder. He had snapped a picture of the alleyway to brag about a recent sexual conquest, and the camera had caught his eventual killer.

The picture was dark. The killer was wearing black, and there was little to go off except that he probably wasn't too short, too tall, too fat, or too thin. And he had a knife. Some were already suggesting that the police should work their magic and find the killer. But this was real life, not *CSI*. No amount of zooming, clarification, and near-supernatural image alterations could help them. For all they knew, the man in black was Scooby-Doo standing on his hind legs and strung out on Scooby Snacks.

Still, that didn't stop the local Facebook groups from going crazy. In the last few hours, the picture had gone viral on Reddit and now it was all over the internet.

Fake as fuck, one commentor wrote.

Definitely Slenderman, said another.

Whoever it was, it made Steven feel uneasy knowing that they could be someone he knew, someone he had met before.

He remembered seeing Michael on the night of his death. He knew that Abi had a connection to him, but he didn't want to tell her about the musician's death. She was scared enough without knowing that she could have been mere feet from the killer.

He heard the final whistle and looked up from his phone. The game was over. The kids could collect their participation medals and receive praise from their parents. Everyone could move on and forget the whole dreadful affair. Steven smiled, opened the camera on his phone, and pointed it at the girls as they dispersed from the pitch, shaking hands and hugging their opponents as they did so.

He zoomed in on one of them—blonde hair, blue eyes, the most beautiful thing he had ever seen.

She immediately ran to the opposing goalkeeper to praise her, having made several big saves. She then shook the referee's hand before quickly doing the same with everyone else on the pitch, leaving no hand unshook.

It was sweet. It showed a level of maturity not usually seen in seven-year-olds, and it made Steven happy. He hadn't taken many pictures during the game itself, but he took several of these humble gestures.

The girl ran over to one of the spectating couples and Steven's smile disappeared. He groaned, turned off his phone, and dropped it in his pocket. Putting out his cigarette, he trudged over to where the girl was, his smile returning when she saw him and ran to him.

"Daddy!" she yelled. "Did you see that? Wasn't that great?"

He picked her up, kissed her cheek, her forehead. "Yes, sweetie. It was. But you lost . . . you know that, right?"

"Yes, but did you see that shot I had in the second half?"

He nodded. He had seen it. She had intercepted a pass from the full-back, but rather than taking it in her stride and dribbling through on goal, she'd hit it the first time, crashing it against the crossbar as everyone—goalkeeper included—looked on in awe.

"Mommy said they should have given us the win because of that shot. That's how good it was."

Steven offered a meek smile in reply.

That's because your mother is a fucking idiot.

"Speak of the devil . . ." he muttered under his breath.

"Lilly, remember to shower when you get to your father's house." The sour-faced woman and her stone-faced husband regarded Steven with a cursory glance. "And Steven, remember that she has a sleepover tonight. A few hours. That's all you have."

"Yes sir." Steven nodded, eliciting a frown from his ex-wife and a warning glare from her new male victim.

"No funny business," she warned.

"That's a shame. I was going to suggest that we watch a comedy. Should we stick with horror instead?"

Lilly found that amusing. No one else did.

"Don't be late," she warned again.

Steven stood to attention and saluted. She shook her head, gave her daughter a kiss, whispered something in her ear, and then left without saying another word to Steven.

Steven watched her go, waited until she was out of ear shot, and then said, "I'm not joking. We're totally watching a horror film."

"Awesome."

"And then we're going to play some violent computer games, listen to satanic music, eat fast food, and if we have enough time, we'll get out the Ouija board."

Lilly looked disappointed. "Oh, you're joking."

He took his daughter by the hand. "What did your mother say to you? Was it one of her witchy incantations? Saying a prayer to her lord and savior, the antichrist?"

"She said that if I get bored or you get too annoying or weird, I should give her a call."

Steven nodded. "Of course she did."

SMOKER

A plume of smoke left his lips and dispersed in the air. The wrinkles at the corners of his mouth and the harshness of his cough suggested he had smoked for a long time. The fact that he did it out of view of his child, even though she clearly knew, suggested he was embarrassed by it or worried that he would influence her.

He claimed that he wasn't a smoker. But he claimed a lot of things that weren't true. The liar was older than he said he was and not quite as much of a catch as he claimed. Single, he claimed; childless, he said. But you can't hide from the truth when the truth trolls your social media accounts, insists you spend more time with your children, harasses you for financial support, and reminds everyone what a sheer and utter cunt you are.

He was a charmer; a handsome, sweet, kind and loving man. He'd had his issues—a past he wasn't comfortable talking about, a career that hadn't worked out—but he knew how to hide them, to use them to his advantage and to keep them away from prying eyes. Smoker spent his days on dating apps, searching for a new wife to ignore, a new family to neglect. He preferred them soft, supple, sweet, and weak—all the easier to manipulate to his will.

Smoker wasn't as bad as Neckbeard. No one was. Neckbeard was a pimple on the asshole of humanity, a despised, unwanted, eyesore that served no purpose and was grossly unappealing to anyone he encountered. The Queen of Instagram was vainer, more narcissistic, and if she had survived our encounter, she would have no doubt gone on to hurt more people, negatively impact more lives, and generally be as much of an obstacle as possible. Wannabe was the same—a societal drain who collected one-night-stands and STDs like children collect baseball cards. Smoker wasn't on their level, but he was still a heavily flawed human being.

And a liar.

He finished the cigarette, stubbed it out, and then reentered the back door of his home, back to his daughter and their rare father-daughter evening.

26

Abi was convinced that Robert was up to no good. It all began to click into place, and the more it did, the more convinced she was of his guilt. Nothing about the situation made sense, nothing was normal. And even if she dismissed everything that had happened in the last few days, and everything that had happened on and after their date, she couldn't shake the memories of being inside his home.

It had been empty, devoid of life, as if its only purpose was to get closer to her, to keep her near.

It was devious, it was twisted, and it was elaborate, but it worked. It also worried Abi. Not only was she living next to someone with bad intentions, someone who likely spent the day spying on her and the night thinking about her, but he had gone to great lengths to get close to her.

He was a disturbed individual, but he was also a committed one, and his commitment was to Abi.

Abi sat in her home office all morning; her phone on the desk next to her, her eyes on the expansive windows that looked out onto the street below. She watched people come and go, crowding around the deceased woman's house like flies around shit. The scene sickened her—all those people, all that excitement, all that intrigue. Someone had been stalked and killed mere feet from where they stood, but all they were interested in was snapping a few pictures for their Instagram or piecing together a story they could tell their friends.

"I was there," the young mother would say, babe in arms as she stood at the school gates, waiting for her other offspring to trundle forward. "Just an hour or two after the body was found. I didn't see anything, but you could almost sense the death in the air. It was like nothing I have experienced before." On her pedestal she would stand, enjoying her fifteen minutes of fame courtesy of someone else's misery.

Her story would likely change over time as she went from being a casual, retrospective observer, to someone who had heard the screams, seen the body being carried out, and even caught sight of the killer. Whatever made her story more interesting.

"It was gruesome. Blood everywhere," the middle-aged man would say, telling his story to his friends down the pub. "It was like a horror film. Never seen anything like it. It changed me. It would change anyone."

The policeman had done the rounds and taken impromptu interviews from all bystanders. He looked like he was ready to call it a day when one of the interviewees pointed to Robert's house. The deputy, the same youngster who had interviewed Abi—his face a picture of tranquility, as if set in stone, his heart and mind no doubt racing under the calm exterior—checked his notes, nodded to himself, gave a signal to his colleague, and then trotted over to Robert's house.

Abi perked up, the disgust on her face switching to intrigue. She retrieved her coffee mug and reveled in the searing taste of the milky drink. The deputy remained rigid and professional in his manner as he rang the bell and waited patiently. The front door wasn't visible from where Abi sat, but she saw the officer talking and gesturing, indicating that Robert had answered.

Robert had been there all along, no doubt peeping through his curtains and watching the chaos unfold on the street, his eyes fixed on Abi, studying her every reaction. The thought sent a chill down her spine, and she shook her head as if to empty it.

Dirty little creep that he is.

The deputy moved to the side and Robert stepped outside. He wore a brown fluffy dressing gown and matching slippers, his attention on the house opposite as he made a show to the officer, feigning surprise and seemingly pretending he had slept through the ordeal. The officer acknowledged the reaction and made a few notes in his book before departing.

Abi heard the faint sound of the officer's voice as he reached the end of the driveway and then shouted back to Robert, "If you think of anything else, be sure to let me know!"

Else? What does he mean? What did he tell them?

Abi took another sip of coffee, checked her phone. Steven hadn't replied to her message and it was now nearly dinnertime. He was at work, she knew that much, but she had hoped he would have seen it and replied by now.

One of her biggest clients had sent her an email, checking that she was prepared to meet a deadline, but the work was days away from completion and she didn't feel up to the task. She made a mental note to send them an excuse later.

Robert was still standing in his driveway, his arms folded across his chest, his eyes on the commotion opposite. There were still several police cars and a forensics unit outside, with even more tape surrounding the house. Abi assumed that the body had been taken away, but—

The sound of screeching tires interrupted her thoughts and she turned to see another van pull into the street. It stopped at the end of Abi's driveway, getting as close to the action as it could. The doors slid open as soon as the brakes were applied, and a news team filed out like excitable clowns in a circus act.

The cameraman came first, lugging a large camera fixed to a tripod. The soundman came next, followed by someone Abi assumed was the producer. They shut the sliding door with force, caring little for the noise they were making or the people they were upsetting. They were joined by a reporter from the passenger seat.

Abi recognized the reporter from the local news station, the same woman who had reported on the previous deaths. A local celebrity of sorts, on a mission to elevate her status and become the figurehead of this local crime spree. Excitement and anticipation seemed to follow her wherever she went, from the eager, bright expression on her face, to the erratic way she moved and ordered her colleagues around.

The "producer" turned out to be a lackey, tasked with setting up the equipment and keeping police and onlookers away and out of shot. The driver assumed the same role and immediately began arguing with a nearby officer while the reporter did her bit to the camera. Abi was tempted to turn on the TV but assumed they weren't live.

Abi couldn't hear what the reporter was saying, catching only glimpses of her words when she shouted, often in anger and often directed at the soundman, who seemed to have little control of the overhead microphone. The reporter took her time in delivering the piece, moving in and out of shot, fixing her hair and makeup between takes, and even pausing to use her phone.

"Yes, yes, I know!" Abi heard her yell at one point, rolling her eyes to the cameraman as she directed her impatience to the person on the other end of the phone. "I'm on it!"

The news team didn't stay long, but more reporters took their place. There were women with digital recorders, men filming on their phones;

one woman seemed to be writing a real-time journal, going from officer to officer and from bystander to bystander and frantically jotting down their responses on a bulging notepad. Abi initially thought she might be a detective, but the readiness with which the other officers dismissed her, and the contempt that she expressed, suggested she was a reporter or blogger.

Plainclothes officers appeared later in the afternoon, by which point Abi was on her third cup of coffee. They didn't stay for long and didn't seem to do much, merely spending a few minutes inside the house before gathering some tidbits of information and then departing just as hastily as they had arrived.

By that time, very few onlookers remained. They had gone back into their homes, to their friends' homes, or to their nearest place of gossip, eager to tell their stories for the first time and to break the story before the local news network did. Of course, it had already broken on social media within minutes of the body being discovered, but they would have the details, they were eyewitnesses and, as a result, they would be in high demand.

As noon gave way to afternoon and then to evening, the street cleared. Robert had been inside his house for the last few hours; the woman with the baby had gone back inside after he woke and began screaming for attention, food, or warmth; the police had returned to their daily duties, leaving only trails of tape and warning signs in their wake. The house had been sealed, the relatives had been informed, and although Abi hadn't checked, she knew the local news would have broadcast the story in all its gruesome details.

Abi still hadn't received a call or message from Steven, but she didn't worry, and didn't doubt that he would contact her when he was able.

Her bones creaked and her back stung as she rose—the first movements she had made in hours. She stretched, groaned, and squeezed her eyes shut as blue stars danced around the corners of her vision.

"Too much caffeine, not enough movement," she told herself. "And if I don't go to the toilet soon, I'm going to wet myself."

She allowed herself a smile, but that smile quickly faded when she heard a door slamming. Her eyes immediately fixed on Robert's house, just in time to see him locking the door behind him and shooting suspicious glances over his shoulder. He had changed into a pair of jeans, a padded jacket, and a baseball cap, with the bill arched down over his eyes.

He turned to look in Abi's direction and she froze. There was no light in the office, nothing to illuminate her from the outside, but somehow, he knew she was there, he was staring right at her, and Abi was sure he could see her. A deafening, pulsing, rushing sound echoed through her head and she held her breath. For the briefest of moments, time stood still.

He stuffed his hands in his pockets, lowered his head, and walked away, allowing Abi to breathe again.

Where to now, you creepy fucker?

HER

She seemed preoccupied, anxious, Her deep green eyes darting this way and that, reacting to the slightest movement, the briefest sound. She was on edge, highly strung or highly caffeinated— Her mind on something dark, something upsetting, something distracting.

I watched Her through my phone, Her every move recorded by the webcam on Her laptop, Her desktop, Her phone—a panoramic view of Her life in real time. It was amazing what you could find on the internet, from instructions on how to make bombs to beheading videos, snuff films, and elite hackers willing to do anything for a few hundred bucks and no questions asked.

She lived a simple life, a miserable and dull life, but there was something so fascinating in the way she lived it, from the grace and elegance of her movements—the way she would almost glide around the room, silent and ethereal, the way she would stare off into the middle distance, lost in some transient, deep, and meaningful train of thought.

Of course, she didn't live alone, and the webcam hacks gave me an insight into Her homelife, Her friends, Her closest family members, Her savior—Her protector.

On the surface, they lived more of an interesting life, from candid conversations about the opposite sex—lurid encounters that probably never happened but were interesting nonetheless—to big business deals, asshole bosses, and hushed claims of sexual abuse. But she had her own stories to tell and lived a life filled with arguments, controversy, animated phone calls, gossip. It was because of Her that I learned the intricate truths of countless people I had never met, from the ever smiling, always "on" Andrew O'Neil, who was deeply depressed and had once tried to top himself with a bottle of painkillers, to the quiet, humble, and introverted Mary Connor, who, despite being nearly seventy-two, had a very active sex life and went through more lubricant than General Motors.

I had no idea who these people were and would never meet them, but their lives were laid out for me on a silver platter, discussed and debated at length. It was a real-life soap opera, reality TV at its very best, with no dramatization, no scripts, and absolutely no commercials cutting in every five minutes.

It was dramatic, funny, and never dull, but the stories didn't interest me as much as the reactions they incited; the drama didn't excite me as much as the quiet times, the alone times, the times when it was just Her alone with Her thoughts, Her regrets, Her dreams. And me.

You can learn a lot by watching someone in their downtime, by spying on them when they think no one can see. It's their time to be themselves, their time to watch the world without it watching back. There are no fake smiles, no forced small talk; they're not trying to please colleagues by engaging in inane conversation, to win favor with bosses by agreeing to demeaning tasks or appeasing passersby with half-smiles and nodded greetings.

It's just them, left alone with their angst, their misery, their happiness, their quirks—everything that makes them human, the good and the bad.

I had wasted countless hours watching Her already and I could have wasted many more, waiting for the next episode of my daily soap opera, to discover whether O'Neil had finally given up, whether Mrs. Connor had finally found a partner who could keep up with her, but I had things to do—places to go, people to kill.

THE PIG

The man with the strong shoulders, shifty eyes, and hunched posture had been on my radar for some time. On the surface, he looked innocent, harmless. But those beady eyes hid a ruthless mind; those thin lips had delivered endless pain.

On the surface, he looked harmless. Another face in the crowd. But he was deceptive, devious. He wasn't just another nobody. He was a wolf in sheep's clothing.

Or more aptly, he was a swine among sheep. A pig in more ways than one.

He was happy-go-lucky most of the time, always making jokes, always smiling, always trying to please people, even if his anxious demeanor meant he wasn't always successful. But deep down, there was nothing good about him. He was evil—pure, unadulterated. More importantly, he was in my way, and he had to go.

I tracked The Pig down to one of the tenements in town, a stone's throw from where Neckbeard had met a fitting end, dying in a pool of blood, piss, and excrement. He met someone outside one of the tenement blocks, a man who looked even shiftier and more suspect than he did. The individual wore an oversized hoodie, its equally oversized hood enveloping his features like the cloak of the grim reaper. He greeted The Pig with a handshake—an exchange of drugs, an exchange of information, a meeting of old friends, it was hard to tell. They spoke for several minutes, shooting furtive glances over their shoulders and doing their best to hide their faces when two teenagers left the tenement block and walked straight past them.

The Pig checked his phone several times during the conversation—making notes, sending texts, looking at porn. They shook hands again and finished with a fist-bump, their knuckles pressed together for interminable seconds as the conversation finished. A nod of understanding, a reciprocated gesture, and The Pig was on his way again.

He stopped by newsagents on his way home. He picked up a local newspaper and a refill for his vape and exchanged pleasantries with a young woman who looked like she would rather be somewhere else and talking to someone else. I kept my distance, pretending to be on my phone as I waited around the corner, a baseball cap covering my face, hiding my features.

The Pig's attention was also on his phone when he stepped out of the newsagents.

"Yes, she has," he said. "I saw her yesterday and the day before. But I haven't seen her today."

He spoke calmly, quietly, but I was close enough to hear most of what he said.

"I'm close. I'll get what I want. But—no, maybe. Maybe tomorrow, maybe next week—look, it'll happen. I'm not wasting my time here, trust me. It'll happen."

He hung up and I felt my anger flare, realizing that my suspicions were correct, and he was up to something. He looked over his shoulder, his eyes fixed directly on me for the shortest of times. I must have said something under my breath, must have made a noise that attracted his eyes to me. I lowered my head just in time, my hands in my pocket, the cap covering my face, using the chilly day to protect me from his prying eyes.

When I eventually lifted my head, I saw that he had stopped staring and was once again walking at a leisurely pace, his suspicions eased. I took an alternative route, nonetheless, going through a housing estate, walking, almost running, to stay ahead of him. There was no need to follow him anymore; I knew where he was going, and I wanted to make sure I got there before him.

I made it to his house before he did and crept around the back, knowing I had between two and three minutes before he was in view, another thirty to forty-five seconds before he was in the house.

The back doors were locked and there were no open windows or loose latches—nothing to tempt me inside, nothing to make my life easier. Defeated, I picked up a large brick sitting by the back door, positioned myself by the window, and waited.

He approached the front door mere seconds later, heavy footfalls slapping the tarmac, crunching the scattered gravel. He cleared his throat, complained about something under his breath. The sound of jangling keys carried on the wind, hollow but vibrant, loud but welcome. Moments later, he was in the house, the front door slammed behind him.

That's when I threw the brick. It hit the glass with enough force to damage it, a spiderweb of cracks spreading from the point of collision to all four corners, but it didn't break. The brick bounced and landed with a dull thud on the patio, chipping the white stone slabs underneath.

The wall next to the window hid me from view as I slipped a bowie knife from under my jacket and waited, head pressed against the cool wall, eyes to my left, where a short passage led to the back door.

First came the sound of an internal door opening, then the sound of him yelling, something loud, but incomprehensible, then the sound of the back door opening, feet slapping on concrete. A man on a mission, ready to face whatever mischievous teenager or hopeful burglar had thrown the brick. There was haste and malice in his steps and vengeance on his mind as he focused his attentions on the connecting yards, expecting to see a group of mischievous kids hopping fences.

He must have heard a noise because he stepped out, ready to shout, to yell, to warn, but nothing left his lips.

He didn't expect the assailant to be much closer to home, and as he raced past my location, I slipped behind him, raised the knife above my head, and drove it down as hard as I could. It sunk into the flesh between his shoulder blades, crunching bone, crushing cartilage, and scraping along his spine as it disappeared almost to the hilt.

He turned to face me as I yanked the blade free, hearing a suction noise, feeling it contact bone.

His mouth was agape, horrified, his words choked. I expected a scream, a violent, angry, verbal assault, but he reacted with surprising speed and calm. He swung for me, finding a degree of strength and agility that the wound in his back should have taken away.

I stumbled back, avoiding the knuckles on his right hand by sheer instinct as a rush of air whizzed past. He also stumbled, but quickly righted himself and threw another punch, and another, windmilling toward me, each swing more erratic and poorly timed than the last.

One punch landed on my shoulder. I blocked another with my forearm, felt a third clip my chin, mere inches from a potential knockout blow.

Blood had soaked his shirt. And the pain must have been immense, but he wasn't giving up that easily.

I moved back and let him swing. He fired off another half dozen lazy and breathless punches before I moved into the line of fire, shifted sideways, and then stabbed him again.

The blade drove into his upper arm just as he was swinging. It lodged in his flesh. I held tight and he followed through, drawing the blade through his triceps and into his shoulder.

He stopped swinging and tried to grab me, desperate to draw me toward him, and when he couldn't make contact with his flailing hands, he charged.

It was a staggered, sloppy, and almost drunken movement, and it was just what I needed.

I threw my own punch, an uppercut, a haymaker. The knife punctured the flesh beneath his chin and drove up through his skull, emanating a wet, crunching sound like someone ripping open a packet of fresh meat.

His eyes rolled into the back of his head, his mouth hung open, the bloodied blade visible through the yawning gap. He flopped to his knees. The blade was jammed, lodged in its fleshly sheath. I gripped the handle with one hand, grabbed his hair with my injured hand, and pulled.

It was like he wanted to come with me. The chaos of broken neurons that fired madly in his brain either tried to activate his fight-or-flight response or begged me to finish him off, because as I pulled, he staggered forward on somewhat willing knees. His brain leaked an assortment of fluid through two gaping holes, his eyes flickered maniacally as if trapped in a waking REM state, and he gurgled a series of instinctive obscenities, but he didn't drop, he didn't die, and that made it easier for me to lead him into the house and the kitchen.

When I relinquished my grip, taking away the support that had kept him stable, he flopped again, first onto his knees, his hands by his side, his face on the floor as if in prayer, then on his side, kicking, twitching like a diseased rabbit gurgling its last breaths. I shut the door behind me and watched over him until he died, a slow and painful process that took at least twenty minutes. He may have already been dead, operating purely on electrical impulses like some temporarily revived frog in a high school science experiment, but I liked to think that he felt every second of it, that he was conscious and aware as his gaze fixed on mine and he realized I would be the last face he would ever see.

27

"Is he in?"

Abi shrugged.

"His car is still there."

"He didn't take it with him," Abi said, recalling how Robert had walked straight past the vehicle after leaving.

"You said you've been watching him all day, so—"

Abi shook her head. "I went for a shower and a nap after he left. I was away for two hours, three at the most. He could have returned during that time." She held an empty cup of coffee in her left hand, her phone in her right, but her eyes were fixed on the table in front of her, lost in contemplation.

"Well, it's getting dark, most of the other houses in the street have their lights on. I can't see his house from here, but the lights were off when I arrived."

"So?" Abi wondered, her attention fixed ahead as the heard the curtains ruffle behind her.

"So, I think we should break in and see what he's up to."

"Are you kidding me? We can't—"

"Why not? Let's say he's not the killer, which is looking like a slim chance at this point, he's still up to something, right? He still has something on you. At best it's an unhealthy obsession, at worst he wants you dead."

Abi nodded, "I suppose."

"Then we have to do it."

"I can't do that. That's not me."

"You don't have to, I will."

Abi looked up as Steven stopped twitching the curtains and stood in front of her, a comforting smile on his ever-friendly face. "You're going to break into Robert's house?"

Steven nodded.

"And what am I going to do?"

"You're going to wait here, keep an eye out, and let me know if he returns. Drink some more coffee, stay alert—that's all you need to do." He grabbed the empty coffee cup from her hand and paused, staring at her wrist.

"What's that?" he asked.

"What, where?" Abi said dismissively.

"Your wrist."

"It's nothing."

Steven's expression suggested that he didn't believe her. He reached for her hand again and peeled back the sleeve of her jumper before she pulled away.

"Jesus Christ, Abi, that's some pretty bad swelling."

"It looks worse than it is."

"Does it hurt?"

She shook her head and rotated her wrist. "It's fine. Just a niggling pain, and it's a little sore to the touch, but I'll live. As my gran would probably say, 'If it doesn't stop you from wanking or writing, it's all good.'"

Steven recoiled at that.

Abi shrugged. "She has a way with words."

Abi took her cup to the kitchen with Steven hot on her heels.

"So?" he pushed. "How did you do it? If that's a writing or masturbation injury, you're doing it wrong."

"I had a bad dream," she told him. "I dreamt that my alarm was going off and I kept hitting my phone to turn it off. I must have been doing it for real because when I woke—" She turned to him, peeled back her sleeve and exposed the swelling. "I saw this."

"You need to get that seen to."

"I told you, it feels fine. It looks worse than it is."

He wrapped his hands around her wrist and squeezed, studying Abi for a reaction. She didn't flinch. He rubbed his fingers over the bump that had formed on her wrist and carefully felt each bone on her finger. "I don't think anything's broken, somehow, but it looks painful."

"I don't feel it, and I have a drawer full of painkillers if it starts to give me problems. I'll be fine."

"A *drawer* full?"

"Doctors these days, eh? You enter with a headache and leave with an opioid addiction." She pulled away, allowed her sleeve to fall, and then hit the switch on the kettle. "So, back to the plan, what are we doing?"

"You've seen *Rear Window*, right?"

Abi's eyes lit up. "I love that film."

"Perfect!" Steven took the cup from Abi's hand and gestured for her to take a seat as he took over. "Well, I'm going to sneak over there and see what he's doing and you're going to ring me if you see him returning."

"This sounds like a bad idea. Shouldn't we just phone the police?"

"And say what? We suspect our neighbor is a serial killer, so can you please search his house?"

"Good point."

"We need proof, something substantial, something—" He paused just as the kettle reached its roaring crescendo. "Where's your gran, anyway?"

"Asleep upstairs. She was out most of the day, gallivanting."

"Gallivanting? How old are you?"

"Underneath these youthful good looks and energetic exuberance, there is a dull, old woman."

Steven gave a gentle shake of his head.

"If this is *Rear Window*, doesn't that make you Grace Kelly?"

"Pretty much," he said. "Lots of milk, no sugar, right?"

"Black, three sugars."

"Oh." He looked from Abi to the cup and back again, shrugged, and then continued, "I only want to have a peek, maybe take some pictures. As soon as you see him return, ring me, I'll put my phone on vibrate and—"

"You lost your phone, remember," Abi told him. "That's why you ignored my calls all day and scared me half to death."

"Oh, shit, good point," he said, not making eye contact.

Steven placed a steaming cup of black coffee in front of Abi, which she graciously accepted with a nod and a wink.

"I'll take your phone in case I need to call the police," Steven said. "If you see him and need to warn me . . ." He shrugged.

"If I see him, I'll make a noise."

Steven looked concerned. "We're going old-school, eh? What kind of noise?"

"A bird noise?"

"You know, it doesn't instill much confidence when you phrase it as a question. Do you know any bird noises?"

Abi cleared her throat and gave her best rendition.

"That's a no then."

28

The day had been long, difficult, tiring, and as he stepped outside and embraced the evening air, Steven knew that it could get a lot worse from here. He hadn't lost his phone. He hadn't been at work. What Abi didn't know was that he'd been sacked months ago. She also didn't know that his "job" had been part time at a call center, had only lasted for a few weeks, and had ended when he lost patience with a customer and swore at them.

In truth, it had been years since he'd had a stable job, which is why he simply told Abi that he "worked in IT." Technically, he spent his days browsing the web and playing video games, so at least he hadn't lied about working with computers all day.

That wasn't the only thing he'd kept from Abi, but it wasn't out of malice. Their relationship was still young. He liked her, and he didn't want to scare her away.

By playing the hero now, he felt that he could somehow make it up to her and impress her. Maybe then he could tell her the truth—the job, the ex-wife, Lilly.

Steven wasn't the macho type, but he wanted to impress Abi, to make her think he was capable of looking after her. The more he thought about it, the more he wondered whether he should have confronted Robert sooner, whether he should have punched him or, at the very least, insisted he gave him answers when they had argued in the yard.

He couldn't let another regret slip him by, couldn't allow Abi to think that he was weak or incapable.

With the imprint of her glossed lips still on his cheek, Steven crossed the back yard, going from the back door to the fence that separated Abi's house from Robert's. There were other houses, other yards, all connected, but Abi had disabled the security light so even the most eagle-eyed of voyeurs wouldn't see him as he stalked across the grass.

As he awkwardly scaled the fence, wishing he was younger and fitter and hoping that Abi wasn't watching from the patio door, he shot a glance at the second story of Abi's house. He looked at what he knew was the grandmother's bedroom, half expecting to see signs of life—a flickering TV, a lamp, the unmistakable blue glow of a phone or laptop. For a moment, he thought he may even see the old lady staring down at him, a suggestive smile on her face as he twisted into and then out of a very suggestive and awkward pose. But he saw nothing. The window was dark, uninviting, empty—the curtains were open, but there wasn't even a suggestion of light beyond.

He landed on the other side of the fence, the concrete patio absorbing the fall and sending shockwaves through his legs, threatening to blowout an old knee injury he'd received playing rugby.

His ears pinned toward the house ahead of him, searching for any sound in the house—a TV, a computer, a snore. He shuffled forward, taking great pains to ensure his steps wouldn't be heard. The night was silent, unnervingly so. Abi had decided that the best way to warn him of Robert's presence was to play music on full volume. It would be brief but loud—enough to dismiss as a mistake and more than enough to get his attention.

She was waiting with her hand on the remote and Metallica on her playlist. But Steven reasoned that if the noise of squelching grass beneath his feet and the shuffling of his pants were anything to go by, a low-volume Leonard Cohen would suffice.

Steven took a deep breath and edged toward the patio door.

Abi waited calmly by the office window. All the lights in the house were off, and she had fetched an old pair of binoculars, allowing her to see everything that happened on the street. The high-powered antique was her gran's. The irreverent granny insisted that her neighbors were dull as dishwater and tried her best to avoid them, but in the comfort of their own homes, when the lights were low, everyone became interesting.

"Everyone has an interesting story, dear, but sometimes you have to discover it for yourself."

The street was lit by sporadically placed streetlights; four glowing orange—radiant, soft, warming; one glowing white—stark, bright, unforgiving.

The light had been smashed by some of the local kids several weeks ago. The council, in their infinite wisdom, had replaced it with a brighter, whiter, and more energy-efficient bulb. It saved them a few pennies on their electricity bill but lit up street like a hospital corridor, eliciting a deluge of complaints from the locals.

Abi often found herself staring at the solitary white light. Lost in a sea of orange, it shone brighter, stronger, and with more force than the others, but it was out of place, unwanted, alone.

Most of the houses in the street were active, buzzing with lights and life. In the house to the left of the dead woman's, which stood dark and empty, a young boy played computer games in one of the bedrooms. He stood upright, rigid, controller in hand, screen mere feet from him, as he engaged in the action. Downstairs, the curtains were drawn, dark silhouettes merged on the sofa as a TV screen flickered.

On the other side, a young woman exercised on a stepping machine in the living room, the windows open to cool her down. Two doors down, a man sat on an armchair with a ginger cat slouched on his lap and a smartphone in his hand. Behind him, on the back of the chair, a brown tabby tested its balance and tried to attract attention from both human and feline.

Abi turned her attention down the street, her heart skipping a beat when she saw a figure in black approach. He moved slowly, almost cautiously, his footsteps staggered, his movement methodical. She reached for the knob on the stereo and waited. The figure seemed to stall, as if aware—maybe he knew he was being watched, maybe he knew someone was prowling around his house.

Abi hovered a finger over the play button and then withdrew it. The figure stepped under the halo of a streetlight, and she saw that it was an old man walking his dog. The fluffy mutt was frantically inspecting the grass, its nose pinned to the ground and its tail in the air as it looked for a place to relieve itself, its owner getting more and more frustrated by the second.

The discriminating canine finally settled on a flower bed nestled between big bunches of foliage and slowly lowered its rear. The old man looked away, checked his watch, tapped the dial, and muttered something, possibly telling the dog to hurry up, possibly moaning about something under his breath. Abi watched the dog for a moment, its bulging eyes, its lolling tongue, before sweeping the binoculars over the yard and onto the upstairs window.

A middle-aged man stood in the window, the curtains open, the light on, his stature prominent and ominous. His arms were folded across his chest, and he wore a menacing glare as his attention focused on the little dog and its mumbling owner. He waited until the dog finished and the man dragged him away before he exploded into life—banging on the glass, gesturing outside, no doubt focusing his angst on his neighbor and on the canine that had just befouled his flowerbed.

Abi swept the binoculars to the dog owner, who held up his free hand in apology and reluctantly slugged back to the offending excrement, retrieving a small plastic bag from his pocket.

The drama of suburban life.

Abi didn't know the dog walker, and as much as she loved dogs and made a point of focusing on them more than their human owners, she had never seen the dog either. She didn't know the man in the window, who watched with something bordering sadistic glee as his neighbor grabbed a handful of excrement, and she had yet to meet his wife, who came up behind him to see what all the fuss was about.

Abi had also never met the man with the cats or the woman on the exercise machine. She had bumped into the boy playing video games after he nearly ran into her one day when riding his bike, but her knowledge of her neighbors was negligible and her interactions scarce. She put it down to being a hermit, to working from home, having very little social life to speak of and spending her days in a self-imposed prison.

Abi sighed deeply, lowered the binoculars, and checked her watch. Steven had been outside for nearly five minutes, she realized. It would surely be a matter of time before he found something, and they could begin piecing this crazy story together.

Steven tried the patio door first, but it was locked. Abi had told him that the doors were poorly fitted and the locks often jammed open, but it was definitely locked. There were no lights inside the house, but the curtains at the front were partially open and they allowed some of the lights from the street to filter inside.

Cupping his hands against the glass, he peered inside, blocking out what little light shone from behind him. He could see the dining room clear as day and the living room beyond that. The layout was almost the same as Abi's house, only it looked a little bigger because it was empty. Where she had a bookcase stacked with end-to-end books, Robert had an old wooden chair; where she had a dining room table, there were just cardboard boxes. Robert had a sofa, an armchair, a small coffee table, and a TV, but that was it.

Steven moved to the back window, the kitchen window. The entire back wall of the kitchen was connected to the garage, separated from the living room by a door, which was firmly shut. There was minimal light inside, a slither of moonlight. He thought he saw someone sitting on a chair near the window and the silhouette startled him, causing him to pull away from the glass and to contemplate a quick retreat, but it could have just as easily been a doll, a coat, or a piece of furniture.

He pulled his face away from the glass, squeezed his eyes shut and breathed deeply, waiting for his rapidly beating heart to slow. When he opened them again, he noticed that the middle panel of the window was cracked, the first layer of the triple-glazed glass had been all but shattered in the center, with thinner cracks spiraling outward. A brick lay at the foot of the window, and Steven assumed it was the offending object, no doubt thrown by mischievous kids. He stepped over it and moved to the back door, hoping the glass panel in the upper part of the door would be more illuminating than the kitchen window, but before he pressed his face against the glass, he decided to test his luck.

He reached for the door handle and pushed.

Abi was growing increasingly agitated, worried—her right foot tapped a techno beat on the floor, her fingers drummed staccato rhythms on the table.

Too much coffee. Not good for my nerves.

The binoculars had been a good idea, in part. They allowed her to see down the street, to catch sight of whoever was approaching long before they became a threat, but they also gave her an excuse to spy on her neighbors, to watch the people she knew little about, to scan the faces she had seen only in passing or not at all.

The little boy playing the video games had been told off by a woman Abi initially assumed was his older sister, but then realized must have been his mother. Her mouth flapped aggressively as she thrust her finger at him and then at the screen. Abi couldn't read lips and she couldn't hear a word that was said, but the conversation played out in her head.

"I told you, no computer games on a school night!"

"But mum, it's just one—"

"But nothing, young man, no means no."

"Can I please just finish this one?"

"What did I just say?"

"I'll only be a few minutes."

The conversation culminated with her turning off the computer and him getting upset. Abi couldn't see the offending act, but she could see the boy, and by the horror on his face, the way he pointed, screamed, and then jumped up and down like a child possessed, she knew that his mother had taken it upon herself to end his night of gaming.

Abi found it all very amusing, and the woman had the same reaction. After the child stormed away, no doubt running to his bedroom as he screamed the house down, his mother grinned like a Cheshire cat as she slowly closed the curtains.

Abi found herself studying the woman's features at that point, noting how young she looked, how innocent she seemed. She was younger than Abi, yet she had a child old enough to play computer games, fight back, and storm off to bed—already she had more experience with children and families than Abi ever would have.

That depressed her a little, but her attention was quickly diverted when she saw movement down the end of the street and focused her binoculars on the source once more. This time the silhouette moved quickly, determination in their step, but when they stepped into the light, she saw that it was a teenage girl talking on her smartphone, her giggles growing more audible the closer she got. She wore a thick, black padded jacket and had equally thick dark hair, but she also wore a short skirt, her pale legs like ghost limbs hovering in the darkness every time she moved away from the glow of the streetlights.

Abi checked her watch for what must have been the tenth time in the last couple of minutes.

Where are you, Steven?

The back door was unlocked and offered little resistance as Steven pushed it open. He had expected, hoped even, that it would be locked. That way he wouldn't have to face whatever was inside, he wouldn't have to ask himself why the door was unlocked and face the consequences of what that meant. Because who, in their right mind, would leave a door unlocked if they knew there was a murderer on the loose, who would allow such a lapse in home security after discovering that someone had been brutally murdered a few feet from their front door?

He had seen enough horror films to know the answer: In a world of chaos, the only one truly at peace is the one responsible.

The door creaked open and immediately Steven was met with a strong stench. It was something he hadn't smelled before, something unusual, but there was a touch of familiarity to it. It was metallic, inhuman, but it reminded him of childhood nosebleeds, of burst lips. His attention immediately focused on the floor, where a slick black patch lay in wait.

"Blood?" Steven mouthed slowly. He reached for the light switch, slapping madly at the wall until he found it, pressed it, and felt his stomach climb into his throat.

The smell hit him more than ever and he knew exactly what it was. There was a coppery stench of blood, that much was unmistakable, but it was overpowered by the stench of excrement, of decay, death. The linoleum floor was slick with crimson—a large human-sized smear ran through the center, parting the red waves all the way to a wooden chair that had been tucked under a small table.

Robert was propped up on the chair, his face a picture of carnage, every inch of flesh coated in crimson, a large knife skewed through his head. He looked like a beaten, bloodied, human kebab, and what scared Steven most of all, what terrified him more than the pool of blood mere inches from his feet, or the grotesque way that his mouth hung partially open, was his eyes—big, white, wide open, and staring right at him.

Steven stood and stared for several seconds, unable to turn away, unsure of what to do. Many thoughts had entered his mind since he had left Abi's house. He thought he might be attacked, his assailant lying in wait and preparing for an opportunity just like this; he thought he might be trapped inside the house as the homeowner returned; he even considered the possibility that he would stumble onto a gang of occultists and find himself the target of their morbid curiosities. But for all the thoughts that entered his head, some plausible, many improbable, he never thought he would encounter Robert dead in his own house.

With his feet glued to the floor, his entire body shaking, Steven retrieved Abi's phone. He pressed the Home button and waited, but the phone didn't unlock.

"Shit," Steven hissed. He tried again, at which point the device asked him if he wanted to use his PIN instead. Remembering the number Abi had given him, he gladly accepted and then tried to type the code she had given him, but his hands were shaking violently, and he struggled to hit the correct numbers. He tried again and failed again.

The phone warned him that he had one more try before it locked, one more try before he lost his chance.

"Come on." A deep breath, eyes closed—he tried again. His trembling digits pressed the wrong number several more times, but he quickly deleted the digit and corrected himself. Just as he pressed the final digit, the door creaked on its hinges, rocked by a breeze, and he jumped, pressing the wrong number again and locking the phone.

"Fuck!"

He locked eyes with Robert once more—those unblinking, unmoving, lifeless eyes. The blood on the floor still looked slick, like a sheet of red ice, but the blood on Robert's face was thick, dark. A congealed blob ran from his mouth and coated his beard, hanging from his chin like a cherry popsicle.

He lowered the phone and slipped it back in his pocket, but three words flashed into his head, words he had read at the top of the locked phone but hadn't immediately registered. "Emergency Calls Only."

In his haste, he yanked the phone out of his pocket, and it slipped out of his sweaty grasp. He juggled with it, bouncing it from one hand to the next, struggling to grip it, his eyes bulging as they witnessed this brief but heart-dropping spectacle. It collided with his right palm and flew forward, out of his reach, into the brightly lit kitchen.

The phone landed in the pile of blood, splashing some of the thick, viscous liquid before resting among it, the blood now gradually enveloping it like some insidious, sentient being. The screen was still glowing as the blood slowly covered it, turning the bright white glow to a dull red.

The pool of blood claimed the phone, covering the screen, glowing red like a lava lamp before flicking off entirely, either succumbing to liquid damage or entering standby. He shook his head in disbelief and then turned to Robert. The human kebab was still staring at him, his dead eyes fixed firmly, but Steven could have sworn he was now smiling, mocking.

29

The back door flew open and rattled in its frame, shaking, vibrating like a leaf caught in a breeze. Abi had been making a cup of coffee at the kitchen counter—the noise caused her to jump, raining sugar granules over the worktop.

Steven stepped out of the darkness and stood in the doorway.

"Oh shit," Abi uttered, hand on chest. "You scared me half to death, what's—" Her mouth dropped open, her eyes widened. "Shit, Steven, what is it? What's wrong?"

His face was white, his chest heaving, the vein on his temple throbbed.

"I—I—I—"

Abi dropped the spoon. The metallic clatter reverberated throughout the room, catching Steven's attention as he glared at the object and then slowly dragged his eyes to the floor in front of him, the dining room table next to it, and then eventually to Abi.

"What's wrong?" she pushed. "You look like you've seen—"

"Don't say it." He looked away, dropped his head into his hands. "You have no idea."

"Here," Abi took him by the arm, noted how he flinched, how his horrified eyes met hers for a moment and sent a chill down her spine. "Sit down, over here." She guided him to one of the dining room chairs, but he froze, locked in position, his eyes even wider, his breath even heavier.

"No, no." He shook his head, stepped back. "Not there. I—I—" His gaze met hers again and this time remained. All the calm and the gentility that had been there before, had remained there throughout the short time she had known him, had gone, replaced by a hardened, cold edge. It scared her and told her all that she needed to know—whatever had happened, it was bad, and it was going to change both of their lives. "I need to use your phone."

"Why?"

"Where is it?"

"I gave you it," Abi reminded him. "You took it with you."

"No." He shook his head. "Not your cell. It fell. I lost it." There was panic in his movements. They were haggard, short, frantic. He looked like he was under the influence of some drug.

"You lost my phone, where?"

"In the house. It's not important—"

"Yes, it is. Steven, please, tell me what's wrong."

Abi tried to grab him, her hands on his shoulders to steady him, to get him to look her in the eye and tell her what had happened, but he shoved her off, his attention elsewhere.

"Give me your landline phone. I need to call the police."

"I don't have one."

His gaze finally focused on hers. The whites of his eyes were slightly bloodshot and moist with tears, something that hadn't been there before. It was as if he was breaking down in front of her.

"You don't have a landline?"

Abi shook her head, feeling her anxiety grow, her panic escalate. She hadn't known Steven for long, but they had been intimate together, they had shared secrets, family histories, likes, dislikes—he was the first man she had slept with that she actually had a connection with. The first man who wasn't just using her. But now, everything that she thought she knew about him was fading, replaced by questions, paranoia, concern.

Had he lost his mind? Had he done something bad?

"We need to phone the police," he said eventually, his eyes on his own feet, lifting them slowly, looking at the soles. It was as if he could see something that she couldn't. He pulled his attention back to her, placed his hands on her shoulders, locked his gaze in hers. "Robert is dead. Someone has killed him."

"No," she shook her head. "That can't be. That means—"

"That means he's not the killer," Steven finished for her. "And whoever is the killer, they could be targeting you."

Abi was suddenly very aware of the darkness that lay in wait behind the open door, the hairs on the back of her neck raised as she pictured someone lurking there, waiting to seize their opportunity and dive inside. She closed the door, locked it, and sat down at the table.

"They're not after me," she said softly.

"Why would you say that? What makes you so sure?"

Abi shrugged. "Robert was the weird one. He was watching me, keeping tabs on me, taking pictures. We thought he was the killer. If he's not, and it's someone else, then what makes you think they are interested in me?"

"Don't you get it?" Steven said, still animated, but a little more tuned into reality. "They killed your neighbor after you argued with her, they killed Robert after we accused him of stalking you, and then there's your ex-boyfriend."

"What?" Abi looked up, surprised. "What ex-boyfriend?"

"Matthew Graves."

She remained speechless, her gaze locked on his, her eyes looking right through him.

"He was murdered in an alleyway behind the Queen's Head," Steven explained. "He was playing the night that we had our first proper date, the night that we came back here and . . . you know."

Abi still didn't reply. She turned away, rested her hands on the table and twiddled her thumbs.

Steven remained standing, mere feet from the door. "You told me about him that night. We'd had a lot to drink, you admitted that he took your virginity and that you hated him for it; you told me that you bumped into him."

"That doesn't mean anything," Abi said, distantly.

"It means someone is killing people that hurt you, people that wronged you. Someone is obsessed with you and—" He paused. The final syllables almost choked silent in his mouth. Abi turned to look at him and noted that he was staring blankly into the middle distance. A spark seemed to ignite behind his eyes. "Your gran," he said. "It's your grandmother."

"What?"

"Your grandmother is the killer."

"Don't be stupid."

"No, it's not stupid," he said, shaking his head, his eyes elsewhere, his mind drifting. "It makes perfect sense."

"She's in her seventies."

"So? They were weak and she took them by surprised. It doesn't matter how old you are if they can't see you and you have a big fucking knife."

"Didn't see her? They would hear her knees creaking from a mile away. And what about Robert? He wasn't weak. He wasn't as easy to kill."

"You said she was fit for her age."

"For her age, yes, but that's setting the bar pretty low, don't you think?"

Steven didn't look convinced. "Where is she?"

"I don't—"

"Is she upstairs?"

Abi stood quickly, moved in front of him. "Listen, this is crazy, you're not—" She placed a hand on his face, rested it under his chin and looked deep into his eyes, but as soon as her hands touched his chin, he snapped.

He shoved her off, a quick, instinctive, jerk reaction. She felt herself falling before she even knew what had hit her, and as she fell, she saw his face light up with surprise, regret—he looked just as shocked as she was.

Abi fell into the chair she had been sitting on, hitting it with her chest first. The wooden seat slipped underneath her rib and the force of the impact sent it sprawling backward, where it slammed into the radiator and toppled over. Abi collapsed to the floor, using her uninjured hand to protect herself, to stop her face impacting the cold linoleum.

"Shit, shit, shit," Steven mumbled above her.

She rolled onto her back, her arms tucked under her ribs, protecting the area, soothing the dull pain that radiated outward. He bent over her, his face a picture of regret, sorrow. "I'm so sorry," he said. He moved to grab her, to hoist her up, and then thought better, instead holding out his hand. "I just—I had images of Robert, his body, the knife in his chin." He shook his head. "It's not important, and I'm sorry, I didn't know what I was doing."

Abi stared at him for a long time. There was fear in her eyes. They remained in that state for several moments: he proffering a hand in hope and regret; her staring into his eyes as if seeing right through him.

Just as he reached his wit's end and felt like he had lost her trust, Abi's expression softened. She smiled and extended her hand, allowing him to pull her up. "That's okay, dear," she said, sucking in a deep breath. "I understand."

She laughed softly and waited for Steven to retrieve the chair and guide her into it.

"I'm so sorry, do you need—"

"I'm good, honestly," she said. "Don't worry about it. Let's get back on track, shall we?"

Their gazes locked; a smile on hers, confusion, regret, and intrigue on his.

"You think my grandmother is the killer?" Abi asked.

Steven nodded.

"You're insane."

"Think about it—"

"I don't need to; I know my gran."

"You know what she wants you to know. But you see her as a granddaughter sees her. Think about it for a moment," he insisted. "It all makes sense."

30

Abi laughed softly. She stood, straightened, groaned at the residual pain in her rib, and brushed past her boyfriend. "Don't be so stupid," she told him. She returned to the kettle, boiled it again, and retrieved a second cup to add to the one already there.

"Think about it," Steven said, following her, hovering near her. "She was out that night. You couldn't get hold of her, you said it was strange of her."

"That doesn't mean anything, Steven, and you know it."

There was an air of indecision around him. Abi retrieved the sugar from the cupboard and he watched all the way, before stating, "It means everything. Think about it—where was she when the old lady across the road died?"

Abi shrugged.

"And what about the troll?"

"The troll?"

Steven nodded. "Simon Turnbull, I read the case online. He was found butchered in his own home."

"And?"

"Maybe you'll recognize him by his screen name: TheMarvelBuddha."

Abi paused, looked straight ahead and replied, almost to herself. "Sounds familiar," she noted, before scooping a third sugar into her cup.

"That's because your gran had been arguing with him for weeks!"

"Oh," Abi replied, nodding slowly. "I see." They locked eyes for several seconds as Steven tried to stare his point into her, to make her believe what he was seemingly convinced of. "How do you take your tea again?" she asked eventually.

"What? What are you doing?"

"I'm making us a hot drink so we can relax and discuss this properly."

"Discuss? *Discuss?*" He shook his head, took a step back. "There's nothing—what is wrong with you?" He ran his hand through his hair, exposing his thinning hairline, the deep-set wrinkles in his forehead, and the stark plainness of his skin. "This is serious."

"I know it is, but that doesn't mean—"

"Where's your gran?" he interrupted, cutting her short.

Abi sighed heavily. "Let's leave her out of this." She finished pouring hot water into the two cups and slowly began stirring the contents. "Would you like some biscuits with your tea?"

"Where. Is. Your. Gran?" Steven reiterated.

"I think we have some chocolate biscuits if you're—"

Abi's words caught in her throat as Steven rushed forward and grabbed her, one hand on either side, his large, strong hands wrapped around her arms. He pulled her around, forcing her to face him, to stare into his eyes.

"I don't know what's going on in there," he told her. "I know this must be hard for you. I know it must be scary, but this is serious. Where is your grandmother?"

"You should moisturize more, dear. Those wrinkles are unbecoming."

Steven groaned and released her, almost knocking her over as he did so. He slammed his fist against the counter and grunted in her direction, adding, "This is fucking ridiculous. I'll go get her myself."

"You do that," Abi called after him. "I'll have the tea and biscuits ready for you when you get back."

He stormed off, his heavy boot-clad feet racing across the living room and then up the stairs, each step reverberating throughout the house, shaking the foundations.

—

Abi finished making the drink and then calmly placed a selection of biscuits—some topped with chocolate, some plain, some still in their wrappers—on a small plate. She took the biscuits into the living room and placed them on the coffee table, followed by the two cups—tea, two sugars, lots of milk for Steven; coffee, three sugars, no milk, for her.

She turned on the television, tuned into a repeat of a soap opera, turned the volume up, and then nestled into the edge of the sofa, cup in one hand, biscuit in the other, an audible sigh on her lips as she sunk into the soft material.

"This is the life," she muttered to herself.

But just as soon as she sat down and began to relax, the chaos started. A thundering noise from upstairs drowned out the sound of the television, forcing her to pause her relaxation and search for the remote. By the time she found it, nestled underneath the cushion, the noise had increased, more banging, more shouting, each noise louder than the last.

She sighed, shook her head, and then hit the Volume Up button, keeping her finger pressed until the noise was drowned out by the sound of scripted gossiping. She lay the remote down on the arm of the couch, lifted her feet onto the coffee table with another audible sigh, and then picked up her cup.

Seconds later, the banging increased, heavy footfalls on hollow wood.

"The door is locked." Steven stood between her and the television, his arms folded across his chest, which heaved with each breath he took. There was a thin film of perspiration on his forehead that he wiped with the back of his hand.

"You're in my way, dear."

He looked behind him, to the TV, and then back again, his mouth agape. "What the fuck is wrong with you? Are you listening to me? The door is locked."

"I can't help you with that."

"It's a padlock."

"Yes, and?"

"It means that it's locked from the outside."

She turned to meet his questioning gaze, their eyes locked again, the desperation, shock, and confusion evident on his face. "You're sweating like a fatty in a cake factory, dear. Maybe we should open a window."

"I—I—" He ran a hand through his hair again, uttered a short burst of laughter, unsure what else to do. "I don't know what this is, but I—" He threw his hands up in the air. "You know what, fuck it—it doesn't matter. I'll get help from one of the neighbors."

"It's a bit late to start waking up neighbors, isn't it? The poor sods might have work in the morning."

"What? Someone is dead."

"Still, you can't start knocking on doors and crying blue murder at this time. People have lives to lead. Shit to do." She paused and allowed herself a smile. "Except Robert, of course."

"What the hell, Abi?" Steven shook his head. "It doesn't matter. If they don't answer, I'll drive to the fucking police station myself."

"You do that," she noted with a nod. "Good night for a drive. I think I'm going to go lie down. This is all getting a bit too much. First the surprise, then the fall, now I have a headache. A rest will do me good."

He acknowledged her with a slow, cautious nod and watched as she slowly, methodically, climbed to her feet, flashed a warm smile in his direction, and then left the room.

31

Steven's first thought was to return to Robert's house—images of the phone disappearing into the blood, enveloped and lost to the darkening and congealing crimson. He thought about retrieving it, or even stepping over it and seeing what else he could find, a landline, a mobile, something. But he couldn't go back there. The thought of seeing Robert again—propped on the chair like the centerpiece of a Halloween-themed storefront—was too much to process.

It didn't seem real; it almost *couldn't* be real. Here he was, in the midst of a murderous crime spree, the gruesome scene of a massacre one way, a potential murderer the next. He didn't agree with Abi. It wasn't preposterous that her grandmother was the killer; it made perfect sense. It was the only thing that made sense, the only thing that—

A thought occurred to Steven, one even more disturbing than the image of Robert, even more pervasive. He shook it away, ran his shirt sleeve across his forehead. The moisture stuck to the fabric and soaked in, like the blood had soaked the welcome mat, like the brain matter had soaked Robert's sweatshirt, like—

Another shake of his head, another thought he didn't want.

"Pull yourself together," he said to himself, his words cracking.

He looked back at the house as an image of Abi invaded his thoughts once more. He thought about the way she was acting, the strange things she had said.

"Can't be," he said to himself. The thought wouldn't leave him, but he was right. He had to be right. He *knew* he was right.

It couldn't be her.

Abi had been with him that night. They had made love for over an hour and had slept, flesh-on-flesh, her legs wrapped around him, his flaccid cock pressed against her, both soaked with sweat, stinking of intercourse and alcohol. He had drunk more than her, much more, and his memory of the events had been fleeting at best, but she had still consumed her fair share.

She had also been asleep.

You can't kill in your sleep, he told himself. You can't follow your ex-boyfriend down an alleyway and butcher him in cold blood. He shook his head and allowed himself a laugh, amused that the thought had even entered his head, that Abi, a prudish, gentle, and anxious girl could have done something so insane, so gruesome, so—

And then he remembered being woken up by the sound of the front door, only to realize that Abi wasn't next to him. "You must have been in the bathroom," he had told her, but she hadn't seemed convinced, had barely acknowledged what had been said.

He remembered how dismissive she had been, how quick she was to get rid of him to—

And then there was the encounter with the old lady. It happened the morning after—what was it she said?

I've seen you. In and out at ungodly hours.

Get out while you can. Wrong in the head.

"We weren't even that late," Steven had told Abi later that night. "She's probably one of these old ladies whose bedtime is 8 p.m., the minute her favorite show finishes." They had both laughed at that, but had he been wrong?

He thought about the victims. The callousness. The brutality. He didn't think she had it in her. She was sweet, innocent, shy—

But as soon as those thoughts entered his mind, they were banished by memories of when they first had sex. She was drunk, yes, and so was he, but she was like a woman possessed. She had pounced on him, pushed his head between her legs and held it there. He remembered wanting to lift his head, to pause and kiss her breasts or lips, but he couldn't, and she followed that with a vitriolic response to the old woman the following morning.

Steven shook his head, ridding those thoughts. He had to be realistic.

It could have been anyone. In his panicked, paranoid, and traumatized state, he could have easily found reason for it being the mailman or even a spate of particularly brutal suicides.

He reminded himself that none of that mattered, this wasn't *Columbo*, it wasn't a case of whether Abi *could* or not—it was a case of whether she *did* or not, and he knew she wasn't a killer. He had only known her for a few days, but that was enough. They had spoken together, they had kissed, hugged, embraced, made love—she had cried over films, shed a tear when he told her the story about how he accidentally killed his childhood hamster, a story he had intended to be funny.

She wasn't a killer, and maybe her grandmother wasn't either, but she was at risk, they all were, and he needed to get help.

I

It was late. Dark. The witching hour, my favorite part of the day.

You can't beat the tranquility of night—the mystery, the fact that anything, anyone, could be lurking in every pocket of pitch-black. The darkness hides everything—faces, feelings, intentions. And tonight, the darkness was just as reliable as ever.

The curtains were drawn, the windows open, the glass reflecting the light from inside the room, showing my haggard, tired features.

I needed to freshen myself up, but first, I needed to check my Twitter and see what argument I could get into. The only thing better than a night on the tiles is a night spent pissing off trolls and arguing with idiots.

Several direct messages waited for me in my account. The first was a man who seemed very proud of his genitalia, even though he had very little to be proud of. He was standing in front of a webcam, his little todger proudly displayed for the camera, hanging between the hairiest set of testicles I have ever seen and thighs that looked like two bear arms. He was more gorilla than man, his hairless, cocktail-sausage-sized penis standing to attention like a bald, naked soldier in a thick, dense jungle.

I thanked him for his picture and replied with something special of my own: another penis, this one taken from a porn site, accompanied by the words "That's not a penis. THIS is a penis."

The second was an attempt at foreplay from a greasy troglodyte who had probably never met a female human, let alone had sex with one. I told him I wasn't interested in the most obscene and gratuitous way that I could think of and then signed out for the night.

I moved on to my vanity mirror just as the sound of banging filtered through the open window. The night was empty, still, and although far away, the noise was loud, each bang like a clap of thunder from some distant, steadily approaching storm.

Several bangs were proceeded by a short silence, and then by more bangs, this set louder than the last, more desperate. More silence, followed by an even louder, cacophonous series of thumps.

I fixed my hair, my attention focused on my reflection and not the chaos outside my window. I was careful to place every strand, to make sure it looked perfect, because I knew this was going to be a big night.

The banging was interrupted by the sound of shouting, a man's voice, a desperate man.

I moved on to my makeup. A long and thankless task, but one that needed to be done. I simply wasn't myself if I didn't wear makeup. No one deserved to see me without my war paint. Years of careful application had turned me into a master, an artist sending sweeping strokes over a canvas, paying little heed to the technique but knowing exactly what the outcome would be.

The banging began again several minutes later, followed immediately by the sound of shouting, screaming almost, a hoarse, desperate, pleading sound. It was distant, the storm drifting and not encroaching, but it still roared with the same intensity as before, if not more.

The noise gradually died down and I finished my makeup. I was ready to embrace the night. I gave myself one last look, tilted my head this way and that and admired how easily I had covered the many wrinkles, how expertly I made my tired, old eyes pop, how I added color to my thin, aging lips.

I stood slowly and headed for the door.

32

Steven avoided Robert's house and ran to the other next-door neighbor. The lights in the house were out, but so was every other house in the street. If someone was going to help him, and he would make sure they did, he was going to have to wake them up.

There was a bell on the front door, but when he pressed it, he couldn't hear a noise on the other side. Instead, he reached for a large brass knocker, a goblin-face with a detachable smile. He grabbed the thick goblin lips and slammed.

Once. Twice. Three times.

He waited, but he heard nothing. Another round of banging. Louder this time.

He waited again, but still, he heard nothing. He was growing impatient, rocking from foot to foot, constantly looking over his shoulder, aware that he was exposing himself to the mercy of the street and whoever lurked in the darkness beyond the streetlights.

Three more bangs. This time he put all of his might into them, forcing the knocker down so hard that an outline of the goblin's smile printed on his palm. He thought he heard voices on the other side of the door and his thoughts were confirmed when he stepped back, looked up, and saw a light in the bedroom window, a light that hadn't been there before.

The curtains ruffled just as he looked, a dark silhouette stood behind them, no doubt wondering what this crazy man wanted and why he was knocking at their door in the middle of the night.

Steven had no time for pleasantries, no time for social convention. There was a dead body just a couple houses away and a chance that everyone's life was at risk.

He knocked on the door again, giving them another opportunity. When they didn't respond after a few more moments, he screamed at the top of his lungs: "Please, I need your help! Open the door!"

He stepped back again and saw the curtains ruffle for a second time as the occupant disappeared out of view. "I know you're up there!" he yelled, his voice cracking halfway through. "Someone has been murdered!" he tried to say, only for his voice to crack again.

He was tired but filled with adrenaline, sick but determined. His body no longer felt like his own as desperation took over and he yelled again, this time his words coming through clearly. "Go fuck yourself!"

Steven moved on to the second house. It had been in darkness when he started banging, but he could now see a lit room to the side. He rang the bell several times, happy to hear that it sounded loud and clear on the other side of the door, a sharp, stinging ring that would have been irritating at any other time.

He rang several times, waited, and then rang again, this time pressing his finger on the ringer for several seconds, rocking from side to side as he did so.

A middle-aged man appeared from the side of the house, a cigarette in his mouth, a dressing gown maintaining his modesty. Despite the chaos and the late hour, he didn't seem perturbed. He wore an assured expression on his wizened face, his forehead set with deep wrinkles.

"What's going on here?" He took the cigarette out of his mouth and tightened the belt around his dressing gown, covering a beer belly that seemed to project several feet from his body, preceding him everywhere he went.

"Oh, thank God," Steven said. He moved toward the man, acting on instinct and desperation, but the man quickly took a step back and held up a hand.

"Keep your distance," the beer-bellied neighbor instructed, using his warning hand to calmly take a puff of his cigarette, during which he studied Steven intently.

"I need your help," Steven said. "There's been a murder, a horrible, gruesome—"

"Old Lady Hunt?" he replied with a nod. "Yeah, tragic, but that's old news. All over Facebook apparently."

"No." Steven shook his head, cleared his throat. "Another one. Robert, his name is."

"New guy, couple doors down?"

"That's the one. I need you to phone the police. Tell them to hurry. He's dead already, but the killer is still out there."

"Okay then." The man calmly took another draw of his cigarette, still studying Steven intently. He blew a stream of smoke toward him and then asked, "Who are you then?"

"What? That doesn't matter. We need the police, we—"

"Don't worry about that," he replied. "They're on the way. I phoned them before I came out, on account of the crazed stranger running around banging on people's doors and screaming obscenities at half-past midnight."

"Sorry about that."

The man shrugged. "Not to worry. I best get back in there, let them know the stranger may not be so crazed after all."

"Thank you," Steven said, a weight lifting off his shoulders. His eyes were drawn to the cigarette in the man's hand, his nostrils having already picked up the sharp scent of burned tobacco. "Before you go, can I steal a cigarette off you?"

The man looked at the glowing stick in his hand. "These things will kill you, ya know?"

"Not if the local psychopath gets to me first."

"Good point."

SMOKER

A cloud of smoke billowed into the night air—the stench of burnt tobacco, the fizzle of burning embers. A satisfied sigh, an utterance of exasperation. Smoker stood at the end of the driveway, a cancer stick in his mouth, a toxic plume drifting into the dark.

He seemed to be enjoying it with a relish usually reserved for the first cigarette of the day or that satisfying smoke after sex. The excitement, the adrenaline and anxiety, the stress—all of his emotions had reached a peak and then descended to exhaustion. I didn't smoke, but even I could appreciate how good it must have felt.

He coughed, the harsh noise like a clap of thunder in the silent night; a pillow of smoke erupted from his lungs. Unperturbed, he took another draw, then another, and another, all in a quick and hungry succession. He smoked it right down to the filter before he finally flicked it away, watching as it hit the wet tarmac and instantly fizzled out. Only then did he turn, his eyes coming face to face with mine.

"What—" A grunt, a groan, another cough. His eyes lowered from mine. He took a half-step backward. I moved with him. He looked at the knife lodged below his rib cage—the hilt pressed tight against his torn sweater, the blade angled upward—and then back to me.

There was a question on his lips, in his eyes, but he was incapable of processing it. He just stood there, immobile, idle, dumb. I drove the knife in further, my knuckles pressing against the moistening wound around his sweater, the blade piercing his lungs.

"You told her you didn't smoke." I yanked the knife out, a move that required force, a move that hooked more flesh and organ tissue on its exit. "Whatever happened to honesty, eh?"

I stabbed him again, the sharp blade driving into his abdomen, piercing his stomach, his intestines; and again, aiming for his chest, cracking a floating rib, sucking the air out of his lungs. He grasped at the knife and at the blood gushing from the wounds, his eyes on mine, his pupils wide.

It was as if he was caught in a nightmare, unsure what was happening and how to react. Desperate to wake up.

I shook my head, showing him my disgust, and then stepped back. I expected him to drop to his knees, to look me in the eyes—a pleading, despairing, questioning look. But his attention turned to his wounds, his hands lapping up the blood as if desperately trying to stop a leak, his panic intensifying with every passing second. Moments later, his body gave out from underneath him, and he dropped to the side, folding like a paper doll and collapsing into a heap.

"Did you just stab him?"

A potbellied man wearing a dressing gown and holding a lit cigarette stood at the side of one of the houses, his eyes switching from me to the body on the ground. I shrugged, making little effort to hide the knife from him as I slid it into its sheath under my jacket.

"You did—You—you."

I dug through Smoker's pockets, looking for his keys and my escape as the neighbor continued to fluff his lines and glare in disbelief.

"The cops are coming, you know?"

I straightened and stared at him, smiling as he took an almost instinctive step back, even though we were separated by at least twenty feet and he was closer to his house than he was to me. "Now, why would you tell me that?"

"I—I—" The neighbor was dumbfounded, even taking a break to puff on his cigarette. "They're going to arrest you."

"Uh-huh." The keys were in Smoker's back pocket. I rolled him over and noted that there still seemed to be life in him, a flickering of electrical activity, a faint whisper of breath, but he was on his way out. He was a brain without a body; a husk without a soul.

"Such a shame. You had promise," I said with a wink, tapping the soon-to-be-corpse on the backside.

I noted that several houses in the street were alive, even at this late hour. Curtains twitched; nosy neighbors made brief appearances. Only one of them had the gall to stand outside and face me, but all of them had probably called the police and I didn't have a lot of time to waste.

As if to confirm my suspicions, the sound of distant sirens cut through the still night air as I entered Smoker's car and quickly made my escape.

HER AND I

She was asleep, dead to the world, her house in darkness, silence. The sirens and the chaos I left behind were a distant memory—the noise failing to break the wall of serenity that cloaked this quiet, secluded farmhouse. Animals rustled in the trees and emitted random vocalizations in the barn, but nothing disturbed the house itself or the occupants within.

The night was gradually turning into day by the time I slipped inside. There was no alarm, no security, and I had a key. It didn't take a skilled cat burglar or a serendipitous thief to enter this particular residence. The house was pitch-black, darker than it had been outside, with no streetlights for miles and no moonlight breaking through the thick curtains. But for the stark red standby lights that littered every room like idle fireflies, there was no hint of light or life. I used a small flashlight to break the wall of black, directing the beam ahead of me. As soon as it fell upon the interior of the house, my jaw dropped.

The decor homey, comforting, welcoming. A short hallway, decorated with oak-paneled floors and vintage wallpaper, led into a large living room. An open fireplace stood as the room's focal point, strewn with a string of twinkling lights, littered with framed pictures. A three-piece suite encroached around a large television and a small wooden coffee table.

I walked through the house taking everything in—the artwork, the detritus of family life. An archway at the back of the open-plan living room led into a large country kitchen, complete with Aga, breakfast table, and the leftovers of a large family meal. At the end of the kitchen was a partitioned door leading into a utility room and what was most likely a garage or storage room; on the other side a hallway, leading into a playroom and downstairs toilet. It was huge, a veritable country palace, but the more I took in, the more despair I felt. The joy and amazement gave way to anger and frustration; the comforting warmth to bitter, chilling cold.

A knife rack stared at me invitingly from the counter. I had come prepared, but the way that the light caught the glint of the blades, the way they gleamed and glistened, called to me. I took out the largest one and sniffed the handle, breathing in the scent of its owner, of a million cuts and dices—the scent of a hardworking mother preparing countless meals for her family.

I walked back into the living room, into the hallway, and to the bottom of the stairs, a winding, twisting staircase bordered by an antique banister and surrounded with more paintings, more pictures—images of a happy, loving family. The handle of the knife threatened to crack in my hand as I squeezed tight, leaving its mark on my skin.

—

The flashlight glinted off photographs and paintings, a spotlight crawling over each stair, each potential obstacle, but the bright white light diffused when the hallway light snapped on and the house came alive.

A tall, slovenly figure emerged into the sudden glare, a slow, staggering, groaning figure who shuffled on bare feet, hunched like a middle-aged zombie. His eyes were fixed on his own feet, barely focusing on the hallway around him, the stairs ahead of him, or the killer below. Bare feet slapped the wooden floor, soaking up the cold, making him more alert, more awake with each step.

He was at the top of the staircase when I backed away, his eyes never once focusing on me—too tired, too blurry, too docile. They wouldn't have picked out the shadowy figure at the bottom of the staircase even if they had been focused.

His hand slapped the banister, gripped tightly, and then shouldered the burden of his entire weight as he leaned into the twisting, wooden railing and descended with the rapidity of a sloth. He yawned, he groaned, he mumbled to himself, and eventually, what seemed like an entire minute later, he made it to the bottom of the stairs.

Only then did I realize that my flashlight was still on, the beam pointing directly at his feet, wrapping him in a florescent halo, his tartan pajamas taking the spotlight. I froze; he did the same. He seemed to stall as if processing something, eyes down, back arched, neck almost horizontal.

Fuck. Fuck. Fuck. Fuck.

I readied the knife, waiting to explode out of the darkness, to cut him down where he stood. The spotlight around his feet wobbled in my increasingly unsteady grip. He straightened his head, and for a split second he looked right at me, but his head continued to rise, until he tilted it back and unleashed a loud yawn that seemed to shake his entire body.

I turned off the flashlight and tucked myself behind the corner; he finished with a grumbled expletive and a high-pitched crescendo and then continued to shuffle his way to the kitchen, walking from the silvery light of the stairs into the graying darkness of the hallway and then the pitch-black of the kitchen. I followed close behind, my footsteps measured, careful and quiet, but unnecessarily so as he continued to grumble, shuffle, and groan his way to the kitchen.

He snapped on the light, an instinctive, accurate punch, as if casually swatting a fly. Zombie kept his head down, eyes low, avoiding the bright, burning light, and made his way to the fridge. He paused again in front of the fridge, one hand on the door, the other lofted in the air like a composer preparing for a dramatic climax.

His Adam's apple bobbed enticingly as he swallowed the air hungrily and more grumbling noises escaped his mouth.

Zombie didn't react when I placed my left hand on his chin; barely flinched as I quickly dragged him back until his head rested on my shoulder. But he did react when he felt the steel tip of the blade on his throat.

The reaction was sudden, instant, explosive. He threw himself forward, breaking out of my grasp with ease. A couple staggered steps to the side, a quick maneuver, a turn, and then our gazes met, his eyes wide with horror, mine wide with surprise.

There was a split second in which we just stared, a moment in which a million thoughts must have run through his head. He raised his hand, pointed it at me accusingly, and then he opened his mouth to voice his anger.

His words caught in his throat. He coughed, his entire body seemingly in spasm, and brought a hand to his mouth. When he pulled it away and looked at it, he saw that it was covered in blood, the same crimson substance that now covered his chin. His eyes, still wide, still worried, slowly followed his hand as he reached for his throat, expecting, hoping, to find a small wound, but instead encountering the hilt of a large kitchen knife.

Death often came quickly and with little fanfare, but there was always an element of surprise, a realization that it was really happening, and it wasn't a dream or a joke. The mind had a funny way of ignoring what it couldn't face. As Zombie dropped to his knees and desperately clawed at the handle of the knife, the realization now sinking in, I wondered whether they genuinely were surprised and oblivious, or if the brain just went walkabouts—deprived of oxygen, of life, of rational thought—to save it from itself.

Zombie eventually pulled the knife out and there was a sense of relief on his face. In that split second, it was like he believed he had done what he needed to do, as if removing the offending weapon had saved his life. But the blood quickly gushed out of the open wound, painting his hands and the floor in a sticky crimson, and then the realization set in. He stared in horror at the blood in his hands, his face twisted, his glassy eyes—once tired and caught between dreams and reality—now stuck in the reality of his demise.

Zombie's hands fell limp, the blood splashing onto the floor, and his face followed, meeting the hardwood with audible force, loud enough to cause concern, heavy enough to crack his skull. I waited, watched, and then reached for the knife, which rested by his side. Just as my fingers gripped the handle, moist with his blood, he sprang back to life. His upper body arched back, his feet began to kick, his throat emitted a high-pitched, strangled whine.

Zombie began to convulse—his dying throes, his desperation, I wasn't sure which, but every twist, turn, and kick brought with it more chaos. The toes of his naked feet slammed repeatedly into the floor, bending, twisting, breaking under the impact; his arms swiped at my legs, scooping the pooling blood and spraying it around.

I stumbled and dropped the knife as he slid closer to me, like a dying dolphin desperate to lash out at its murderer. A bottle of wine fell from the wine rack near his legs, breaking on the hardwood floor; a cupboard repeatedly banged open and closed, open and closed; his fist slammed against the fridge, a pounding, ominous beat.

My boot made rough contact with the top of his head, skimming his forehead and nearly causing me to lose my balance as my standing foot struggled to gain traction on the blood-soaked floor. His face fell against the floor again, his body no longer arched, but he continued to struggle, to wail, to fight. I kicked again, this time making a cleaner contact, breaking his nose, the appendage crushed under leather and laces. His whole body felt the force of the impact, skidding on the blood-soaked floor, slamming against the counter.

I stepped forward and kicked again, and again, and again, breaking his jaw, his teeth, and leaving his face a bloodied, beaten, pulp. His body continued to fight, to struggle, but it faded with each effort and then disappeared completely.

I stared and waited, almost expecting him to spring back to life. His choking breath accompanied the steady glug of blood pouring from the wounds on his neck and his face. My breaths were short and raspy, but when I eventually calmed down, when my heartbeat slowed and my breathing steadied, the house had returned to almost complete silence.

"Fucking hell," I whispered under my breath, "That was intense."

I left the kitchen knife where it was—the handle and blade now dripping with blood—and retrieved my blade from its sheath.

Part 4

33

Lauren Mathers-Brown awoke with a start, her heart pounding out of her chest, a slick of sweat on her forehead. She'd dreamt that she was on a boat, lost in some vast, postapocalyptic world, escaping from zombies, gruel-covered creatures, and other horrors back on the shore. An explosion had woken her, a sound that seemed to penetrate every fiber of her being as a mushroom cloud of brilliant white exploded from the shore and enveloped the boat, her, and everything she held dear.

Her breaths left her lungs in short, raspy waves—a measured, controlled panic attack. She placed a hand to her head, noted the moisture that rested there, and the moisture that had already soaked into the duvet, sheet, and pillowcase.

"I had another bad dream," she whispered, her voice breaking, but remaining clear. "That Valium, I swear—it'll be the death of me." She tossed the covers away from her, relished in the momentary rush of cooler air on her exposed legs, prickling lines of goosebumps, little hairs standing tall from her ankles to her thighs.

"If it's not a postapocalyptic wasteland, it's a plague of monsters, a serial killer, an explosion, an—" She turned and saw that she was alone. The space so often occupied by her husband, John, a light sleeper who woke when she did and shared in her frustrations, was empty. There was just an empty space where he usually lay, his body no longer molded to the memory foam mattress, his shape no longer visible.

Then she heard the noise again, the same one from her dream, the one that had accompanied the nuclear blast and forced her awake. But this time it was real and coming from directly underneath the bedroom, in the kitchen.

Lauren thought about shouting downstairs to her husband. A light sleeper, but a heavy drinker. When he woke, dehydrated, and desperate for some sustenance, he was like the walking dead, complete with bad breath and a staggered, moaning gait worthy of the silver screen. There was a good chance he had just bumped into the fridge, dropped a carton of juice or—

Her thoughts were cut short when she heard another worrying sound, one of breaking glass, followed by repeated banging. Lauren quickly jumped out of bed, slid into a pair of slippers, and threw on her gown. The bedroom door stood ajar and looked onto the pitch-black hallway. More noises—heavy, forceful bangs, like when her son, Ethan, played soccer against the garage door.

"What the hell is going on?" she whispered to herself.

She shuffled across the room, out into the hallway, and bumped straight into someone. For a moment, it felt like her heart dropped out of her body, the same feeling she had when Ethan insisted that she take him on a roller-coaster, the one she often got when he watched too many horror films and tried to scare her by throwing plastic spiders in the bath or jumping out from behind the sofa.

Her fears faded and her heart ascended when she saw that the figure was Ethan, her thirteen-year-old son and the source of many of her jump scares.

"Oh my God, Ethan, you scared me half to death."

"I scared *you*? You're the one who bumped into me, Mom. If anyone has a right to be—"

"Was that you banging?"

Ethan shook his head. "Someone's downstairs." Lauren could hear the fear in her son's voice, but it was layered with curiosity. "Maybe we should phone the police?"

"It's just your dad."

"I know, but I don't think he's alone." Ethan's reply was enough to give Lauren another shock, only this one didn't fade quite as quickly.

The banging stopped, prompting them both to stand and listen in silence, waiting for the next noise, the next clue as to what was happening in their house. But there was nothing—no banging, no breaking, no shouting. Whatever had caused the commotion, it was over.

Lauren had images of John fighting with a burglar and losing; of him tripping and falling, lying in a pool of his own blood, desperate for help. But she was quick to dismiss her paranoias, telling herself that if he had fought with a burglar then there would have been more noise, with at least some shouting, and reminding herself that if he had fallen and hurt himself, there wouldn't have been so many bangs.

"What do you think all that was?" Ethan said, asking the same question that was running through his mother's head.

"I don't know, but I'll find out." She placed a hand on his shoulder. "You wait here. I'll go and see."

"Not a chance in hell," Ethan quickly replied.

"Excuse me?"

"If something is happening down there, it's best that we face it together. That way, I can rugby tackle the big one while you eye-gouge the little one."

"We need to start monitoring your Netflix account." Lauren sighed. "Okay, come on, let's go. But slowly—try not to make a noise."

34

Lauren took the lead, walking ahead of her son, her steps slow and methodical. She thought back to when she was younger, to the house she had grown up in. In that house, she had memorized a detailed blueprint of every single stair. Which ones creaked, which ones groaned. She would play her own game of hopscotch as she moved up and down late at night or early in the morning. This house was new and didn't creak or groan in the same way, but she applied the same level of care and attention now as she had done when she was a child trying not to wake her grandmother.

Ethan's hand rested on her shoulder as she descended, a process that seemed to take several minutes. The light at the bottom of the stairs was on and she could see the front door, part of the passageway, and part of the living room. She scanned every visible inch on her descent but didn't notice a single thing out of place. At the bottom, she turned toward the kitchen, to the source of the noise.

The light in the kitchen was off, as was the light for the hallway leading to it. A little voice at the back of her mind told her that something was wrong—if it was John and if he had fallen, why would the lights be off? She pushed this to one side, keeping her head clear just in case someone was lurking around the corner, just in case her husband had hurt himself.

Ethan's hand moved from her shoulder to her back, as if urging her forward, pushing her toward the kitchen door, which was slightly ajar, the gaping blackness beyond sending Lauren's heart racing when she imagined herself walking through and discovering something that she didn't want to discover.

She pushed the door open with her lead leg, listening to the squeak of unoiled hinges as it rocked this way and that. Ethan removed his hand from her back as she stepped inside, swallowed thickly, and prepared for whatever chaos awaited her, from a sleeping or unconscious husband, to broken plates and more.

When the light eventually snapped on, Lauren came face-to-face with a sight unlike anything she had seen before, a sight that hadn't even haunted her disturbing dreams. She also saw someone she never thought she would see again for as long as she lived.

"Martha," Lauren mouthed slowly. "What—what—what the fuck is going on?"

Lauren hadn't noticed the stench at first, but as soon as the light snapped on, as soon as she saw the twisted, bloodied portrait of her former husband on the hardwood floor, it hit her. It was a coppery, sewage smile that invaded her nostrils and made her sick. Her stomach acid rose, her gag reflex activated, and while the stench alone wasn't enough to bring her to her knees and force her to vomit, the image was.

Lauren gagged once, twice, thrice, before she finally vomited. But there was nothing in her stomach, nothing waiting to be purged except bile and acid. The pain of gagging was all she felt and all that the vomit produced initially, but then yellow bile surfaced, dribbling out of her mouth like a strand of spaghetti and drooping to the floor. A sour, burning taste remained in her mouth—her throat on fire, her stomach in agony, her eyes watering, both from the pain and from seeing her dead husband.

"You finished?" Abi stood between Lauren and her husband, moving off to the side to allow Lauren to glimpse every inch of the carnage. A knife hung loosely in her right hand, her left rested lazily on the counter. She looked like a teenager waiting idly for a friend, and not a sick killer who had just butchered someone in cold blood.

"What did you do?" Lauren asked, trying to tear her eyes away from her husband but finding herself unable.

"He got in my way, dear." Abi shrugged, checked her nails. "I would say that it was either him or me, but he never stood a fucking chance." She chuckled. "It was like *Dawn of the Dead*. I don't know what you saw in him, to be honest."

Lauren finally dragged her eyes from her husband and fixed them on her sister, a woman she hadn't seen in years, a woman she barely acknowledged. "What are you wearing?"

"Excuse me?"

"The wig, the makeup, you look like—"

"A much younger woman? A mature model? I know, I still have it, don't I? Even at my age."

Lauren shook her head. "What are you doing here, Martha? Why are you dressed like an old woman?"

"Firstly," Abi pointed the knife at her sister, the tip of the blade thrust menacingly toward her. "Old woman? I raised you to respect your elders. God knows what this loser has been teaching you." She glared at John Mathers, kicked out in his general direction, but missed him by an inch. "But it's not too late to relearn some of that respect."

Lauren found herself just staring, a thought slowly occurring to her, a thought that should have been obvious the moment she stepped into the kitchen and found her long-lost sister wielding a knife, standing over a dead body, and wearing a gray wig. "You've lost your fucking mind."

"Language!" Abi yelled, advancing on her sister. "I've always told you girls—just because I swear, doesn't mean you can!"

"*You girls?*" Lauren mimicked. "Do you think you're my—*our*—fucking grandmother?" Lauren shook her head in disbelief and then laughed.

Abi's face twisted with rage, "I told you to watch your fucking mouth!" She grabbed Lauren by the hair and pulled.

Lauren felt strands of her hair rip, felt the pain burn across her scalp. She quickly propped herself up, using her hands and knees to support herself, to avoid her entire scalp being ripped off. "Now," Abi said, pressing the blade to Lauren's throat. "Get in the living room. The night may be over for your late husband, but for you, it's only just beginning."

Abi moved around the back of her sister, keeping a clump of her hair clasped firmly in her left hand while she used the right to wield the knife and press her forward, the blade pricking the skin on the back of her exposed neck.

Lauren took several steps forward, moving closer to her husband's dead body, to the stench that cloyed at her throat, the sight that would forever stay in her memories. Her knees went weak, her body threatened to collapse, but her sister's words and the images they conjured kept her alive, strong.

"And where's this son of yours?"

In the chaos, Lauren had forgotten about Ethan. She recalled feeling his hand on her shoulder as they descended the stairs, then on her back as they walked across the hallway, and then—nothing. He hadn't joined her in the kitchen, had sensed the danger and stayed back.

Lauren couldn't help but smile, and as they entered the living room and she allowed herself a cheeky glance at the kitchen entrance, confirmed that Ethan was nowhere to be seen. "He's not here," Lauren told her sister.

"Don't lie to me, or I'll—"

"He's not, I swear. He's at a sleepover."

Lauren screamed as her hair was yanked back, nearly lifting her off her feet before sending her to her knees, the blade of the knife now firmly in her flesh, drawing a line of blood she felt trickle down her back. "You better not be fucking lying to me, dear." Abi's words were hot and hushed, spoken within inches of Lauren's ears. "If you are, I'll kill him just like I did your husband, only this time I'll make you watch. This isn't my first rodeo; I know what I'm doing. You can't play me like you did your sister. Fuck with me and I will kill you."

"I swear," Lauren begged, tears streaming down her face, her words shouted, screamed, making sure that Ethan, wherever he was, could hear. "He's at a sleepover. You can check his room if you want. I swear he's not here."

That seemed to satisfy Abi. She dragged Lauren to her feet, tapped her lovingly on the back, and then, in a calm, sweet, grandmotherly voice, said, "That's okay, dear, I trust you."

35

"Why are you doing this?"

Abi had wrapped zip ties around Lauren's hands and tossed her unceremoniously onto the sofa, where she immediately sagged down into plush cushions. The plastic ties dug deep into her flesh, cutting off all feeling to her hands, but her own safety was the last thing she cared about. The staircase was off to her right, through an archway that led into the hallway. Abi was standing in front of her, the staircase to her left.

Lauren wanted to look, to check where her son was, to make sure he was safe, but she knew that doing so could expose him, and so she pinned her eyes forward, distracting Abi just in case.

"I raised you girls to be fair," Abi told her, waving the knife at her as she spoke. "To share. To love. If your sister had something, I'd make sure you had it as well; if you had a brand-new computer, I bought one for Martha."

"Martha."

"Yes, dear?"

Lauren shook her head. The makeup. The wig. The voice. Her sister's mind had gone AWOL.

"That wasn't a question."

Abi looked confused.

"That's what you get when you name a kid after their grandmother," Lauren grumbled. "I always said Martha was a stupid name."

"You always had a problem with Martha," Abi continued, choosing to ignore the comments. "You never appreciated her. You never shared anything with her," Abi continued. She gestured around the room. "With your big house. Your expensive things. Your family." She shook her head and made a disapproving tutting sound, her hands on her hips. "And what did your sister have?"

"A screw loose and an obsession with old ladies?"

"Nothing. Nothing is what she had."

"You killed my husband because I didn't give *Martha* any money, is that it?"

"There is more to life than money, dear."

"So, what's your fucking problem!" Lauren spat, her confusion and fear turning to anger and growing with each second, each syllable that left her sister's mouth.

"You're the reason she didn't live the life she deserved. You had everything—friends, family, money, success. She had nothing." There was a trace of bitterness on Abi's face, as if each syllable had come from deep within and delivered on a torrent of bile. "She watched you. Obsessed over you. *Loved* you."

"Then why did she kill my fucking husband?" Lauren spat.

Abi advanced, her footsteps slow, methodical, a malevolent expression on her face. She paused in front of the sofa, leaned in close, close enough for Lauren to smell her breath, to feel its warmth on her face.

"Because now I'm here to even things out." Abi straightened, the sinister smile locked on her face. "After all, fair's fair."

Lauren hated every word that left her sister's lips, struggling to fight back the anger. She wanted nothing more than to spring to her feet and rip her throat out, but for the sake of her son, her future, her life, she restrained herself.

"Wait," Lauren said, squirming, eager to keep her sister, her grandmother—whatever she was—talking for as long as she could. "I get it, I do, but this isn't the only way. Please, let's talk about it."

"What's there to talk about, dear?"

Martha had always respected her grandmother. She was much closer to her than Lauren had ever been. The grandmother-granddaughter pair were two different people—one outgoing and confident, the other timid, shy, and introverted. Her grandmother also wasn't much of a people person, especially not when those people were needy family members. But they had the same name—a mark of respect from Lauren's mother to her mother-in-law, an apparent—and that bonded them.

Lauren locked stares with her sister, her breathing heavy and labored, her chest rising and falling rapidly. "How is my sister these days?"

Abi shrugged, retreated several steps and then turned her back. "She's been better," she said, tossing the knife from hand to hand. "She met someone. Steven, his name was. Nice guy."

"*Was*? She's not with him anymore?"

Abi shook her head. "That one didn't work out. Turned out he was a smoker; you know what Martha thinks about smoking."

Lauren tried her best to muster a smile, reciprocating the one that curled menacingly on her fake grandmother's lips.

"And then there was Robert. He was a little strange though. A bit too obsessive. So." Abi shrugged. "It's really just been me and her. She has her work, of course, and that keeps her busy. If you ask me, she's been a little stressed lately. A lot of people have been getting her down—ex-boyfriends, crazy neighbors, stalkers. She even had a run-in with a crazy little bitch at the coffee shop. Humiliated her right where she stood, just because she hesitated a little." She shook her head, her hands on her hips once more. "Can you believe that? What is the world coming to?"

"Right? Tell me about it. The things that the younger generation gets away with these days, eh?" Lauren mocked.

"Oh, she didn't get away with it. She suffered. She got a taste of her own medicine. The world saw her humiliation."

Lauren nodded slowly, her sister's words not fully sinking in.

She kept one eye on the clock above the mantelpiece as each second dragged by. Ethan would have phoned the police. He was a smart kid, he had a cell phone, and he would have heard the commotion. It would take them roughly five to ten minutes to arrive from the local police station. After that, the situation could get messier, but at least Ethan would be safe, at least she wouldn't need to die with the knowledge that he would be next.

"That's why I am here, after all," Abi said.

Lauren dragged her eyes from the clock to her attacker, noticing the glint in her eye, the smug satisfaction, the malice. "What do you mean by that?" she asked, knowing exactly what she meant.

"Well, I'm her grandmother, aren't I? I'm her protector. It's my job to keep her safe."

"And how do you do that?"

"I make sure they get what they deserve."

It suddenly dawned on Lauren. She realized what her psychotic relative was saying. News stories, newspaper headlines, Facebook posts—the killings she had followed so intently and with such horror, the same ones that had swept the country. The internet troll, the young girl, the aspiring rock star. They occurred a relatively short drive away from the town she called home. They had felt close to home at the time, but she now realized that they had been closer than she could have known.

"You killed them." It was a statement, not a question, one that almost fell from Lauren's thoughts. "How many?"

Abi shrugged. "I lost count. There are a lot of horrible people in this world, you know?"

"And my husband? What did he do wrong? How could he have possibly hurt Martha? He didn't even know she existed!"

Abi looked appalled, once again her hands went to her hips, and she shook her head slowly from side to side. "You mean to say, you didn't tell your husband and your child about your own sister?"

"I. Don't. Have. A sister," Lauren grunted, the anger returning once again. "I haven't had a sister since she killed my parents."

36

"Now. Now," Abi said. "Let's not go throwing accusations around, you know—"

"She killed them," Lauren said, cutting short her relative's monotone statement. "It was her fault. Martha's the—"

"Stop that!" Abi slapped Lauren across the face with the handle of the knife. For the first time, there was a sense of haste and desperation in her voice. "You know that's not true."

Lauren felt a searing pain race through her head. Stars danced in front of her eyes. "You think she was innocent?" A slither of enamel freed itself from a wisdom tooth and rested on her tongue. She spat it onto the floor at Abi's feet. "You can't be that stupid."

"She was young, she was troubled, she—"

"She burned them alive!" Lauren said, laughing from the pain, the anger, the absurdity. "I was twelve years old. Twelve! And I was forced to listen to my parents screaming for help as they burned to a crisp!"

Lauren was slapped again, and again, and again, her head rocking this way and that, the pain growing with each contact. Abi shouted as she hit her, but the words didn't filter through the pain, through the ringing in her ears. When she stopped, Lauren could see only a haze, a fuzzy outline of her psychotic sister as she loomed over her, breathless, angry, struggling to contain herself.

"She was only three years older than you," Abi said, backing away, her voice and her movements more animated, less methodical. "Just fifteen. Still growing. Still getting to grips with the world. And it wasn't her fault."

"You don't think she started the fire?" Lauren said slowly, almost dreamily, as her vision gradually returned.

"No—No—maybe—it doesn't matter. She lost her parents, too, you know."

"I think that was the point, wasn't it?" Lauren asked. "She wanted them dead."

"No, she did not!" Abi screamed. "She loved them. She was just angry. All little girls get angry at their parents, all little girls—"

"Barricade them into their bedroom and then start a fire?"

Abi paused, hands by her side. Lauren's vision was still hazy, the stars still clearing, but she saw the hatred set deep into her sister's heavily made-up face.

"It was a mistake, okay?"

"But that's not what the police said, is it?" Lauren shifted on the couch, forcing herself to sit up straight, to stare her attacker in the face. "They locked her away, didn't they? Too young, they said, but she wasn't a criminal, she wasn't a murderer, she was just mentally ill. That's what they said. That's why they put her in that psychiatric hospital. And that's where she stayed for the next ten years."

Abi sat on the sofa opposite, practically falling into it, her head hung low, the hand that held the knife slung over her lap. "Martha hated it there," she said. "They treated her like a madwoman. I sent her letters every day. I visited her. I kept her spirits up as much as I could, until I just couldn't anymore—" She paused, shook her head. "I did my best."

Lauren rolled her eyes and then turned them back to the clock. A couple more minutes had passed, but time seemed to be moving even slower than before. She allowed herself a glance toward the stairs, free to do so now that she wasn't being watched. A shadow behind the wall caught her attention and she knew instantly that it was Ethan. It was the same place he hid when he was preparing his jump scares, because no matter how many times he did it, no matter how prepared and expectant she was, he always managed to scare her.

The sight of his shadow empowered her, gave her the strength to continue. "They told me the day she was released. They said she had moved down south, two hundred miles away, they promised. Under an assumed identity, they said."

Abi nodded and then returned to mournfully staring at her lap. "She was too young when it happened so her name was never released to the press, but of course, the locals knew. The rumors spread. She couldn't return here."

Lauren shook her head. That wasn't the only reason she couldn't return. There was also the fact that Lauren still lived in the town they had grown up in, and she didn't want to breathe the same air as her sister, let alone live in the same postal code. Her eyes returned to the mantelpiece, but this time they focused on a large ornamental urn.

"She lived a normal life. A quiet life. Under her new name, she made a good living for herself." Abi looked up, catching Lauren's gaze just as she pulled it away from the mantelpiece. "She wanted to be your sister again," Abi continued. "To re-create the family. Just us three. But you wouldn't let her."

Lauren shrugged. "I had my own life to live."

"And you were going to give up on your sister just like that?"

Lauren nodded. "She could have contacted me. She *should* have been in touch."

Abi shook her head. "That's not true."

"Why?" Lauren pushed, waiting for her to admit it.

"You know why."

"It was a long time ago, I forget. You tell me."

Abi rose to her feet. "Because they wouldn't let her, that's why. Because they said she couldn't have contact with any members of her family. She wasn't even allowed to use the family name!" She threw her hands in the air and finished with a short burst of laughter, expressing just how absurd the demand had been. "Crazy that, isn't it?"

"It was a restraining order, if I remember, right?"

Abi nodded. "Restraining order," she mimicked. "If you could believe such a thing. Imagine arresting someone for seeing their own family!"

"Imagine that..." Lauren said slowly, keeping eye contact. "So, did she ever break that restraining order?"

"Of course not. She's a law-abiding girl."

"Except when she's burning down houses and killing her parents, you mean?"

"How dare you—"

"Tell me this," Lauren said quickly as Abi advanced on her again. "If she didn't break it, then what the hell are you doing here and how the fuck were you in her life for so many years?"

Abi stopped still, the anger fading, dripping from her face like warm ice cream.

"You're a member of her family, right?"

Abi didn't respond, her eyes vacant, her expression empty.

"So, tell me, did she break it or not? And while you're at it," Lauren added, "take a look at the mantelpiece there and answer me this question: if you're my grandmother, then why are your ashes above my fucking fireplace?"

37

Abi moved toward the mantelpiece; the knife held loosely by her side. She made a beeline for the large ornamental jar, adorned with a golden plate, engraved expertly with the name of the deceased. Her movements were methodical, distant—she rested the knife on the wooden surface, before a picture of Lauren and her happy family. She reached for the ashes.

Lauren was up quickly, finding strength and bravery that she didn't know she possessed, strength and bravery born of anger, frustration, desperation. She scooted up behind her relative, waited, and prepared.

Abi grunted in displeasure, placed the urn back on the mantelpiece, and turned around. "It says Butch, not—"

Lauren moved her head back and then forward, a pendulum swing that connected forehead to nose, skull to cartilage. The impact rocked her, instantly blurring her vision, sending a screaming pain through her skull and forcing her to stagger, but she had the advantage of surprise, and it did more damage to her assailant. Abi careened backward, her spine connecting with the wooden edge of the mantelpiece and causing her to double over, bringing photographs and the urn of ashes tumbling down as she crashed into a heap on the floor.

"That's because it's our dog!" Lauren yelled through the blinding haze, kicking out in the direction of her attacker's face, reveling in the sensation she felt when the bones of her slippered foot connected with flesh. "Gran was buried, you psycho bitch!" she swung again, this time connecting with her jaw. The impact broke bones in Lauren's foot and caused her to stumble, but she righted herself and swung with her other foot. "She stopped visiting you and sending you letters because she fucking died. Dead people don't write letters, they don't visit people in hospital, and they definitely don't kill people!"

Lauren kicked and kicked, hearing grunts and anguished cries spit and splutter in reply, realizing that her efforts were working. The noise of encroaching sirens filtered through the whistling tinnitus, creating a banshee cacophony. Her body was fueled on adrenaline—shaking, unsteady, dizzy. The chaos around her seemed far away, an alarm clock interrupting a deep sleep and a vivid dream, a film watched through fatigued eyes.

Every kick she threw her sister's way was weaker than the last, causing less damage, making less of an impact, until eventually, Abi caught one of the swinging limbs and, with what little energy she could muster, held it tight. Lauren was too exhausted to fight back. Immediately she lost her balance, shaking on her standing leg, arms flailing, a yelp escaping her lips. She was unable to right herself, unable to prevent her sister from clawing at her leg, twisting her, dragging her down.

Lauren fell sideways, into the fireplace. She threw out her hands to stop herself and prevent the vulnerable appendages from taking the brunt of the fall. Her hands caught on the metal grille of the fireplace, the plastic zip tie forcing her arms upward while the rest of her body fell down.

A bolt of white-hot pain raced from her shoulders to the back of her skull. She heard something crack, and for a split second she thought she had ripped her arms out of her sockets, but then she felt them drop loosely by her side—numb, tingling, and wrapped with the remnants of a broken zip tie.

Lauren fell as a crumpled heap on her sister, her temple clipping the bottom of the grill—another short, sharp shock, another bolt of pain—before her body rested atop the mess of canine ashes that coated her face, her clothes, and the floor.

The pain screeching through her body seemed to stop, if just for a moment, and she felt like the world had slipped out from under her. There was movement, a juggle of bodies, an exchange of positions. Lauren realized that her sister had pulled away, no longer lying beneath her, no longer supporting her. But even as the shadow of her psychotic sibling slowly rose above her, a black silhouette breaking through the white noise of her vision, the only thing she could think about was her son.

Had she given him enough time? Would the police arrive quickly enough?

The silhouette grew. Her sister reestablished her dominance, preparing to kill the one she was most jealous of, the one she hated more than anyone else in the world. The movement in her arms was gradually returning, the blood rushing to where it needed to be, the adrenaline forcing them into action, but her vision blinked in and out. She saw the silhouette of her sister one minute—towering over her menacingly, threateningly—and the welcoming relief of blackness the next.

In the darkness, she felt a weight on top of her. When she opened her eyes, she realized that her sister had now straddled her, taking control. Abi grabbed Lauren by the bangs, pulled her head forward, and then slammed it down. A tuft of ashes rose around her face as it connected with the floor and what remained of her beloved pet.

The ringing in her ears stopped for just a moment, before being replaced by a louder, more alarming noise, as if her mind was screaming at her. Her head was slammed again, and again, but the more pain she felt, the more her body told her wanted to close her eyes and drift away, the more determined Lauren's mind was to stay awake. She couldn't hear the sirens anymore, but she knew they were there, she knew the police were near, and she knew that the more she fought, the more time she bought her son.

Lauren kicked and bucked, trying to throw her assailant off, but Abi rode her like a bucking bronco, holding on tight. She tried to punch and claw, but her efforts were futile as her arms were weak. She tried to bite, but she couldn't reach. And all the while, Abi wore a mocking smile, treating it like a game, a harmless fight between siblings.

Lauren twisted, squirmed, but Abi seemingly lost patience, moving her hands from Lauren's blood-soaked hair to her neck. "Thought you could get the better of me, dear?" Abi scowled, squeezing tightly. There was a menace to her voice that wasn't there before, spittle spraying on every syllable. "I've killed bigger and stronger people than you."

Lauren tried to scream at her, to call her names, to yell for help, but her words were trapped under the tightening grip of her attacker.

"You're just a worthless little girl. You can't kill me."

Lauren thought about playing dead, an idea she entertained for the briefest of moments, but her instincts fought it. She continued to buck, knowing she couldn't force her attacker off, but also knowing that it would distract her. Just as Abi rode another attempt, keeping her hands tight to Lauren's neck as she rocked forward, Lauren swung her fist at her sister's face. There wasn't much force behind the punch, but it was accurate and enough to catch Abi unawares and to knock her off balance. The grip loosened momentarily, but Lauren didn't waste time admiring her handiwork. She used the extra freedom to shift to her left, bringing a toppled picture frame into reach, its solid wooden edges welcome underneath her fingertips. Lauren gripped the frame tightly and swung, connecting with Abi's face just as her sister was recovering from the shock of the punch.

The glass in the frame had already cracked, but on contact with Abi's temple, it shattered into a dozen more pieces and rained over the brawling siblings. Lauren bucked again, this time more successfully, causing her sister to rock and stumble. Her focus, her vision, her strength, and her determination were returning. Adrenaline, desperation, anger—emotions raged inside her and gave her a strength she didn't know she had.

The glass may have broken, but the solid wooden frame was still intact. Lauren repositioned it so that the sharp corner jutted outward and she swung again, making clean contact with Abi's temple, an impact so fierce that it snapped the frame in half.

Abi swayed from side to side and looked unsteady as a wound on the side of her head rapidly leaked blood. Lauren slapped the floor again, looking for another weapon, another opportunity. Her sister, albeit dazed and confused, returned her hands to Lauren's throat, her mouth opening and closing to spit, her face a picture of malignancy, her words dead on arrival, her grip as weak as her mind.

Lauren's eyes lit up when she felt cold steel between her fingers. It was an ornamental art piece, an industrial construct made of recovered wood and iron nails. She remembered the fake gratitude she had expressed when her husband bought it for her; the smile on his face as he waited for her to reciprocate and told her how it had been handmade by a famous industrial artist from Greece. Despite the pain, despite the noise that echoed throughout her skull and despite the threatening presence of her sister on top of her, Lauren swung with all her might.

A sound like a muffled gunshot rang throughout the room as the piece connected with Abi's temple, cracking her skull, rolling her eyes to the back of her head, and sending her toppling to the floor. Lauren held the piece above her, blood dripping from one of the nails, trickling over the composite image of Christ.

Ethan appeared behind the sculpture. Lauren's vision was still hazy, unable to focus, but she could see that he was terrified, visibly shaking. He held a baseball bat in both hands and seemed preoccupied with Lauren's fallen foe.

"Ethan, you're okay," Lauren said, feeling an immediate sense of relief, the natural painkiller that her body had been crying out for.

"Are you?" he asked.

"I'll live."

"Should I finish her off?"

Lauren laughed, the noise becoming trapped in her throat, choked out by a spluttered cough.

"I will, you know. She deserves it."

"She does," Lauren agreed. "But no."

Ethan bent down and extended his hand, but Lauren tiredly shook her head. "If you don't mind, I'm going to lie here awhile. At least until the world stops spinning."

Ethan nodded and looked at the woman, technically his aunt, the woman he didn't know existed. "Is she dead?"

"We can only hope."

"Should I make sure of it?"

Lauren laughed again, a short burst that she immediately regretted. "The police will be here soon. They'll deal with her. Just . . . keep your distance."

"I saw what she did to Dad," Ethan said, not moving an inch despite what his mother told him. There was a pause, a protracted silence through which Lauren heard the sirens again, realizing that they were nearer, much nearer. "I saw what she did to you, as well. I was going to stop her, if you . . . you know."

"I know, son. I know. Now, get the hell out of here in case that crazy cow comes back to life."

EPILOGUE

Lauren felt sick. A sense of dread, of worry, crawled through her bones like some tainted arachnid, leaving its mark on every ounce of her being. Not since that dreaded night, when flames ravaged the house she once called home, when her parents, the people she loved most in the world, were reduced to screams, ashes, and memories, had she felt this sickening sense of dread.

"Are you okay?" A reassuring hand on her shoulder, a kind glance into her eyes.

Lauren took a deep breath and closed her eyes. She fought against the flashbacks, the images of her husband on the kitchen floor, her sister standing above her. She repeatedly told herself that it was going to be okay. It wasn't going to be like it was the other night; this was different.

Her physical injuries had cleared up—a night in the hospital, a visit to the dentist, a week of high-strength painkillers—but the mental impact would no doubt linger for the rest of her life. She had never come to terms with her parents' death, but there were times when the weight of burden had lifted, times when she told herself that her sister had made a mistake. She had acted without complete control. A regrettable moment of madness.

This was different—cold, callous, unforgivable. But despite that, she felt like she had to do what she was about to do. She wasn't going to run away; she was going to face her, stare into her eyes, and tell her how much she hated her.

"Are you ready?"

Lauren nodded and Steven placed his hand gently on her back, leading her down the corridor, their footsteps slow and staggered, as if they wanted to take every opportunity they could to delay the inevitable.

Doctors, nurses, patients—everyone whizzed by them at a frantic pace, a cacophony of noise, an endless march of activity, but they both continued their slow trudge. They followed the signs hanging from the ceilings and plastered on the walls and before long they were walking down a quiet corridor, darker and more subdued than the rest.

They came to a door at the end of the corridor. A deputy sat to one side of it, a paperback novel in his hand. He looked up as they arrived. "The sister and the boyfriend, right?"

"Ex-boyfriend," Steven corrected, turning to Lauren. "And—"

"Former sister," she finished.

"Go inside," the deputy said, leaving them with a smile as he returned his attention to his book. "She's waiting for you."

Lauren entered the room first, with Steven close behind.

She had expected to feel fear, a climax of the dread that she had felt all day and one that caused her to collapse in panic or turn and flee. But when she saw her sister, her *former* sister, all that dread disappeared, and the only thing left was a feeling of relief.

Martha was still breathing, but only with the help of a machine. There were tubes connected to her mouth and nose; patches stuck to her exposed shoulders and arms. A multitude of machines sounded a series of beeps and pings—radar searching for threats and finding none.

"Is she dead?" Steven's words made Lauren jump, lost as she was in the repetitive noise and the image of her sister, who seemed to be enjoying some undeserved peace and tranquility.

"More or less." Lauren's attention had been so fixed on her sister and on the machines that kept her alive that she hadn't seen the other two people in the room. One of them, a male doctor, wearing an obligatory white coat and carrying a clipboard, was the first to speak. "She's comatose. Vegetative state. We're keeping her alive." He returned the clipboard to its holder at the bottom of the bed and approached Lauren. "Lauren, right?"

Lauren nodded and shook his proffered hand.

"We spoke on the phone. My name is Doctor Fraser. As I said, you're the closest thing we have to a next of kin, but—" He shrugged and glanced toward the other person in the room, a middle-aged woman wearing a pinstripe suit. "First, I believe Detective Robinson here wants to have a word. I'll be back shortly. Please, excuse me." The doctor smiled warmly, nodded a friendly greeting to Steven, and then left, his footsteps hurried as he exited the room and made his way toward the buzzing hive of activity.

The detective greeted Lauren and Steven in turn and then told them to take a seat on the other side of the bed. There was only one chair and

Steven offered it to Lauren, but she politely declined, choosing to stand and to keep her distance from her sleeping sister in the process.

Steven sat down with a sigh, holding his heavily bandaged chest and wincing audibly. The detective watched them both, waited until they were comfortable, and then spoke to Lauren. "You're here today to decide if your sister lives or dies. I figured it was only fair that I tell you what I know."

"If it's that my sister was an absolute sociopathic shithead, I already know."

The detective shook her head. "I'm afraid you don't know the half of it."

Lauren and Steven exchanged a concerned glance before turning their attentions to Martha, as if to ensure she was still comatose.

The detective inhaled deeply and exhaled quickly and audibly. "Your sister—"

"Let's just call her Martha," Lauren interjected.

"Or the psycho bitch," Steven offered.

"Martha," the Detective said with a nod, "had been on our radar for some time. She was released from psychiatric care when she was in her mid-twenties. Given a new identity, a new address. She served her time, so the system gave her a fresh start and only her social support team knew her real identity. Within the year, they began reporting some . . . let's call them oddities—"

"She believed she was my grandmother. Bit more than an oddity."

Detective Robinson nodded. "Agreed, but we hadn't quite reached that point at that time, and it wasn't a concern until much later. You see, I didn't find out about this until I was called out to the murder of an elderly couple. They were in their eighties, married for nigh-on sixty years, never a burden to anyone. The wife was bedridden, riddled with cancer; the husband was her caregiver. For some reason," she said with a shrug, "someone took an exception to them being alive and murdered them."

She paused, shuffled on the hard-backed chair, and continued.

"They were your sister's next-door neighbors. At first, we thought it was a robbery gone wrong. Then we did some digging. By chance, we discovered your sister's real identity. At first, it didn't seem that big of a deal. She was a quiet, timid girl. Yes, she'd killed in her youth, but under different circumstances and . . . there wasn't much to go on."

"A murderer lived next to a crime scene, and you didn't connect the dots?" Lauren asked.

"You'd be surprised how many people have horrible things in their past and go on to live perfectly normal lives."

"Why would she kill them? Did she have something to gain?"

"Probably not. But as we know, she didn't always need a reason. There were some rumors about the old man. Despite his age, he had a tendency to get a little *handsy* with the local ladies. Maybe she took exception to that. Maybe they were on to her. Maybe she just got angry and they got in her way. . . . We don't know."

"So why didn't you take her in? Why didn't you charge her? You could have prevented all of this."

"We had to give your sister the benefit of the doubt. Initially, at least."

"Why initially?"

The detective sighed and glanced at Martha. "We discovered that her social workers, the ones who knew about her identity, had also died in suspicious circumstances. Both deaths had been ruled accidental, but only because they could never be certain that a third party was involved. One of them, a man named Victor Dunne, apparently jumped from his balcony."

"And?" Steven said.

"His coffee table was filled with drugs. He'd just bought enough beer for a two-day bender, and he'd arranged for the . . . *services* of an escort for a couple of hours after he died. Sometimes people kill themselves in the spur of the moment, and he had so many intoxicants in his system he could have also done it accidentally, but his death came three days after the other social work fell from a cliff while hiking and broke her neck."

"Jesus."

Martha had only been living here for a year at the time. Not close enough to be recognized by people from her youth, but always within touching distance. She rented a house by paying a year in advance, and the next thing we know, the neighbors show up dead."

"She rented?" Steven asked. "She told me her grandmother owned the house."

Lauren laughed, short and sharp. The detective shook her head. "Her family had never lived there. She had rented for a year before, well, this—" She gestured to the hospital bed. "But she wanted everyone to believe that she'd spent a lifetime there. I suppose it was all part of her game. That way she could hide who she really was, where she came from."

"Jesus," Steven repeated.

"Her grandmother, *your* grandmother." She gestured to Lauren. "Lived a mile down the road, but she died when Abi was in the psychiatric hospital. That obviously affected her."

"Martha adored her," Lauren cut in. "Even after it happened. She forgave her. She was the only one who went to see her. We didn't have much of an extended family, and the ones we did have basically rejected her. And me. My grandmother was probably the only communication she had with the family when she was in there. I certainly didn't want to contact her." She released a long, drawn-out sigh, focused her attention on the detective. "Gran died a few years after the fire. Heart attack. Her friends said it was because of the trauma of losing her child and daughter-in-law and then watching her beloved granddaughter suffer. But she drank like a fish and partied like a twenty-year-old, so that probably had more to do with it." Lauren allowed herself a smile. "What I don't understand, is if you knew this, why didn't you arrest her there and then?"

"We didn't have any proof. She covered her tracks."

"So, you left her to kill?" Steven asked. "That poor old lady, the young girl, Robert, her—"

"Robert was undercover." The detective was visibly uncomfortable. "Tasked with keeping an eye on her, getting as much information as he could." She shrugged. "He was adamant that she was up to something, but he couldn't catch her in the act."

"Shit," Steven said, the color draining from his face. "I—I—didn't know. I mean, she killed him, I wasn't involved, but I thought he was the killer, I thought he was up to something, I may have pushed her into—"

Detective Robinson held up her hand. "It's okay, there was nothing you could have done. You weren't to know. Everyone was fooled. Even when the body count began to rise, we never truly suspected she was behind it. She seemed to live a quiet life. Spent most of her time inside—rarely left the house, never interacted with the neighbors."

"What about the old lady across the road?"

"I think Robert began to suspect her at that point. He contacted us, told us how she had complained about late nights, about her sneaking out in the morning hours. He asked for night-vision cameras, surveillance equipment to monitor her in the early morning hours, but before he had a chance to set them up . . ." She allowed her voice to trail off.

A silence descended over the room, with only the sound of Martha's aspirated breathing and the rhythmic bleating of the machines. Lauren thought she noticed a tear forming in the comer of the detective's eye, but she quickly turned her head, rubbed her face, and hid whatever had been affecting her.

"So, what happens now?" Steven asked.

"Now?" The detective stood. "Now you thank your lucky stars that you survived this crazy bitch, you pray for the ones who didn't, and you sell your story to the highest bidder." She cracked a smile, but it quickly faded when she heard the encroaching footsteps of the doctor. Detective Robinson turned to the windows and watched as Doctor Fraser approached.

"Just one thing," she said to Lauren. "The doctor is going to come in here and ask for your final decision on whether you want to pull the plug or not. When he does, remember that this piece of shit is not your sister, she's not his girlfriend, she's not anyone's friend. She's the one who killed your husband, tried to kill you, murdered an officer of the law, and took the lives of several others."

The doctor entered just as the detective finished her statement. Lauren closed her eyes as she heard the door shut behind her, picturing the chaos that her sister had caused, the destruction she had brought to her family and several others. When she opened her eyes, Doctor Fraser was standing in front of her, a practiced look of compassion on his face.

"Are you ready?" he asked.

"Yes," she said, standing, feeling more assured and more confident than she had since the incident. "I've made my decision."